# *Suddenly, out of the darkness, Noah Rider appeared.*

A gasp escaped Paige, and he spun around at the sound and did something she could never have expected.

He kissed her.

Sudden and fierce and hot, he kissed her. She responded, unable not to, and heat rocketed through her again.

He broke the kiss, and she suddenly realized that he'd kissed her to keep her quiet, to keep her from alerting their captors.

But then he whispered, "I've been wanting to do that for days."

She wanted to say that she had, too, wanted to believe that keeping her quiet hadn't been his only reason.

But even if it hadn't, where did that leave them? Where did they go from here?

Nowhere, she realized, unless they got out of this alive. And there was a very real possibility that they wouldn't….

Dear Reader,

Once again, Intimate Moments invites you to experience the thrills and excitement of six wonderful romances, starting with Justine Davis's *Just Another Day in Paradise*. This is the first in her new miniseries, REDSTONE, INCORPORATED, and you'll be hooked from the first page to the last by this suspenseful tale of two meant-to-be lovers who have a few issues to work out on the way to a happy ending—like being taken hostage on what ought to be an island paradise.

ROMANCING THE CROWN continues with *Secret-Agent Sheik*, by Linda Winstead Jones. Hassan Kamal is one of those heroes no woman can resist—except for spirited Elena Rahman, and even she can't hold out for long. Our introduction to the LONE STAR COUNTRY CLUB winds up with Maggie Price's *Moment of Truth*. Lovers are reunited and mysteries are solved—but not all of them, so be sure to look for our upcoming anthology, *Lone Star Country Club: The Debutantes*, next month. RaeAnne Thayne completes her OUTLAW HARTES trilogy with *Cassidy Harte and the Comeback Kid*, featuring the return of the prodigal groom. Linda Castillo is back with *Just a Little Bit Dangerous*, about a romantic Rocky Mountain rescue. Finally, welcome new author Jenna Mills, whose *Smoke and Mirrors* will have you eagerly looking forward to her next book.

And, as always, be sure to come back next month for more of the best romantic reading around, right here in Intimate Moments.

Enjoy!

Leslie J. Wainger
Executive Senior Editor

Please address questions and book requests to:
Silhouette Reader Service
U.S.: 3010 Walden Ave., P.O. Box 1325, Buffalo, NY 14269
Canadian: P.O. Box 609, Fort Erie, Ont. L2A 5X3

# Just Another Day in Paradise

## JUSTINE DAVIS

# INTIMATE MOMENTS™

Published by Silhouette Books

America's Publisher of Contemporary Romance

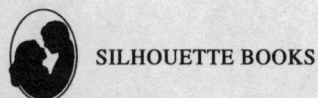 SILHOUETTE BOOKS

ISBN 0-373-27211-1

JUST ANOTHER DAY IN PARADISE

Visit Silhouette at www.eHarlequin.com

**Printed in U.S.A.**

**Books by Justine Davis**

**Silhouette Intimate Moments**

*Hunter's Way* #371
*Loose Ends* #391
*Stevie's Chase* #402
*Suspicion's Gate* #423
*Cool under Fire* #444
*Race Against Time* #474
*To Hold an Eagle* #497
*Target of Opportunity* #506
*One Last Chance* #517
*Wicked Secrets* #555
*Left at the Altar* #596
*Out of the Dark* #638
*The Morning Side of Dawn* #674
*Lover under Cover* #698
*Leader of the Pack* #728
*A Man To Trust* #805
*Gage Butler's Reckoning* #841
*Badge of Honor* #871
*Clay Yeager's Redemption* #926
*The Return of Luke McGuire* #1036
†*Just Another Day in Paradise* #1141

*Trinity Street West
†Redstone, Incorporated

**Silhouette Desire**

*Angel for Hire* #680
*Upon the Storm* #712
*Found Father* #772
*Private Reasons* #833
*Errant Angel* #924
*A Whole Lot of Love* #1281

**Silhouette Books**

*Silhouette Summer Sizzlers* 1994
"The Raider"

Fortune's Children
*The Wrangler's Bride*

## JUSTINE DAVIS

lives in Kingston, Washington. Her interests outside of writing are sailing, doing needlework, horseback riding and driving her restored 1967 Corvette roadster—top down, of course.

A policewoman, Justine says that years ago, a young man she worked with encouraged her to try for a promotion to a position that was, at that time, occupied only by men. "I succeeded, became wrapped up in my new job and that man moved away, never, I thought, to be heard from again. Ten years later he appeared out of the woods of Washington State, saying he'd never forgotten me and would I please marry him. With that history, how could I write anything but romance?"

Once upon a time, there was a genre of books that was sadly misunderstood by anyone who didn't read them. Those who did read, loved them, cherished them, were changed by them. But still, these books got no respect on the outside. In fact these books were belittled, denigrated, held up as bad examples, while their readers and authors were sneered at and insulted by people who, although they never read the books, had somehow arrived at the idea that it was all right to slap others down for their choices. But those readers and authors kept on in the face of this horrible prejudice. Why? Because they found something in these books that they found nowhere else. Something precious, that spoke to them in a very deep and basic way.

Then one day, this beleaguered genre was given a gift. A fairy godmother, if you will, a person with an incredible knowledge of these books and why they worked, and an even more incredible generosity of spirit. A one-person support system who gave so much to the writers of these stories, and was ever unselfish with her time and that amazing knowledge. And her endorsement counted for something; readers took her word and knew they would rarely be disappointed. She was a rock, a pillar on which the genre depended. Her loss has left a gaping hole that can never be filled, and will always be felt by those who love these books—and loved her.

For those reasons and so many more, the Redstone, Incorporated series is dedicated to

## MELINDA HELFER

Lost to us August 24, 2000, but if heaven is what it should be, she's in an endless library, with an eternity to revel in the books she loved. Happy reading, my friend....

# Chapter 1

"It's scary to see that here in paradise."

Noah Rider nodded at Redstone Inc. pilot Tess Machado as they looked out the parked jet's window at the airport terminal. There was something inherently ominous about men in camouflage anywhere, but it seemed even worse in a tropical paradise. Especially when those men in camouflage had automatic rifles slung over their shoulders.

He called up a memo on his laptop computer, knowing he needed to notify the main office that things might be worse than suspected. Redstone had received reports that the rebels were calling it a political uprising, when in fact it was simply a rebellion against the suppression of the drug traffic. But if the government of Arethusa felt the need to guard the airport, it did not bode well for continued peace in this Caribbean island paradise.

"It's a good thing the resort guests coming in next week won't be making this stop," Tess said.

Rider looked at the woman who had been Joshua Redstone's personal pilot for six years, ever since the head of

Redstone Inc. had reluctantly acknowledged he had to work during a flight too often to keep doing all the flying himself.

"Yes," he agreed. "It's not the most welcoming sight for vacationers."

He knew some would arrive at the newest Redstone resort in their own planes, some via Josh's private fleet—probably even the new Redstone Hawk IV he sat in now—but none should need a refueling stop before landing at the new airstrip at Redstone Bay. They had only stopped to pick up a shipment for the resort; the Hawk IV had more than enough range to make the trip from India nonstop.

"Do you know who you're bringing in next week?" he asked her. When Tess wasn't piloting Josh, she was part of the Redstone pilot pool, at her request; she loved flying. She traveled almost as much as Noah, and he wondered what kind of strain that put on her relationship with the stockbroker she'd been seeing. It had certainly been enough to destroy his own marriage, and the one serious relationship he'd had since. He kept his mouth shut, however; Tess was like a big sister to him, and she'd made it clear if there was any advice giving to be done between them, he'd be on the receiving end.

"I'm not sure yet," she answered. "But if we have to stop for any reason, it'll be in Antigua," Tess said, pushing dark bangs back with her fingers as she looked out the window once more.

"Good idea." Her gesture made Rider think of his own appearance, and he rubbed a hand over his bewhiskered face.

As Tess returned to the cockpit he rose and walked back to the head, although it had always seemed ludicrous to him to call something as elegantly appointed as this bathroom a head. Josh had drawn the line at gold-plated fixtures for this, his own personal jet, but everything was still the highest quality. As were all the planes built by Redstone. From the smallest prop to the biggest jet they made, the fleet that was the foundation of Joshua Redstone's business empire was all pure class.

But the quality of the mirror couldn't help the reflection, Rider thought as he peered at himself. He looked like what he was, a man who'd been running too long on too little sleep. His dark hair was tousled and overdue for a haircut, he'd gone beyond fashionable stubble sometime yesterday afternoon—whatever time zone that had been in—and his eyes were as much red as blue. But nobody would really care what he looked like as long as he acknowledged the hard work they'd been doing.

As they began to roll again, loading completed, Rider went back to his seat and glanced out at the military men once more. He wondered for a fleeting moment if his clever boss had done this intentionally, so he'd get a firsthand look at the situation on Arethusa. But he discarded the thought; if that were the case, Josh would have sent Draven, or someone else on the security-and-troubleshooting staff, not him. He was strictly a detail man, and hadn't been this close to serious weaponry since the years spent hunting with his father in the wilds of Montana. He might once have been able to stalk even a wary skunk, but these days boardrooms were as close as he came to throat-slitting violence. And most times, that was close enough for him. He was glad to leave Arethusa behind.

By the time they were approaching Redstone Bay, Rider had his checklist prioritized. First the staff meeting to thank them all for what they'd done so far, then individual meetings. Then he would—

Tess's voice crackled over the intercom. "We're about to land, Mr. Rider."

Smiling at the formality she always maintained once in the cockpit, Rider pressed the intercom button on the console beside the spacious table. "Thanks."

He'd asked for a circuit of the island before they landed, so he could see what the place looked like from all ap-

proach directions. He had a knack—some called it a brain
glitch—for remembering maps and plans, and he could call
up the original planned layout at will. So now he studied
the view below, nodding slowly.

They'd done a good job, kept the disruption of the landscape to a minimum and the buildings in keeping with the
style of this part of the world. Not that there was any lack
of luxury, but there was no towering concrete monolith of
a hotel here—that wasn't Redstone's style. The four-story
buildings were arranged around a large courtyard, and were
low enough to be masked by the inevitable palm trees. A
number of small, elegant and very private bungalows were
scattered among the trees. The swimming pool at one edge
of the courtyard was also subtle, designed to look more like
a natural lagoon and grotto than something built by man.

Even the landing strip, Rider thought as they banked for
the last turn, wasn't a huge scar on the land, but had been
landscaped with exquisite care to maintain the most natural
look possible.

He sat back in the leather seat, nodding with satisfaction.
This, he thought, was going to be smooth sailing.

Paige Cooper turned a page in her leather-bound journal,
ran her finger down the center to make it lie flat, and picked
up her pen. Then she set it down again, caught unexpectedly by a wave of emotion. She closed the journal and
gently touched the cover, tracing the intricate Celtic design
on the teal-green leather. Moisture welled up behind her
eyelids as she fought down a stab of fierce longing for those
days past, when life had been good and her son, Kyle, had
loved her enough to save all his allowance for three months
to buy this for her birthday.

As if her thoughts had summoned him, she saw Kyle out
of the corner of her eye, leaving his room and walking
toward the front door of the bungalow they'd been given
to live in while she was on the staff. She knew the instant

he realized she was there by the way his normal, gangly-fifteen-year-old walk became a slow, dragging shuffle, with his shoulders slumped as if he bore the weight of an unfair world.

She smothered a sigh and tried for a cheerful tone. "Where are you off to?"

He stopped dead. Only his head turned toward her as he gave her a look of such exaggerated incredulity that she winced inwardly. Everything seemed to be over-the-top with him these days.

"Nowhere." His voice was bitter, acidly so. "Since I'm in the middle of noplace, with no friends and nothing to do, I'm going nowhere."

She reined in the urge to order him not to use that tone with her. She knew he was having a hard time just now, and tried not to focus on the superficial symptoms of that.

"It must be awful to feel that way," she said, her voice carefully even. "Especially when lots of people would love to be here."

It stopped him, but not for long. "*Those* people would be here by choice. *They* wouldn't be dragged away from home, forced to leave all their friends and even their own stuff."

She'd known when she'd taken the Redstone job last month that this could be a problem. "I told you," she said patiently, "as soon as we get a little ahead you can have Danny come for a visit."

"Danny? That little geek?" Kyle sneered.

"He's your best friend."

"Maybe when I was seven. You just don't get it, do you? I've grown up, I can't hang around with those little kids."

"He's your age," Paige pointed out.

"It isn't the age," Kyle said haughtily, "it's the maturity. Danny is still a kid. All he thinks about is school and sports and computers. He doesn't have a life."

Paige's patience ran out abruptly. She stood up, not that

it helped much now that Kyle was nearly two inches taller than her five foot four.

"You think it's more mature to have a police record that will follow you the rest of your life? That your life is best spent playing video games endlessly? That it's more grown-up to hurt the people that love you the most?"

Kyle flushed. "The one that loved me the most is *dead,*" he shouted, and ran out the door.

Paige sank back into her chair, blinking rapidly. The truth boiled up inside her, and she was thankful Kyle had gone. She didn't think she could have held it back this time. But telling him would only hurt him all over again, and he'd been through enough. He'd adored his father and now he was dead, and beyond that nothing much mattered.

Except that now, at fifteen, that same loving son hated her. And never let pass a chance to tell her yet again how she had ruined his life and he would never, ever forgive her.

She fought down the urge to cry; she'd wept enough over this to know it was a useless exercise. She straightened her spine, opened the journal and picked up her pen.

Sometimes, she told herself firmly, you just have to do what you know is right, and damn the torpedoes. Or whatever that saying was.

She found her page and glanced at what she had written before: "Nothing much happens here in Redstone Bay."

It suddenly struck her this was very much like the opening of an old, much-loved book her mother had handed on to her. It had been written on a postcard in the story, but the sentiment had been the same. In the book it had also been the precursor to chaos for the unsuspecting heroine.

Paige smiled wistfully at her own whimsy. She lifted her gaze and looked around at paradise. A slight, balmy breeze rustled the palm fronds, but barely stirred the few strands of hair that had escaped her braid. She couldn't imagine a more peaceful place. The strife she'd heard the hotel staff talking about seemed distant and unreal in this haven of serenity.

And that serenity was exactly what she'd come here for. It had been difficult, giving up her home. But she'd had enough of the brutal streets of Los Angeles. And more than that, she'd had too much of what they were doing to her son. She empathized more than he would believe with his struggle to go on without his father, but she simply would not allow Kyle to be turned into one of those street fighters who turned up on the nightly news, either as killer or victim.

The distant sound that had been niggling at the edge of her awareness swelled to a roar, and she looked up to see a sleek jet, painted in the red-and-gray color scheme of Redstone Inc. She thought it looked like the same one that had ferried her here from California, and wondered if Tess Machado was flying it. She had liked the charming woman with dark, pixie-cut hair and the lovely smile. It had been an experience unlike any she'd ever had; the novelty of leaving when it was convenient for her, of knowing the plane would wait if she was late, and sheer amazement at the amenities. And Tess had told her Josh—anyone who'd worked for Redstone more than a year seemed to call him that—hadn't gone for the extreme luxury he produced for other customers; he'd spent his money in the avionics, the instruments and in extra training for his pilots.

Even Kyle had forgotten his anger in the thrill of the ride on the powerful jet, and for the length of the ride at least, they'd been close once more as he excitedly pointed things out to her. He'd even thanked her when she'd negotiated with Tess to allow him a brief period in the cockpit. She knew he would enjoy it, and besides, it couldn't hurt for him to see the pilot was female.

As the jet headed for the landing strip, Paige glanced at her watch. The point man, it seemed, was right on time; the staff meeting was set to begin in an hour. Everything she'd ever seen connected to Redstone seemed to run like clockwork, although she was sure there had to be glitches in at least some of their huge undertakings. But that's what this guy was here for, she thought. To smooth out the bumps in these last days before the Redstone Bay Resort opened for business.

She closed her journal and stood up. The mild breeze played with the hem of her new, tropical-print dress, an indulgence she had allowed herself the day after she'd accepted the job offer that had brought her here. She rarely wore it—she had to be too careful as a redhead in a land of tropical sun—but she'd put it on today because she needed the confidence the flattering dress gave her.

And speaking of that job, she told herself, she'd better take the short time she had to go over her papers once more. She doubted the man would want to delve into her lesson plans, but it had been a few years since she'd taught, and Joshua Redstone had taken a chance on her, so she wanted to be completely prepared just in case. She was happy with how her students had adapted so far.

Except for the one student she'd known was going to be a problem from the beginning, a certain angry, recalcitrant fifteen-year-old. Kyle alone sapped at her energy, and she wasn't sure she was up to adding twenty-six other kids into the mix. But she had no choice.

After one final glance over her schedules and plans, she gathered everything up and put it into her tote bag. It would take about five minutes for her to walk to the main building from their bungalow. She'd let him pick it out from the ones available for staff, hoping it would make him less resistant to being here. It hadn't helped much—she suspected he'd picked this one because it was farthest from the schoolhouse and would be the most inconvenient for her.

But she'd taken his choice gracefully, exclaiming on the lovely view of the water and closeness to the perfect beach, as if it were the one she would have chosen herself. That her reaction only made him angrier seemed proof of her suspicions, and she knew then that when you came to paradise, you could still carry your own hell with you.

Rider studied himself in the mirror for a moment, decided his tie was even enough, and reached for his suit coat. Later he would change into more casual clothes. He'd found it helped loosen people up, that they talked more easily to a guy in jeans or khakis. Maybe he'd even pull out that Hawaiian-style shirt Josh had given him. He'd thought at the time the shirt was a joke, but then wondered if maybe it was his boss's way of telling him once more to lighten up and relax. Of course, it had been Josh who'd had him on the run for three months straight, bouncing all over the globe to keep up with various projects.

He rubbed at his eyes, knowing he'd need about ten hours' sleep to help the redness. But other than that he looked fairly presentable now that he'd had a shower and tried out the hotel barber, who had arrived a couple of days ago to set up shop and get the staff in shape. Not that Josh cared how you wore your hair, as long as it was clean and neat. Rider had seen the single photograph that had survived from the founder of Redstone's mysterious youth, and the teenager with the intense eyes and the long mane of dark hair didn't seem all that far removed from the business powerhouse Rider knew now.

He stepped outside his room just as Barry Rutherford, the cherub-faced, slightly fussy project manager, was arriving.

"I'm sorry I wasn't here to greet you, Mr. Rider. I'll show you to the dining room," he said formally, referring to the large room utilized by the staff. Redstone Bay was specifically designed not to handle conferences or large meetings, it was for people to get away and unwind.

"Just 'Rider,' please, Barry," he said. "And I probably

can find it. I think I had the plans memorized before construction even started.'' He gave Barry a crooked grin. ''Let me try, anyway, since you're here to save me if I get lost.''

Barry smiled tentatively this time when he spoke. ''I really am sorry I wasn't here when you arrived.''

''What fire were you putting out?'' Rider asked with another grin, this time one of commiseration and understanding.

''A small one, really. Our facilities director was called home for an emergency, and I had to assign someone to handle the job.''

Rider headed down the hall toward the elevator. ''Will he be back in time?''

''I don't know, I'm afraid. It's something to do with the problems on Arethusa. So I'm going to work out a schedule to cover in case he's unable to return right away.''

''Good,'' Rider said with a nod, although he was frowning inwardly. Suddenly Arethusa didn't seem quite so distant.

But the resort itself was looking good. True, there were materials scattered about and workers scurrying, but he was used to that. He'd learned long ago to look past the surface chaos and see truly how close they were to being ready. And Redstone Bay was close.

''What's hanging besides polish work?'' he asked.

''Nothing, really,'' Barry said proudly. ''All the major projects are done.''

''What about off-site? The staff housing, the school?''

''The only bungalows not completed are the ones where the occupants can't make up their minds what color they want,'' Barry said with a chuckle. ''The school was finished last month, and is already in operation.''

''Any changes?''

He shook his head. ''None needed. Somebody spec'ed it out perfectly.''

Rider wondered if the man was trying to butter him up;

he must know Rider had been the one who had made the final changes on the plans and equipment list for the small schoolhouse.

"The man's a bit manic about education," Rider said, referring to the passion all of Josh's people knew about.

"It keeps people happy, being able to work here and keep their kids with them."

"And Redstone likes happy people," Rider intoned, quoting the mantra that they all laughed at but lived by, knowing that as far as employers went they were with one of the best. The formula Josh had stuck to for years still worked; he hired top-notch people, paid them well and let them run.

Rider found his way to the dining room as easily as he'd hoped. It was nearly full; the staff would eat at different times, so it would rarely be this packed again. Rider declined Barry's offer to introduce him to the gathered crowd, many of whom had noticed their entrance and suspended conversation.

"I don't want this to be that formal," he explained. "I'm not the boss checking up on the employees."

Barry nodded. "Here's the roster," he said, handing Rider a small sheaf of papers. "And your master card-key." Rider took the papers and slipped the key into a pocket; he knew the key, which would override any lock in the resort, was the symbol that the project manager considered all parts of the hotel ready for official inspection. It had become a tradition of sorts, and Rider knew that as long as he got that key within eight hours of his arrival, chances were things would be okay.

He stepped up to the small podium. It didn't take long for the silence to spread. When they were all watching him he said, "I'm Noah Rider, the project coordinator, and I'm here to tell you if you don't like the uniforms, it's too late."

Laughter rippled through the room, as he'd hoped it

would; they'd all had a chance to give their input and vote on what the uniforms should be.

"I haven't had much time to look around yet," he went on, "but what I can see looks good. That's not to say there aren't some problems, there always are. That's what I'm here to help with. But everything's coming together nicely, you've all obviously done your jobs well, and Redstone Bay is lucky to have you."

A burst of cheers and whistles greeted that.

"That said, anyone have any problems that need to be dealt with before opening day?"

"We need a new movie service," somebody called out. "This one just runs the same old stuff over and over."

Rider grinned. "Just so happens I brought along a really big satellite dish. Anybody know how to set one of those puppies up?"

Laughter and cheers met that as well. When no other complaints arose, he nodded in satisfaction.

On some other level of his mind, beneath the part that was handling the speaking task, he registered that there was a redhead in the back row. She snagged his attention, as any woman with hair of that particular rich, autumn-leaves shade did. Even after five years.

It wasn't that he thought about it a lot. It was not, after all, his finest hour, and he didn't like dwelling on it. In fact, in a life that held few regrets, that one woman stood as an eternal torch of reproach.

He shook off the memory and began again, scanning the room, trying to make eye contact with everyone. "I hope to meet with you all over the next ten days, and I want you to feel free to bring up anything you want. Some of the best ideas come from you, out on the front line, and that's what I'm here for."

It was a motivational statement, Rider knew, but it was also true, and Redstone believed in it. And the staff responded, nodding as they turned and glanced at each other.

There was a reason Redstone was consistently in the top ten on lists of best places to work.

"Doesn't matter if it's business or personal, I—"

Rider was only vaguely aware he'd stopped talking. Or that he was staring. A beefy, broad-shouldered man had shifted in his seat, giving Rider a full view of the woman with the coppery hair.

*It can't be.*

She sat there at the very back table, staring down at folders in front of her. He silently urged her to look up, to face him so he could be sure. But she didn't. Or wouldn't. And he was sure, anyway. He knew he couldn't mistake the long, thick braid of hair, the line of her cheekbones, the tilt of her nose. He knew if she looked up, her eyes would be that rich, cinnamon-brown. He knew it.

*But it can't be.*

He lifted the now-forgotten page of statistics and grabbed at the personnel roster Barry had given him. He scanned it quickly and let out a sigh of relief; her name wasn't there. It was a fluke, just a resemblance. He'd reacted out of guilt, that's all.

Steady again, he moved to slip the roster back beneath his page of notes. It snagged on something, and he reached to free it from the small piece of paper stapled to the back of the roster.

He glimpsed the last few words on the note before his page pulled clear. He grabbed at it, tearing it loose from the staple. And there it was, immutable and real. The news that the teacher had arrived nearly a month ago to get the island school up and running before the opening. The teacher. Paige Cooper.

He'd hoped never to see her again. He'd hungered to see her again. He'd never resolved the contradiction. And now the contradiction was sitting in front of him.

The only woman who had ever made him throw whatever decency and common sense he had out the window.

The only woman who could shame him with just a look.

The only woman who had ever made him ache for her in so many ways he couldn't even count them all.

Paige Cooper, sitting there, refusing to look at him, reminding him all the more of what he'd done the last time he'd seen her. He remembered his earlier assessment, and decided he must have really ticked off whatever god was in charge of his fate at the moment.

The ship he'd thought was going to have a smooth sailing had just encountered a reef.

## *Chapter 2*

He had a roomful of people staring at him, and Rider couldn't for the life of him remember what he'd been going to say. He wasn't at a total loss often enough to have learned how to deal with it well, so he knew he was fumbling now. He took refuge in the numbers and details he could spout without thought and began the rundown while his mind raced.

He shouldn't have been so surprised. It was a very Joshua-like thing to do, to hire the widow of one of his people. Especially since Phil Cooper had been killed while working for Redstone. Even though the man hadn't been one of Redstone's hires originally—he'd been a vice president of a purchased company—Josh didn't make a habit of wholesale firings at new acquisitions.

I would have fired him, Rider thought, anger spiking even after all this time. But he knew his feelings were biased. The Redstone investigation into Cooper's death had been, as usual, thorough and deep. In fact, the deepest one he'd ever seen, because the plane had been brought down over Portugal by a terrorist bomb. After five years they still didn't know exactly who had done it, they'd only succeeded in narrowing down the possibilities. And discovering that Cooper had left his widow in unpleasant, if not dire, straits.

Rider knew the truth about why Phil Cooper had been on that plane. If he hadn't, he would have felt only a vague sorrow at the death of a man he'd hardly known. And only a pity-tinged sympathy for his wife.

But instead...

With an effort he shoved his thoughts aside. He finished acknowledging the impressive list of things accomplished since construction had started. And finally remembered where he'd been before he'd gotten derailed.

"As I was saying before jet lag caught up with me," he joked, "whatever you have to say, I'm here to listen. Those of you who have worked for Redstone, you know I mean it. Those of you who are just starting out, welcome."

He started to move away from the podium, then turned back. "Oh, did I mention the party? We'll be having it two days before the opening." He managed a grin. "Two days, because we expect you to enjoy it so much it'll take that long to clean up for the opening."

A rather raucous round of applause greeted that statement, loudest from those who had worked at a Redstone resort before and knew that they definitely knew how to throw a party.

Rider waved in recognition of the good cheer and left the small lectern. The moment his mind was freed from the task of conducting the meeting, it leaped back to the subject he'd tried to suppress.

Paige Cooper. Here. Unavoidably here.

He let out a compressed breath. He'd long ago given up trying to convince himself that what he'd felt five years before was just sympathy. He'd felt a lot more than that. And what he'd felt had led him to actions so uncharacteristic that he'd shocked himself. He still couldn't quite believe it.

And if his reaction just now was any indication, those feelings had only been in hibernation.

His smooth-sailing ship, he thought grimly, had just run aground.

I should have known, Paige moaned inwardly. How could it not have even occurred to me that it would be him?

She barely managed to gather up her papers, and nearly dropped the tote bag in her haste. She dodged out of the dining room and headed for the outer door at the fastest pace she could manage without running and drawing attention. Once outside she slowed, pressing her fingers to her face, wishing for an icy-cold breeze. Her fingers were cooler than her overheated cheeks, but not cool enough. Ice, she thought. Ice would be good.

"You idiot," she muttered to herself. "You're such a fool."

She knew, had known even back then, that Noah Rider was one of Redstone's premiere point men. That he ran all over the world, setting up new operations, finalizing things. So why on earth hadn't she realized there was a good chance the exec sent to oversee the final stages of Redstone Bay would be him? True, she'd been busy, her classes had started barely a week after she'd arrived so the kids would be in the routine by the time the resort opened, so there had been little chance for her to hear his name mentioned, but still—

"Paige? You all right?" Miranda Mayfield, head of technical services and mother of two of her students, put a hand on her shoulder.

"Fine. Thank you." She sounded completely unconvincing, even to herself. Miranda looked doubtful, and Paige tried to pull herself together. "It must have been the crowd," she said. "I've gotten used to the quiet here."

Miranda smiled. "It is that, isn't it? Almost makes up for those rascals you're trying to teach."

Paige managed a smile. "They're good kids." Except for mine, at the moment, she amended silently.

"They like you. And you're giving attention to all of them, despite the difference in ages. All the parents are pleased. We know that can't be easy to accomplish."

"Thank you," Paige said again, meaning it this time. It was sweet of Miranda to tell her that.

When the woman had gone, Paige took in a deep breath of the balmy air. She was steadier now. Steady enough to marvel at how shaken she had felt just moments ago.

But perhaps it wasn't so surprising. Not when she'd just been faced with the man who'd inspired her to the most impulsive thing she'd ever done in her generally traditional life. Her husband's body not even brought home yet, and she'd shared a passionate embrace with a man she barely knew. An embrace that could easily have led to more, had the arrival of her son not interrupted them. Her recollection of that time wasn't clear, was mercifully lost in a sort of fog, but that one vivid, shocking memory was forever seared into her mind.

She had been able, since then, to rationalize her actions. Given the circumstances—all of them—she obviously hadn't been herself. But there was no analyzing away her reaction to the man. What she'd done, practically throwing herself at him, might have arisen out of her emotional state, but her response to him, to his mouth, to his hands on her, had been purely physical and unlike anything she'd ever known before or since.

And if she'd succeeded over the past five years in pushing him out of her mind, it had been made clear to her just now that her body remembered him perfectly. So perfectly it had nearly forgotten how to breathe when he'd walked into the room.

It made no sense. She knew who he was, what he was,

that he was a globe-trotter of epic proportion. That alone should be enough to send her scurrying; she'd been down that road once and still carried the scars. But instead she had been drawn, aware not only of the piercing blue of his eyes and the male strength of his jaw but the empathy she'd seen in his eyes and the gentle touch of hands that somehow seemed to ease the pain.

And if the jump of her heart just now and the pounding that had followed when she had realized it really was him were any indication, she was still drawn. Powerfully. Painfully.

Foolishly. That above all. Noah Rider was many things, including good-looking, smart, trusted by the shrewd and brilliant Joshua Redstone, and a high-powered executive, just as her late husband had been. What he was not was a man for a woman like her. Or perhaps any woman. She'd heard his work came first, last and in between.

She heard the door open behind her again and wished she'd gone before the motherly Miranda had come back to check on her again. With a "Really, I'm fine" on her lips she began to turn. But she froze; the footsteps she heard did not belong to the petite, usually high-heeled Miranda. They were heavier, more solid. Male. Yes, definitely male.

She should truly have run when she'd had the chance.

The footsteps came to a halt behind her. Every muscle in her body seemed to tighten as she waited, holding her breath. It could be anyone, but she knew as clearly as if she'd turned to look who it was.

The silence spun out for a long, aching moment.

"Paige?"

She let out the breath she'd been holding, in a long, inaudible sigh. It took every bit of nerve she had to do it, but she turned to face him.

"Hello, Noah," she said, softer than she would have liked, but more evenly than she'd expected. And then regretted it, when a faint flicker in those eyes reminded her he was usually referred to as Rider by everyone else.

For a long moment he just stood there, staring at her. He was as big as she remembered, at least six feet, a good eight inches taller than she. His hair was just as dark, and he wore the same kind of conservative gray suit—although because of the tropical locale, lighter weight this time—he had worn the last time she'd seen him.

And he still looked so incredibly strong. She had almost convinced herself that she'd only thought he was because she herself had been feeling so wobbly and weak at the time. But now she knew better.

"I didn't know you would be here," he said abruptly, the words coming out in a rush.

She took another quick, steadying breath to be sure her voice would come out normally.

"And I didn't know the project coordinator would be you. Although I suppose I should have," she added honestly.

Only after she'd spoken did the implication of his first words sink in. *I didn't know you would be here.* Meaning what? That if he had, he wouldn't have come? Would have made them send someone else? Had she embarrassed him that much, made him feel so awkward he would actually let it get in the way of his work? The thought made her so hideously self-conscious that she scrambled to fill the silence.

"I wanted to tell you—the project coordinator, I mean, that the school is really wonderful. You did an excellent job planning the modernization."

He blinked once, his brows furrowed slightly, then he seemed to relax. So he *had* felt awkward, she thought. No doubt he was glad she'd brought up something so…safe.

"Keeping your family with you is one of the perks of working for Redstone."

''So I've been told,'' she said. Phil had never wanted to avail himself of that option.

But she also knew from the staff—whenever they weren't talking about the problems brewing in nearby Arethusa—that the staff housing and the school were directly overseen by the coordinator. ''But I know the coordinator made several changes and additions to the school plans, and they've worked out very well for the children.''

His mouth quirked at one corner. ''I figured the indoor plumbing would be a hit.''

Paige blushed, wondering if he was inwardly laughing at her. Perhaps he always had been. Poor, new widow, throwing herself at the first man who tried to comfort her. Maybe that's all she was to him, a slightly embarrassing, mostly pitiful memory. She couldn't blame him for that. It's how she thought of herself back then, too. But she was stronger now. Much stronger. He'd no longer find much trace of the wobbly, uncertain woman she'd been in those days after Phil's death.

''I had more in mind the computer center,'' she said, making her voice match her more determined thoughts. ''The kids are already using it, even ones who've never seen a computer before.''

One dark brow lowered, as if at the new intonation in her words. ''I'm glad to hear that. There was some…discussion over the extra construction it took for the wiring.''

She read between the lines and said, ''Thank you for fighting for it, then.''

He shrugged. ''Wasn't much of a fight. They knew if it got all the way to Josh, he'd approve it.'' His forehead creased. ''Is your son with you?''

''Yes and no,'' Paige said wryly, then regretted the words. Her problems with Kyle weren't something she wanted to discuss, least of all with this man.

''Does that mean he's here physically but not mentally?''

"Exactly," she said, surprised he'd gotten her meaning so quickly. "He's not happy with me for making him leave L.A."

Rider scanned the lovely vista before them, inviting pathways through gently waving palm trees, stretching down to a pristine white beach.

"One man's paradise is another man's hell," he said softly.

He'd surprised her again. "And L.A. was this mother's hell," she said, her voice rather sharp. "Kyle was headed for serious trouble, and I was not going to let it happen."

His gaze snapped back to her. "He never came around? After he found out…?"

He paused, clearly uncomfortable. She'd been so focused on the stupid things she'd done, she'd forgotten Rider had met Kyle, however briefly, in the days he'd been with her after the crash. And that his concern had stretched to both of them. Perhaps if she'd been more aware of that, she would have seen that he'd merely been being kind, not sending an invitation to the widow.

And suddenly she knew she couldn't go on like this. If she were to get through the time he would be here, she couldn't handle the strain of either trying to dodge him or feeling this horrible knot in her stomach every time she saw him. Not on top of dealing with Kyle and keeping up with her students.

She bit her lip, not knowing how to say it, then finally just blurted it out. "Could we talk?"

His brows furrowed for a split second, in what she thought was a flinch. "Is that talk with a capital *T*?"

The woman she'd once been might have given up. Might have ignored the elephant in the kitchen, hoping it would magically vanish, as she had done with too much else. The woman she was trying to be would not.

"Let's just say—" she looked around at the people who

had exited the meeting and were now milling about, some glancing their way "—that I don't want to do it here."

"Paige, is this necessary?"

She hadn't really considered that this might be as distasteful to him as to her. He'd probably managed to forget all about that night, until he'd walked into that meeting and seen her, the painful reminder.

It would be better for both of them, she thought. She was sure of that. "It's necessary for me," she insisted.

He let out an audible breath. "All right. I've got meetings the rest of the day. What about dinner?"

She frowned; that sounded too much like a social occasion, and while this wasn't really business—except the unfinished, personal kind—she didn't feel comfortable with the implications of a formal dinner engagement.

"I'm sorry," he said stiffly when she didn't answer. "I should have realized you wouldn't want to do that. Later this evening then?"

"Fine," she said, wondering why he suddenly sounded so odd.

He appeared to be thinking for a moment. "The overlook?"

The deck built out over the steepest slope down to the beach would most likely be private enough. And convenient, she thought sourly, if she decided to jump off.

"Fine," she repeated. "You just got here, do you know where it is?"

"Theoretically, from the plans. I need to check it out in person, anyway."

He sounded more natural now, but still stiffer than before. Dreading this, she assumed. "It won't take long," she assured him. "Eight?"

"Fine." He echoed her acceptance.

"All right." She became suddenly aware that several of the people from the meeting were still lingering, and she realized they must be waiting for him. "I'd better go. People are waiting to speak to you, I think."

"Seems to be my lot in life today," he muttered.

She winced inwardly, but said nothing as she turned and hurried back toward her bungalow. After tonight it would truly be over. She would deliver her long-overdue apology, he would hopefully accept it when he understood she was as embarrassed as he, and they could both put that night behind them.

"I'm going with you."

"No," Paige said firmly. "You're not."

Kyle eyed her stubbornly from beneath the old, dirty baseball cap he still insisted on wearing backward despite the brilliant flood of sunlight here. The two earrings that pierced his left earlobe glinted, one gold, one silver and black. The second was a rather grim representation of a skull she hated but hadn't made an issue of, for fear it would make him determined to keep wearing it whether he really wanted to or not.

"Why not?"

"To start with, you weren't asked. Mr. Rider and I have things to talk about."

"You're going to talk about Dad, aren't you? So I want to go. He knew him. I want to ask him some things."

"We have school business to talk about." That much was true; she did want to give him at least a brief report on the school and the students' progress. "Besides, he didn't know your father well at all."

"How do you know?"

"Because he said so. Mr. Rider only met him briefly a couple of times."

"Then why did they send him, after he died?"

She'd wondered that on more than one occasion herself. Wondered what would have happened—or not happened— if they'd sent someone else.

"I don't know. Perhaps I'll ask him."

She gathered up the lightweight blue shawl to toss over her shoulders; the breeze had been picking up at night lately, and while it was hardly cold, it could be cool on bare arms. At the door she paused and looked back at her son.

"Don't forget you've got that history assignment, and the next chapter of *Beowulf* to read."

She thought he swore under his breath, but wasn't sure enough to call him on it. "Bad enough to have to go to school, but living with the teacher sucks."

"You've been living with a teacher all your life," she pointed out.

"Yeah, but you weren't *my* teacher."

She gave him a long, steady look. "I tried to be," she said. "About the things that really count, at least."

He turned and walked away, into his bedroom, without a word. He'd taken to doing that recently, walking away from any discussion he didn't want to have. She was going to have to call him on that soon, convince him that running away from the unpleasant didn't work. She was certainly living proof of that.

As she walked toward the lookout, she rehearsed in her mind yet again what she would say. There was no easy way to apologize for having so embarrassed them both, and having thought about how she would do it countless times hadn't helped.

How did you apologize for something like that? The man had been there as a representative of her husband's company, he'd been doing his job, nothing more. They'd been kind enough to send him to see if she was all right or needed anything they could provide. Her emotional state had been so very tangled and fragile, and she had clung to him. And he had let her, comforting her, giving her his strong arm to lean on and broad shoulder to cry on. He'd helped her through the ugly process, even made the arrangements to have Phil's remains shipped home on one of Redstone's own planes.

For nearly two weeks he'd been there to help. And then, one night after a nasty emotional outburst from the grieving Kyle, a night when she'd felt more alone than she ever had before, she'd leaned on his strength once more. He'd held her, soothed her…but when she'd looked up into his eyes she'd thought she'd seen something more, something warm and hungry.

She'd responded to that look, imagined or not, with a speed and urgency that had astounded her even as it was happening. The next thing she knew she was kissing him. Hotly, deeply, in a way that made her blush at the memory even now, five years later. And the fact that he kissed her back, the fact that after a few moments his strong hands had begun to caress her, to rouse in her startling sensations that made her shiver, didn't ameliorate her own responsibility for what had happened.

And what might have happened, had Kyle not just then slammed back into the house, fortunately through the kitchen door, giving them time to recover before he walked in on them. If she thought he was angry with her now, she could only imagine how he might have felt had he seen his mother kissing another man before his father's body was even home, let alone buried.

Of course, Kyle didn't know what she knew. At least she'd managed to keep that from him. It hadn't been an easy choice, but it was the only one she could make. Her son had already been in agony. She couldn't risk any further damage.

Rider was there, waiting for her. She stopped a distance away, looking at him silhouetted against the fading light. He was leaning forward, hands braced on the railing, staring out at the sea. The light breeze caught his shirt and swirled it. He'd changed into casual clothes, she saw. Khaki pants, it looked like, and a Hawaiian-style shirt in muted colors. Navy-blue and tan, the same shade as the khakis, she thought. And realized with a little jolt she'd never seen him, this man who had taken up permanent residence in her memory, in anything other than a suit. Until now.

He seemed to sense her presence and turned. She started up the last few steps and walked out onto the deck. Just say it and get it over with, she told herself. Just apologize. Just do it.

Instead, when she reached him she found herself asking inanely, "So, does it meet your standards?"

There was a second before he answered, and she wondered if she'd startled him, if he'd been expecting her to plunge right into the emotional depths. Since that had been her plan, she couldn't blame him; it wasn't his fault that she'd chickened out at the last second.

"It's solid. Well built, good materials."

She couldn't help the half laugh that escaped her. "Most people would be raving about the view."

He shrugged. "It takes advantage of it."

She sighed. "I suppose when you've seen views all over the world, it takes more to impress you."

He gave her a puzzled look. "You must have seen a place or two."

"Nope. Never been out of California, until now."

His puzzlement shifted to a frown. "But your husband traveled extensively."

"Yes. Alone." Maybe, she added bitterly to herself.

"You never went with him?"

"No. With Kyle so young, I preferred it that way." Not that he would have wanted me along, anyway.

"And now you've traveled halfway around the world."

"I had no choice."

He looked at her for a long, silent moment. "So you gave up your life to move your son. That's quite a sacrifice."

Her eyes widened. "Not many would see coming here as a sacrifice."

"Sacrifice is in the reasons not the setting," he said.

She considered what he said. "That's rather profound."

He only shrugged. For a moment the only sound was the rustle of the palm fronds and the more distant sound of the surf from below. It was time, she told herself. Time to get it done. She opened her mouth to speak, to at last say she was sorry.

"Okay, let's get it over with," he said, before she'd gotten a word out. "I'm sorry. It should never have happened."

She gaped at him as he spoke the words she'd opened her own mouth to say.

"What?" she finally managed.

"I'm apologizing, all right?" He nearly snapped it out. "It's been eating at me for five years, so I'm apologizing. I took advantage. I'm a jerk and a slime and an idiot, and all the rotten things you've probably been calling me all this time."

She stared at him. "That," she barely managed to squeak out, "is what I've been calling *myself* for the past five years."

# Chapter 3

$P$aige felt utterly bewildered. But there could be no doubt—he'd said it so adamantly. The man she'd wanted to apologize to for so long was instead apologizing to her.

She heard an odd little chiming sound.

"Damn," he muttered under his breath. "Excuse me," he said to her; she wasn't sure if it was for the curse or the interruption. He reached into a shirt pocket that had looked empty and pulled out the smallest cell phone she'd ever seen. He pushed a button and said sharply, "Rider."

He listened for a moment, his mouth tightening. Finally he advised the caller he would be down in a few minutes, and disconnected. He slipped the tiny phone back into the upper pocket.

"Bad news?" she asked.

"Minor problem. I'll deal with it after...we're finished here."

That brought her back sharply to the realization that had so startled her. "Noah, I can't believe you're apologizing to me after what I did! I'm the one who jumped all over you, when all you were trying to do was be helpful.''

"Helpful?" Both dark brows shot up. "Is that what you thought?"

"I know you were just trying to comfort me, and then I—"

"I knew you were vulnerable, I knew you were confused, and I let it happen, anyway." He grimaced but went on flatly. "It was my fault. I was supposed to take care of you, not…" His voice trailed off as he shook his head in obvious disgust.

"But I started it," she protested.

"You weren't thinking straight. Under the circumstances you can hardly be blamed."

"But you can?" she asked, steadier now.

"I hadn't just been through an emotional meat grinder. Yes, I can be blamed all right."

Paige felt as if her world had tilted slightly on its axis. She'd worked up to this, had planned it for the day she might see him again, had even considered making it happen, even if she had to call Redstone and make an appointment. Only to find now that he had felt the same way. And suddenly she realized the reason he'd looked so odd when he'd suggested dinner and she'd reacted negatively—when he'd said he should have known she wouldn't want to do that, he'd been thinking she wouldn't want to have dinner with a man who had, in his view, treated her so badly.

If you only knew, she thought. On her scale of being treated badly, that kiss didn't even make the top million.

"You're right about one thing, though," he said after a moment. "This should have been done long ago. I owed you that much."

"I owed you a lot more. I don't think I'd have gotten through that time if you hadn't been there."

His mouth twisted. "Nice to know I didn't completely fall down on the job."

That reminded her. "Tell me something, will you? Why did they send you back then? Why not somebody from, I don't know, personnel, maybe?"

He shrugged. "I'd just been in Portugal a few weeks before. I knew some people, people I could call if there were any problems with...arrangements. But there weren't, really. They were as horrified as the rest of the world, more so since the plane had gone down in their country. They went out of their way to help."

As simple as that. As simply as that a practical choice was made, and her life was changed forever.

Paige drew in a deep breath of the night air, savored the scent of the night-blooming flowers that had been carefully planted around the grounds. Some sweet, some spicy, it was the kind of perfume that would never be matched by the hand of man in a laboratory.

Somehow the knowledge that he had felt nearly as bad as she enabled her to finish what she'd come here to do.

"If we're going to work together while you're here, we have to put this behind us," she began. "We can't both go on feeling guilty about it."

"Wanna bet?"

The words were negative, but his tone was much lighter, and Paige nearly smiled. "Can we forget about it and go on?"

"Forget that I took advantage of you?"

"You didn't, but I'll allow you that if you accept I was the initiator and a willing participant."

He closed his eyes, as if her words had caused him pain. After a moment he opened them again. "I suppose it's going to be impossible to do what we have to do here if we can't get past it."

"It will be for me," she admitted.

"So we both made mistakes, now we go on?"

"Right."

He turned to look back out over the calm, warm sea. She heard him take a couple of deep breaths.

"All right. We start over," he said finally.

"Hello, Noah Rider. I'm Paige Cooper," she answered.

He turned back to her then. An odd expression was on his face, and an odder half smile curved his mouth. That mouth she'd spent five years trying to forget.

"Hello, Paige Cooper," he said. "Nice to meet you."


Rider walked down the long hallway to the administrative offices of the hotel. He'd kept Barry waiting longer than he'd wanted to, but he'd had to finish with Paige.

*Finish with Paige.*

That was something he'd been hoping for for five years now. To conclude what had felt like unfinished business. Or at the least, unatoned-for business. So why didn't he feel relieved, now that the air had been cleared, apologies—however unexpected hers had been—made, and an agreement reached that they would forget and move on?

Forget. Right. Not likely. He had thought it would be over now. That after he'd apologized to her, she would have forgiven him, and they could have gone on, comfortable in the knowledge that they would rarely, if ever, see each other again once he left here. It should have been easy.

But it wasn't. Not a damned thing had changed. Except now she was right here, within reach.

So now what? He was supposed to just smile and walk around cheerfully as if it had never happened? Pretend he'd never met her before this day, that she hadn't been a warm, taunting image in the back of his mind since even before the night he'd made himself walk away from her?

His cell phone rang again.

"Rider."

"Sir?" The voice was tentative. "This is Miranda Mayfield, in tech services? I know it's after hours, but you did say to let you know when the test data on the standby generators was finished.''

"Relax, Miranda. There's no such thing as after hours for me while I'm here. Drop it off in my temporary office, will you? Then go home.''

"Thanks, Mr. Rider.''

He slipped the phone back in his pocket just as he reached Barry Rutherford's office. The door was open, and the man was still at his desk. Out of courtesy Rider tapped on the doorjamb rather than just striding in. He might outrank the man in the general scheme of things, but Redstone Bay was Rutherford's bailiwick, and would be long after Rider was gone.

"So what's that bad news?''

"I just hung up with Bohio's family,'' Barry said. "What I'd feared is true. He's not coming back.''

"Because?''

"Sadly, that emergency he left for was the death of his brother.''

Rider frowned. "Did you tell him we'd hold the job for him, as long as he needed?''

"I'm afraid I wasn't able to speak to him directly. He's no longer there.''

Rider studied the older man's face for a moment. "Do I need to sit down for this?''

"As you wish. It's not pretty, but not unusual of late. Bohio's brother was in the army. He was killed in a skirmish with the rebel forces on Arethusa. Bohio has decided he must help the army hunt down those responsible.''

Rider's mouth twisted. In all his travels he'd more than once been close to a restless part of the world. He hadn't liked it then and he didn't now. He dealt with it when he had to, but that didn't mean he enjoyed it.

"And he's already gone?'' he asked.

Barry nodded.

So, no chance to try to talk him out of it. Not that he

could have, but it would have been nice to try. But he could understand—intellectually, anyway, because he'd never had to face such a decision himself—that Bohio had felt he had to do this.

"See if the family needs anything," he told Barry.

"I will. As for his job, we'll need somebody fairly soon to replace him."

Rider gave the man a wry smile. "You're a master of understatement, Barry. I'm sure Redstone has someone they could send out temporarily. But first, are there any possibilities already here?"

Barry frowned. "You mean, someone who could take over? No one with his training and credentials."

"What about any bright lights? Somebody who's shown some knowledge or initiative?"

Barry thought for a moment. He opened his mouth as if to speak, then shut it again.

"What?" Rider asked.

The man shook his head. "No, he's too young."

"Who?"

"Elan Kiskeya. A local. He's been helping Bohio, so he knows the systems, and he's got a knack for mechanical things, but…"

"Does he have the drive?"

"He's always asking for more to do, but he's only twenty-four."

"I was twenty-six when Josh Redstone gave me a shot at your position on the San Juan Islands project," Rider said. "I'd never done anything that big before. I worked harder than I ever had in my life, to prove I could do it."

It had also been nerve-racking as hell, San Juan being Redstone's first resort venture. But now it was a cornerstone of the resort end of the business, and Rider knew it was why he was where he was today.

"He would have to learn a great deal very quickly," Barry warned.

"Is there a good staff in place? I haven't gotten to that part of the report yet."

Barry nodded. "Very good. Bohio picked good people. Including Kiskeya. Do you wish to talk to him?"

"Let's bring him in tomorrow so we can discuss it. But it's going to affect you the most, since you may have to help him along, so the final decision is yours. If you don't think he can cut it, we'll send for help."

Barry looked a bit relieved. "All right."

Rider smiled. "Steamrollering people from the top isn't the Redstone style."

The man chuckled. "Did I look that worried?"

"Just a little."

"I'll have Kiskeya come in first thing in the morning, if that works for you?"

"Sooner the better. He's going to need all the time he can get. And let's hope we don't lose anybody else."

On his way back to the small suite set aside for visiting Redstone personnel, Rider's thoughts played back those moments in the dining room meeting when he'd seen Paige, doubted his own eyes, then seen her name undeniably written before him. But it still hadn't quite sunk in until he'd caught up with her outside. But there, with her hair a fiery beacon in the setting tropical sun, he was sure. She looked just as he remembered so vividly. She'd been standing with her arms drawn in tightly, as if she'd been as shaken as he by the unexpected encounter. And when she'd begun to chatter about the improvements to the schoolhouse, as if desperate for any diversion, he'd been sure of it. She was as rattled as he was.

He should be fine now, he argued to himself as he closed the suite door behind him. They'd talked it out, it was over, time to move on. He still felt utterly responsible for what had happened that night—he supposed there were worse things than kissing and pawing a distraught widow, though it was surely one of the worst things he'd ever done—but was at least relieved to know that she didn't hate him or blame him.

He pulled off his shirt and tossed it over the back of a chair. He should be exhausted; his day had become a marathon. But instead he felt strangely wired. He kicked off his shoes, then looked at the stocked minibar consideringly. He was more inclined to put on his running shoes and go out for a late-night jog. But he decided against it; his memory for plans and layouts was good, and there was nearly a full moon, but he'd only physically been here once before, and inadvertently running off a cliff wasn't his idea of a good way to end a day that had already been trying enough.

He resorted to pouring a small amount of Amaretto into a glass, then wandered out onto the lanai. From here he could just see the overlook, where he and Paige had stood. He sat down on the edge of one of the chaises, then gave in to the lure, swung his legs up and leaned back. He had a lot to do in the next few days, but for now, just for now…

He woke up in the same place the next morning feeling more rested than he had in days. He wondered if it was the balmy outdoor air, the Amaretto or the simple fact that a large load had been removed from his conscience.

This island, Paige thought as she walked along the immaculate beach, watching the lap of tiny waves on the sand and the break of larger swells far beyond on the reef, had never seemed so small before. You'd think in nearly a thousand acres—and when you spent half your day in a single room with twenty-six kids—you wouldn't run into one person quite so often. But she seemed to have run into Noah Rider quite a bit in the past two days. True, it was a weekend, and once she'd graded some essays and corrected some math papers she'd had the rest of Saturday and now all of Sunday free to wander, but she'd never seen any one person as often and in as many places as she'd seen him.

So maybe it was just that he was everywhere. Anywhere there was a problem he showed up. And from what she'd heard from other staff, he managed it without stepping on any toes or coming off as the big cheese so many had expected.

Paige wasn't surprised at that. Not after the gentle, kind way he'd dealt with her in her time of need. Tact was something he clearly had in abundance. She supposed it was a requirement to reach the level he had.

And she had to admit that the times she had seen him hadn't been difficult, if you didn't count her own silly anticipation anxiety. He was acting just as she would have wished, treating her just like everyone else.

And if she didn't completely like that, it was her problem. She could not—*would* not—make it his, too.

She glimpsed some activity down the beach, a gathering of people and a small boat in the water. She headed that way, curious. She knew at this late date, so close to the scheduled opening, there was no such thing as a weekend off, so whatever it was had to be related to the resort. She was still about fifty feet away when she heard the sound of a motor, and the people gathered began to back away from the boat. She saw a flash of bright colors, red, blue and yellow, and it was a moment before she realized what it was.

And then it became obvious as the colors billowed up into an arc of fabric that then soared into the air. Parasailing, she thought, and in that instant the passenger, attached by lines that seemed too insubstantial to her unpracticed eye, soared upward.

It was Noah.

She stared, certain she must have seen wrong, but she knew deep down she hadn't. She couldn't mistake his size, his solid build, and the economy of movement that had been one of the first things she'd ever noticed about him.

But why on earth? Surely this wasn't required of him.

Did he really carry his oversight so far as to risk his neck trying out the recreational offerings? He had to be hundreds of feet up by now.

Although she had to admit, as she came up to the group of spectators, it did look exciting. Very. It looked, in fact, awfully close to flying, and she wondered if it felt like that, too.

She noticed Miranda among the watchers, and the woman smiled and walked over to her.

"My boy can't wait to try that."

Paige grimaced. "I'm sure Kyle will want to do it, too. In fact, I'm surprised he's not here."

"I saw him earlier, talking to Lani over by the pool."

Paige smiled. "Well, that should keep him happy for a while."

She knew Kyle was taken with the exotically lovely island girl whose family had lived here for generations. Her mother had died at Lani DeSouza's birth, but her father had been there for her all her life, and Paige knew the girl loved him dearly. That father had also been the local population's representative at the time Redstone had bought the island a decade ago. He had been a persuasive voice then, and, she'd heard, a shrewd bargainer. And a wise one. The people all agreed, because so far Joshua Redstone had kept every promise he'd made, including a school that would accept every child on the island.

And Lani was as clever as her father. She was a pleasure to have in class, absorbing every bit of knowledge Paige provided her with an eagerness that made Paige regret the years she'd been away from teaching, although she knew students like Lani were rare. She was secretly delighted that Kyle was interested in the bright, sweet-natured girl. Of course he was far too young to be serious, but Lani couldn't help but be a good influence on him. She hoped he would follow the girl's lead; Lani could hardly wait until this summer, when she hoped to work as one of the many personal assistants, or PAs that Redstone hired to help all their guests with any and everything, from scuba diving the reef to nature hikes to finding a book in the small but well-stocked library.

"Now there's a man," Miranda said as the boat maneu-vered to bring its airborne passenger back to the beach, "to keep a woman happy."

Paige nearly blushed, then silently called herself an id-iot—from now on he worked for the same company she did, that's all, she told herself.

"Mr. Rider?" she asked, trying for an innocent tone.

"I sure didn't mean ol' Rudy," Miranda said with a grin, nodding toward the round, bald, very tanned head of the executive chef.

Paige giggled in spite of herself. "I don't know. He's kind of cute, in a grandfatherly sort of way."

"Well, he does make a mean fricassee, I'll give him that," Miranda said.

Paige knew Rudy Aubert had been at a large five-star hotel for years, but had jumped at the chance to oversee this smaller but no less exclusive operation. And, judging by his tan, he was soaking up island life in a big hurry.

Unlike herself, she thought, always checking that she wasn't inadvertently exposing unscreened skin to the sun that was so deadly for her fair complexion. On this lovely day she wore leggings and a long-sleeved, gauzy blouse. Even then she'd had to put sunscreen on, knowing she could burn through the fabric if she spent too much time— for her that meant anything over half an hour—out in the sun.

"So, how long have you known him?"

Paige blinked. "Mr. Rider?" Miranda gave her a look that reminded her of the way she sometimes looked at Kyle when he didn't—or refused to—see the obvious.

"Oh." She glanced over to where Rider was now safely ashore and getting out of the harness. He was grinning widely and then he laughed, clearly exhilarated. She turned back to Miranda and said carefully, "What makes you think I've ever met him before he got here?"

The look was even worse this time. "Oh, maybe because he about swallowed his tie when he spotted you in the staff meeting. And you couldn't wait to get out of there."

She considered lying, but it seemed pointless, and she didn't want to lie to this woman who was becoming a friend. There had been more than enough lies in her life.

"I knew him from…a bad time in my life. Redstone sent him to help when my husband was killed."

Instantly contrite, Miranda put her hand on Paige's arm. "Oh, honey, I'm sorry. I didn't mean to pry."

"It's all right. It was a long time ago. And it was only that I didn't expect to ever see him again. I was…startled, that's all."

Miranda patted her arm comfortingly. "Still, I'm sorry. But, my, he'd be enough to wake up any breathing woman. So tell me, why does he only go by Rider?"

"I don't know. Maybe he just doesn't like Noah."

She liked the name, and that's how she thought of him, but now she wondered why she persisted, when he'd asked everyone else to call him Rider. Maybe because he hadn't asked *her* to call him that. And her mind skittered away from figuring out the motivation behind that particular choice.

As if satisfied that Paige wasn't really a source of details on the man in question, Miranda gave up on the subject. They chatted for a couple of minutes about how her two children were doing in class, and then the woman excused herself to go find said kids and stop them from whatever trouble she knew they were up to.

Paige watched her go, feeling oddly wistful. Once she'd said similar things, said them in that same light teasing tone, knowing it was just that, teasing, and that there was little chance her sweet boy would really be in any kind of trouble.

Now there was every chance, every day, and what she'd thought would help—extricating him from the environment that had had him skating on the edge of real problems—only seemed to have made it worse. He was angrier than ever, and it showed no signs of abating. Most days she could barely get a civil word out of him.

"Paige?"

Her breath caught at the unexpected sound of his voice so close behind her. She took a half second to steady herself before she turned around. He was wearing jeans and a blue T-shirt with the Redstone logo, and she was startled at how the casual clothes suited him even better than the executive look. He looked windblown and exhilarated, his blue eyes brighter than ever.

"Have fun?" she asked.

He grinned. "It was great. Want to try?"

She glanced toward the water again, saw that somebody else was taking a turn now. The urge was there, but so was a little tingle of fear. She looked back at Rider. "I don't know," she began.

"I saw you watching. You looked like you were wondering how it felt."

"You saw me from up there?" she said, not quite believing him.

He reached out, touched her hair with his fingertips. "You stand out."

In an instant the air between them seemed charged. She held her breath, afraid to move. He drew his hand back, looking at it in surprise, as if he hadn't even realized what he was doing. He curled his fingers to his palm, and shoved on the sunglasses he'd been holding in his other hand.

"Come on," he said. "Catch a ride before they wrap it up for the day."

She looked at the current flyer, who suddenly looked

much higher than before. She wanted to try it, but a bit of shiver down her spine stopped her from immediately jumping at the chance. "I'm not sure," she said.

"You'll love it. I promise."

"And if I don't?"

"Dinner. On me. Rudy has a new dish he wants to add to the menu."

Dinner again, she thought. As neatly as that he'd put her in a corner. If she said no, he'd think she hadn't forgiven him, that she wasn't sticking to their agreement to put it behind them. And if she said yes...

If she said yes, she could end up marooned at a table with him, truly testing the strength of her resolve to not think about what had happened between them anymore.

So, you'd better love this little adventure then, she thought. "All right," she said.

As she walked beside him down the beach, Paige had the strange but persistent feeling she'd done more than just say yes to a physical flight of fancy.

# Chapter 4

Noah didn't help as the operator got her into the harness, and Paige wondered if he was avoiding touching her again. He seemed to have gotten over his tense reaction. He was cheerfully encouraging her, treating her like anyone else here.

"Tomorrow we'll hook up the tandem rig," the man was telling Noah.

"Fine," Noah said, "but right now you've got one of our most valued people."

The man took the hint and concentrated on her rigging.

"Pay attention here now," Noah said with mock sternness as the man began to give her safety instructions. "I doubt very much that doing a nosedive, or drowning because you can't get out from under yards of wet fabric is in your plans for the day."

She wrinkled her nose at him. "Charming. Are you trying to make sure I don't enjoy this?"

He grinned. "Don't put it past me. Maybe I really want

that dinner. In fact, if I'm right and you do love it, you can buy. Employees' rate, of course.''

''Gee, thanks.''

And then it was time. The man signaled the driver of the boat, and the engine changed pitch. For an instant she wanted to yell at them to stop, she'd changed her mind, but it was too late. She was committed now.

She thought it would take more time or speed, but before she even realized it, she was on her way, her feet lifting off the back of the boat. Lifting so easily it stunned her. It *was* like flying, she thought, finally remembering to breathe. Or at least close to flying. The sensation without the work. But tethered to the boat below—frighteningly far below—it was also without the control.

But the sensation was amazing, the wind of their passage whipping at her braid, the literal bird's-eye view of the resort and this side of the island. She hadn't realized the coast curved so much, she thought as she looked down through her dangling feet. She could see the variations in color in the water from here, how it changed from green to aqua to deeper blue in undulating lines. And Redstone Bay Resort itself, looking as if it had always been here, subtle, blending with the landscape.

By the change in her view she realized the boat was heading back toward the beach. She could see the group of people, all staring up at her. She thought of what Noah had said, that he'd seen her from up here, and began to look for him.

It took her only a moment. Even though he wasn't the only one in a Redstone T-shirt, he stood out to her immediately. Something about the way he held himself, or the way he was watching her so intently and not chatting with those around him. Rather inanely she thought of waving, then realized she wasn't about to let go of her grip on the lines.

Even from up here, she realized rather glumly, he fascinated her. Phil had been a high-powered businessman, but for a much smaller company. In essence Noah held a much higher position, and yet he was so much more at ease with it and with himself. He didn't seem driven, just good. Nor was he arrogant, as Phil had been with people under him. Noah treated them with respect, making it clear their contributions were valued.

And for a few days, during a ghastly time of her life, he'd made her feel valued. He'd made her feel as if she were someone who deserved to be taken care of, as if there were truly people who cared about her and wanted to help her get through this. He'd been there for Redstone, but he'd made it personal, believable.

Her mind wanted to swerve down that old track, drag up again the memory of how she'd repaid him for that, but she quashed it. She felt too wonderful to tread that old road again. They'd made a pact, and she'd keep her word. Maybe she would even pay off on that bet.

This was wonderful, she thought. Indeed exhilarating. She couldn't think of anything she'd done that was more exciting than this.

Except maybe kiss Noah Rider.

She was not having much luck keeping her promise to put that behind her, she thought wryly. But at least she could make sure he didn't know that.

She felt the change as the boat began to slow. She was sorry it was over, but that passed as she concentrated on what the man had told her about landing. As it turned out, she drifted down easily, slowly enough that she could even enjoy it. She ended up a bit off target from where they'd told her she'd land, but Noah was there, waiting. And when she hit, barely hard enough to stagger her, he was there to steady her, to keep her clear of the chaos of lines and sail.

Just as he had five years ago, he kept her balanced and safe.

She drew in a deep breath, knowing she was grinning like a kid.

"How was it?" he asked.

"Looks like I'm buying dinner," she said.

Rider ran a hand through his hair wearily. It wasn't that anything was really going wrong. In fact, the most important things were progressing right on schedule. It was the little things that were not quite coming together and driving him nuts.

The best thing he could say was that it wasn't because of any of the Redstone people: it was people on the outside who were falling down on the job. The man who was supposed to have run the final test on the air-conditioning system had been delayed. And two important shipments of extra bedsheets—Redstone Resorts always triple sheeted the beds, so no blanket ever touched a guest's skin—and the last of the gym equipment were held up in Arethusa, something about a bomb scare. He made a note to put that in his next report to Redstone. If the unrest kept escalating, they might have to make other arrangements.

He glanced at his watch as he'd been doing all afternoon. Still plenty of time before dinner. His mouth twisted wryly; he was acting like a teenager with a hot date. But he couldn't deny he was eager—and apprehensive—about dinner with Paige tonight. They'd kept it light, under the guise of a bet being paid off, but he knew she could have gotten out of it if she'd wanted to, since she'd never actually agreed to that part of it.

But she hadn't. And he wasn't sure why. Was she only trying to show him she was keeping to their agreement? Or did she want to—

"Mr. Rider?"

He glanced up to find Elan Kiskeya, the young man they'd decided to give a shot at replacing Bohio, in his doorway.

"Come on in," he said, glad enough of the interruption.

"I won't keep you," the young man said. "I just wanted to tell you the elevator system is ready for you to check."

"Already?" Rider asked, surprised.

"Yes, sir." Kiskeya's voice was full of pride. And rightfully so, Rider thought.

"Good job, Elan. I figured we were a couple of days away on that."

"Thank you. And thank you again for taking a chance on me."

"No...thank you," Rider answered. "You're making me look good. I'll be sure they hear about you at Redstone."

"Thank you. I already enjoy working for them."

He liked it when a gamble paid off, Rider thought as the young man hastened away, off to work even harder, he guessed. When Josh had first given him the power to make field promotions, he'd been wary; personnel wasn't his field. But he'd been right more than he'd been wrong, and that was all Josh asked.

In a way, Rider thought, he was in a unique position to understand the vast scope of Josh's vision. He'd come directly from an earthquake-ravaged part of the Middle East, where Redstone was helping finance a massive rebuilding effort, to this place catering to the movers and shakers. He found it to be an education in itself. And after nearly fifteen years Rider was as impressed as he had been in the beginning.

He decided abruptly that three hours in this office dealing with paperwork and details was enough for today, and got to his feet. He needed to check the generator tests, and then he'd stop by and sign off on Kiskeya's work. By then Barry would be waiting—and probably fussing—to start the final check on the rooms in the north building, and after that he'd head back. He'd already told Rudy to fire up the grill for his special meal.

By the time he finished, including some reinforcement

of his appreciation for Kiskeya's good job, he was running late. He took the shortcut back to the main building where his room was, cutting through the garden.

He froze in front of a hibiscus bush when some leaves rustled off to his left. A much more definite rustle than just the current slight breeze. In a burst of idiocy his brain ran through the list of creatures native to the island—iguanas, the odd but harmless mastiff bat, tiger beetles—even though he already knew none of them were particularly threatening to humans.

He held his breath and listened with a hunter's ears. The old, long-unused skills came back surprisingly well. Something large, and tall, the sounds were coming from at least a couple of feet above the ground. Only one thing fitted that description on the island. And then the breeze shifted slightly, he caught the smell of cigarette smoke, and he knew he was right.

He turned and took a careful step, then another, moving silently, in the old stalking way, past the hibiscus and into the tropical grass that was the flowering bush's backdrop. There he found his quarry; a boy crouched hiding in the thicket of tall grasses, smoking a cigarette.

Or trying to; the face he was making and the sudden burst of smothered coughing told Rider he hadn't been at it long.

"Get rid of the butt of that cancer stick somewhere else," he said.

The boy let out a strangled yelp and scrambled to his feet. His baseball cap fell backward off his head. The sunglasses he wore slipped to the end of his nose. The cigarette dropped onto his shirt, and he swatted it wildly. It hit the ground, glowing orange. The boy instinctively moved his foot to crush it out, but stopped abruptly, apparently remembering shoes hadn't been in his wardrobe today.

Rider stepped on the cigarette, but didn't grind it. He picked it up, and handed it back to the boy.

"Tell me you didn't get that here."

"Huh?"

Rider tried again. "Where'd you get the cigarette?"

"Oh. I brought it from home."

"Good."

"Huh?"

"I didn't want to have to fire somebody."

The boy looked blank. "Fire somebody?"

"For selling them to an underage kid."

The boy stiffened. "I'm not a kid."

"Prove it. Be smart enough not to smoke."

"Yeah, yeah," the boy muttered in the tone of one who'd heard it all before. As perhaps he had. Then he gave Rider a sideways look. "You're Rider, aren't you? The big kahuna around here?"

"I'm Rider, at least," he agreed.

"I remember you."

Rider blinked. He hadn't met any of the children on the island yet, so how could—

It hit him then. "You're Kyle?"

The boy nodded. "I remember when you were there. When my dad died."

He said it levelly enough, but Rider could hear the lingering pain behind the words.

"That was a tough time."

"My mom said you made sure he got brought home."

"I did what I could."

The boy stood up straighter. "Thanks," he said, and held out his hand. Startled, Rider took it. While the boy's grip was firm, his palm was sweaty. But the gesture was very adult, and Rider treated it that way.

"You're welcome, Kyle. I wish I could have done more."

And in the next instant the boy was back. He plucked a leaf from the hibiscus, and nervously started to fold it into a tiny square. "You going to tell my mom? About me smoking?"

He had been only ten when his father had died, and when Rider had first seen him he'd been dazed by what had happened, not quite comprehending yet that death truly did mean forever. He'd changed a lot, of course, since then, but Rider could still see traces of the child in the teenager, although the sullen set of the mouth was new, as was the half-shaved head with the thick mop of slightly maroon hair above it, and the earrings piercing his left lobe.

"Well? You gonna tell her?"

"I'm not sure." He drew in a breath; the smell of smoke was fading now. "How much will it hurt her?"

The boy flinched but recovered quickly. "Probably none. She doesn't care what I do."

"Oh?" If there was one thing about Paige he was certain of, it was that this boy was her life.

"She doesn't care about me at all. If she did, she wouldn't have dragged me here, away from my friends."

"So why did she?"

"She *says* it was to keep me out of trouble. But I wasn't really in trouble, she just doesn't understand. She never does."

"At least she cared. Maybe you should be glad of that."

"Yeah, sure," the boy said sarcastically. "Look, she doesn't like my friends, doesn't like what I like to do, doesn't like my video games. She doesn't like anything!"

She liked flying, Rider thought, picturing her face this morning and the huge smile she'd given him when she'd landed.

"And now she's my teacher, too, and it really sucks."

"I can understand how that would be tough," Rider said neutrally.

"She just wants me to work and study all the time." Kyle added a four-letter word that succinctly pronounced his opinion of that.

"You know, swearing doesn't make you an adult any more than smoking does."

"Oh, yeah, and I guess you never swear?"

"Me? Oh, sure I do, when provoked. In fact, I can say what you just said in about nine different languages."

"Nine languages?" Kyle looked intrigued. Then he frowned. "So why are you on my case?"

"Swearing is best saved to make a point. If you use it all the time, it becomes meaningless."

"Huh?"

Rider smothered a sigh; he'd never realized talking to teenagers was so much work. "Look, if you wanted to…say, scare somebody with a firecracker. You set one off and they jump. You set off a whole string, they jump at the first one, but by the end of the string they're used to it and it doesn't scare them anymore."

"Oh."

Kyle said nothing more, but at least he looked thoughtful. Rider glanced at his watch and winced. He wondered if the boy knew he was going to be having dinner with his mother in less than ten minutes. He started walking again, and to his surprise the boy followed.

"Have you seen your mother this afternoon?" he asked.

"Nah. I try to avoid her." Kyle grimaced. "She's probably hunting for me for dinner by now, though. If I don't go back she'll be really snarly."

"Actually, maybe not," Rider told him. "She and I are having dinner at the restaurant in just a few minutes. Chef Aubert is using us as guinea pigs for something new."

The boy looked startled, then shrugged. "Rudy's cool. He's been just about everywhere in the world."

"I know. I ate at his restaurant in London, and then in Rome. After that I went on a campaign to get him for Redstone."

"You've been to London? And Rome?"

Rider nodded. "And just about every place in between."

"Wow." The boy was genuinely impressed now. "My dad used to travel a lot."

"I know." He said it carefully, not wanting to open up a subject he had no desire to get into.

"Once he brought me back something, too. A model of the Eiffel Tower, from Paris."

Odd, Rider thought. The boy spoke as if he'd had the perfect father, with nothing but love and sadness at his loss in his young voice. As if it didn't matter why his father had been on that plane when he died.

And you'd think a traveling father would bring something back for his only son more than once.

On impulse he said, "You're welcome to join us for dinner, if you want. You have to eat, anyway, and Rudy always has some good stories to tell when he's got a captive audience."

The boy hesitated, and suddenly Rider was anxious for him to come. "Of course, it'll be kind of adult discussion, so if you'll be bored…"

"I won't," Kyle said instantly, as Rider had thought he might.

And so he had company when he walked into what would be the main restaurant at the resort. Rudy had only been expecting the two of them, but a single extra body, even with a teenage boy's appetite, was but a minor obstacle for someone with Rudy's experience.

Paige was already seated at the table when they arrived. She was toying with her silverware, as if too nervous to simply sit still. Rider noticed she had a stack of folders on the seat beside her. They looked like the same ones she'd had at the meeting the day he'd arrived.

"I invited a friend," he said as they got to the table. She looked up quickly, apparently so intent on the fork that she hadn't realized they were there. "Hope you don't mind."

"No, of course not…"

Her voice trailed away and her eyes widened when she saw her son beside him. "Kyle?"

"He invited me," he said almost angrily, his chin jutting out slightly.

Rider wondered if Kyle remembered that they hadn't really settled the question of whether he would tell Paige he'd caught her son sneaking a smoke. If he did, it didn't show in his attitude, and Rider suddenly wondered why on earth he'd done this, invited the kid. He was clearly furious with his mother, and Rider doubted he himself would be able to stay out of it if Kyle continued to talk to her in that tone.

"Then sit down," was all Paige said.

Kyle did, glancing at the folders on the chair. He rolled his eyes. "You even brought school stuff here?"

To Rider's surprise, Paige blushed. "I thought Mr. Rider might want to see how things are going."

Rider was puzzled as he took a seat across from her, and then it struck him. The school papers were protection, so she could make this seem like a business dinner, not a personal one. He felt oddly disappointed by the realization.

It wasn't until Rudy arrived and muttered something in his ear about bringing your own buffer, that he realized he'd done the same thing. Inviting Kyle hadn't been for the boy's sake, it had been for his. Nothing could get too personal with Paige's fifteen-year-old son at the table with them.

He almost laughed aloud at the absurdity of it, both of them so busy protecting themselves from the possibilities.

He wondered if that meant she was as tempted by them as he was.

Paige got over her nervousness rather quickly, if only because she was wondering who this kid was sitting at the table. The sullen, snippy teenager she'd almost grown used to was nowhere in sight. This Kyle wasn't the outgoing, friendly boy he'd once been, but he was considerably more civil and sociable than he'd been with her for longer than she cared to remember.

He seemed more than willing to talk to Noah, and listened to what he said with every appearance of rapt interest. When their food came, he even ate like a normal person, instead of shoveling it in as fast as he could in order to escape. And when Rudy sat down for a few minutes, to get their reviews of his experiment—fresh mahi grilled with his personal choice of spices that had given it a wild combination of flavors that somehow worked—Kyle was downright friendly to him, as well.

Paige was aware she wasn't sharing in the conversation very much, but it had been so long since she'd seen her son act like a human being she didn't want to waste it. Even though she realized that to Noah he probably seemed like a normal, even likable kid.

Eventually Kyle asked Noah what time it was, and when he said nearly eight, the boy stood up.

"I gotta go. Thanks, Mr. Rider."

More courtesy than I get, Paige thought. She was curious about where he was going, but knew if she asked she would only get that pained look he did so well, accusing her of treating him like a child.

"Be home by ten. School tomorrow."

He glared at her. "This isn't—" He stopped himself, as if aware that what he was going to say—This isn't my home—might insult his new friend. "Later," he muttered, and left.

Paige smothered a sigh.

"How long has the attitude been going on?"

Paige looked at him in surprise. "I thought he was perfectly nice to you."

"He was. It was you he was treating like a pariah. When he bothered to acknowledge you exist at all."

She was surprised again—this time that he'd noticed and had bothered to mention it.

She tried to shrug as if it didn't matter. It did. And she knew there would come a time when she was going to have to start demanding respect from Kyle. But tonight had made it clear that that time was here and now. She didn't like being humiliated ever, but in front of this man it was unbearable.

"He's still hurting," she said. "I know it's been five years, but they're very tough years for a boy."

For a long moment the silence spun out. Noah seemed about to speak twice, but stopped. Then finally, slowly, words began to come.

"After my mom was killed in a car accident when I was Kyle's age, my dad came down on me hard. He was tough on my sister, Michelle, too, but he really caged me. Stopped me from doing everything except going to school."

Paige frowned. "That must have been hard."

"It was. We'd always been close, hunting, fishing together, that kind of thing, so it hurt."

"He even stopped that? Why?"

"For a long time, I didn't know. I heard people tell him he should cut me some slack, I'd just lost my mother. He ignored them."

That one hit close to home; she'd been giving Kyle slack for five years, and look where it had gotten her.

"Finally one day, when I wanted to get my driver's license and he wouldn't let me, we had a huge fight. I yelled at him, he yelled back at me, it escalated, and I...put my fist through a wall." He flexed his right hand as if at the memory.

"And is that when you found out?"

He let out a compressed breath, as if for that moment he truly had been back in that painful time.

"Yeah. He finally said something that made sense out of it. I realized he was scared to death of losing me, too, and the only way he could think of to keep that from happening was to keep me where he could look out for me.

Michelle was less trouble, she was younger and still home most of the time, anyway. But he wanted me in sight all the time. If I wasn't, he got scared.''

Paige felt the sting of moisture in her eyes. ''I know the feeling,'' she said, her voice tight. ''I wanted to do the same thing with Kyle.''

''I guess my point is…once I understood that, I didn't mind so much. In a way it was my dad showing me how much he loved me.''

If she'd needed any encouragement to do what she'd been putting off, it had just been given to her. ''Thank you,'' she said. ''That helps me…know what to do.''

Noah shrugged then, leaning back, looking at his glass, his empty plate, anywhere but at her face, as if he was now sorry he'd opened up quite that much.

''Did you and your dad make up?'' she asked.

He nodded. ''We're fine now. I get back to see him two or three times a year.'' Given his traveling schedule, Paige guessed that was more difficult than he made it sound. ''He does most of his hunting with a camera now, but we still head out into the backcountry at least once a year.''

''Did he ever…remarry?''

''Not yet.'' Noah grinned. ''But there's a woman down the street who's got her eye on him, and she's a pretty smart lady. I may get a stepmother yet.''

Paige smiled, took a sip of the excellent wine Rudy had recommended, then stopped with the glass still to her lips when Noah asked, ''What about you?''

''Me?''

''You haven't remarried.''

''No.''

''Must be some likely candidates.''

''No.''

''I find that hard to believe. Are the guys in L.A. blind or just stupid?''

She told herself it was the alcohol causing her flush, but

she knew better. "Maybe I'm just not in the market to get married again. What about you?" she asked, hoping to divert the conversation.

For a moment he looked as if he were sorry he'd started this, but he did answer. "Married once and almost a second time. Both of them bailed for the same reason."

"Your work?" Paige guessed.

His mouth quirked. "Am I wearing a sign? Something only women can see?"

"Maybe only women worry about whether the man in their life will put them first or not."

"I do remember the phrase *second fiddle* being tossed around." His tone was wry, but Paige sensed there was genuine regret behind the words.

Paige grimaced. "I would have settled for second. Fourth or fifth was a little tougher to take."

Noah's gaze fastened on her, his eyes full of some emotion she wasn't sure she could name, and she had the oddest feeling that he knew more than he could possibly have guessed about her marriage.

"You should never have to settle," he said.

The intensity of his look rattled her, as if they had turned some corner she'd known was there but hadn't expected to reach just yet.

"Doesn't everyone settle in one way or another?" She said it lightly, trying to move this back to safer ground.

"It shouldn't be that way," he said flatly. "I understand now why Carrie left, and Linda practically ran from the altar."

A vivid image of Noah Rider waiting at a flower-bedecked church for a woman he loved enough to ask to marry him flashed through her mind. And for that instant none of the reasons she'd believed so strongly for so long seemed important enough that she would run. Not if he was the one waiting for her.

# Chapter 5

*She'd known. He'd tried to get there before she heard on the radio or saw it on TV, but he'd been too late. The woman who'd answered the door when he rang the bell had that hollow-eyed look people got when death has struck close.*

*He'd only had to do this a couple of times—Josh spread it out so that nobody got the unpleasant duty too often—but that didn't make it any easier.*

*"Mrs. Cooper, I'm Noah Rider, from Redstone. We met last year, briefly. I'm here to help," he'd said. The standard, simple opening, a truth that did nothing to change what had happened or what was to come.*

Rider awoke with a start. It had been a long time since he'd had that dream. But this time was no different from all the others—the memories flooded him. That night was so vividly etched in his mind. He remembered thinking about the last time he'd seen her, at the dinner given when the deal between her husband's company and Redstone had been finalized. That woman, dressed sleekly in a deep-blue gown that had turned her red hair to fire, bore little resemblance to the woman who had opened the door of the home whose family had just been forever changed.

He'd been seated next to her at dinner that night, and he'd thought she was lovely. They'd talked, and he'd found he was enjoying himself more than he ever did at those things, even laughing out loud more than once at her easy wit.

And then he'd been given this awful job, simply because he'd had the misfortune to be in Portugal three weeks before Flight 78 went down.

He'd handled the calls, both incoming and outgoing, so she didn't have to go through it over and over. He'd fought through the red tape of bringing Phil home from a foreign country. He'd handled every detail, down to providing catered food for the inevitable stream of visitors offering condolences. He'd helped wherever he could, including with the heartbroken Kyle.

And when she'd finally broken down late one night, he'd held her. He'd let her cry, she'd thanked him, and pulled herself together with a strength that made a mockery of the idea of women as the weaker sex.

She'd gotten through the funeral, and the gathering after, with that same strength. But early that evening, as he'd been preparing to leave, his job finished, something changed. He didn't know what, but thought it might be some kind of post-traumatic stress. She'd had a fight with Kyle earlier, the boy had stomped out of the house to a friend's, and he was worried about her being alone. She seemed dazed at first, then wobbled back and forth between anger and tears. He supposed it was part of the natural process, and wondered if he should stay.

He had tried to ask her. When she whispered, "Stay," he thought she'd wanted his shoulder again. But she'd made it clear in the next few minutes that she wanted much, much more.

As vividly as if it had just happened he remembered the heat of her kiss, remembered the hot, surging response of his body, remembered the soft, luscious feel of her clinging to him, remembered the feel of her breast against his palm. She'd begun it, and he'd lost all sight of reality in the fire she kindled. Only the noise Kyle made, returning unexpectedly, snapped him out of it. And only then did it really hit home what he was doing.

And the image of himself, his hands roving over her body, his mouth dancing against hers, of himself allowing that to happen, had haunted him ever since. It had both taunted him and berated him, adding to his utter confusion; up until that night, he'd been seriously considering trying to mend the breach with Linda. The only thing that saved him was the thought that he'd likely never see Paige again.

And now here he was.

He sat up, rubbing at his eyes. He'd left the slider open, and the night breeze brought him the scent of the sweet, warm tropical air. He tossed off the sheet that was all he needed in this balmy locale, and stood up. He didn't bother to dress—it was night and he wasn't going to go beyond his own lanai, which was in shadow anyway.

He stood there in those shadows, letting the breeze wash over him.

All he had to do was get through ten days. He should be glad he'd had the chance to apologize and that she'd not only accepted it but had insisted on lifting some of the blame from him. That should have changed everything, should have freed him from the dream.

It hadn't. He was glad, but it hadn't helped a bit.

She had tried to start this reasonably, to talk to Kyle in a sane, courteous manner. But when she broached the subject in the morning at their small kitchen table, he shut down immediately.

"I hate you for bringing me here. I'll always hate you."

All right, she thought. If he truly hated her for removing him from all that—including his precious video games— then so be it. Even if it meant she sometimes felt even more alone than she had after Phil's plane had gone down, leaving her with a ten-year-old boy, no job and the devastating knowledge that they were nearly broke because the husband who had promised he would take care of everything had in fact taken care of nothing. If it hadn't been for Joshua Redstone...

She drew in a deep breath. She stood up, needing the tiny extra edge of looking down at him.

"All right. You hate me. That's a distinct change in our relationship, and therefore the rules will now change."

She saw the word *rules* had caught his attention, but he still refused to look at her.

"Obviously it's impossible for you to be pleasant to me, but as of now you will no longer show me disrespect. You don't have to love me or even like me, but you will show me the same courtesy you show any other adult."

"That's—"

"Be quiet."

Kyle blinked, startled.

"You will do your schoolwork without protest and on time. If it is not done, you will remain after school until it is. You now have half an hour to socialize after school, then you will be home until your homework is completed. If you leave the house after that you will either tell me or leave a note about where you're going, with whom and when you'll be back. If you want to go somewhere outside of the resort itself, you will ask permission first, and you will tell me where you're going and who you will be with and when you'll be back. And you will do it without being rude and without dramatics."

Kyle stared, his eyes widening. "That's not fair!"

"Neither is how you've been treating me. Now, the consequences of violating these rules will be immediate. First, you will return here and complete the work you've not done, or think about what you have done that landed you here—for the remainder of that day. And for the next week you will be limited to the grounds of the resort, not including the beach.''

"But—"

"Quiet. You have no say in this. A second violation will result in grounding to this bungalow until I say different. Got that?"

Kyle scrambled to his feet. She could see he was ready to bolt.

"And if you run away now, you will be very, very sorry. I am legally in charge of you for three more years. If you would like to see how awful I can make them for you, just keep pushing.''

Slowly, gaping in shocked disbelief, Kyle sank back down into his chair.

"One last thing,'' she said. "You say you hate me. Fine, that's your choice. But know this. Somehow, some way, you're going to become the best person you can be, no matter what I have to do.''

She leaned forward, hands on the table, and it was a measure of Kyle's stunned state that he didn't pull back from her.

"And remember this. I love you. And nothing you can ever do will change that. I will never, *ever* give up on you.''

*Shell-shocked* was the phrase that came to Paige's mind. He looked shell-shocked. Deciding her point was made, she headed back to her room to gather up papers for the school day and left him there.

He never looked at her the entire day in school, but Paige was grateful he'd shown up at all. He left the moment class was over, and she saw he was headed for the bungalow. She purposely didn't hurry. She'd laid down the rules, it was up to him now. It had hurt her to do it, more than Kyle would ever know, but they simply couldn't go on the way they had been. He'd been headed nowhere good, and it had to be stopped.

And Noah had given her the strength to do it. The strength and the direction. She didn't know if he'd intended to, but she did sense it wasn't like him to pour out his past to a near stranger like that.

Even if it was a stranger he'd once kissed like a long-lost lover.

She shivered inwardly at the memory that never seemed to lose any of its power, no matter how long it had been or how much she tried to stifle it.

"Are you all right, Mrs. Cooper?"

She looked up to see Lani DeSouza standing before her. "I'm fine, Lani. What did you need?"

"I wanted to give you my extra-credit history paper."

Paige smiled as she took the pages from the girl. "I'm going to have to invent something higher than an A-plus for you."

Lani giggled. "I love the way you teach it, especially when you translate it into modern speech."

It was one of her favorite things to do, to translate what was usually a stuffy or dry historical event into modern-day terms; it seemed to get through to the kids in a way nothing else did.

Lani, she thought as the girl left, was a beautiful girl now; as a woman she would be beyond stunning. Paige finished gathering her papers and headed out of the now empty schoolhouse. But she stopped in the doorway when she heard Kyle's voice. She couldn't tell what he'd said, but Lani's voice was quite clear.

"You Americans, you think you're better then everybody."

Kyle said something else she still couldn't hear.

"No, you're not bad, you're just like…like a big puppy, good in your heart but clumsy, and sometimes hurting people when you don't mean to."

She wished she could have heard what had started *that* conversation, Paige thought. Perhaps Kyle had again let slip his opinion of Lani's home. She'd heard the girl once telling him he was foolish for preferring "silly video games" to a good life here on her island. It made her glad she'd made him leave the video games behind.

The voices got fainter as the two moved away and she headed back to the bungalow. But once she'd arrived and changed clothes, she felt too restless to stay there. She grabbed her wide-brimmed hat and started out on a walk, choosing a direction she'd not taken before, up the slope away from the resort. The path wasn't as well delineated as the ones on the resort grounds, but it was clear enough as it wound through the trees and bushes. She saw the occasional lizard and several darting crested hummingbirds. And every few feet she caught a glimpse of the water, each time from a different angle.

At the top of the slope the path became more difficult and overgrown than she wanted to tackle, and she needed to see that Kyle was following the new rules, so she turned to go back. Something caught her eye out in the water, and she leaned forward to look. Three small boats sat in the distance, one of them larger than the other two. It wasn't unusual to see a boat out there, but she'd never seen three together before. The larger one appeared to be a fishing boat, and she wondered what they were catching. Marlin, perhaps? That's what she always thought of, films of the huge, graceful fish leaping its length and more out of aquamarine water. But for all she knew, they didn't even live around here.

She should send for some books on the local wildlife and plant life, she thought as she headed back. It would be good for her own sake to know, and also in case the kids who weren't native to the island wanted to know. She'd go online tonight and see what was available.

She was lost in thought as she walked back across the

resort courtyard, until for the second time she heard Kyle's voice. Snapping back to herself, she looked around and saw him sitting on a bench with his back to her. Next to him sat Noah.

Another conversation I'd love to hear, she thought. She wouldn't stoop to eavesdropping, but there was, she decided, no reason she couldn't just keep walking as she had been. So she did, and as she got closer she began to hear bits and pieces.

"—go places, like my dad," Kyle was saying. "I'm not going to be afraid to go anywhere, like my mother."

Paige winced, but Noah pointed out reasonably, "She came here."

She didn't hear what Kyle said then, and it was probably just as well.

"Did you ever stop to think that maybe she didn't want to leave, either? That she gave up her own life for your sake?"

She wanted to hug him for his support.

Kyle snorted. "Yeah, right." Brushing off the possibility he asked, "So, when you were in Egypt, did you see the pyramids? And the sphinx?"

Noah grinned. "I don't think they let you out of the country until you do."

"Someday I'm going to see them. I'm going to see everything, as soon as I get out of school. And my mom can't stop me. I'm going around the world, just like my dad!"

Paige felt something cramp up inside her. For years she'd fought through the shambles of the life left her by her globe-trotting husband, and now here was her son wanting to do the same thing. She didn't think she'd made a sound, but Noah looked up. When he did, so did Kyle, and the boy's exuberance vanished.

"I suppose you came to tell me I'm late and in violation?" he said with a sneer.

She sensed Noah stiffen, but didn't look at him. She

glanced at her watch and said, her voice as calm as she could manage, "Actually, you have three minutes left. However, since you've just been extremely rude, yes, you're in violation. You'll go home and stay there until school tomorrow."

Kyle turned to Noah, disbelief clear in his face. "Can you believe that?"

"I can," Noah said, his voice cold. "If I'd ever spoken to my mother in that tone of voice, I'd have been grounded until I was forty. And I probably wouldn't have been able to sit for most of it."

Looking as if an idol had betrayed him, Kyle threw a last angry glare at Paige and then took off toward the bungalow at a run. Once he was out of sight, Paige sank down onto the bench, her knees a little wobbly after this first test of the new management.

"Thanks," she said after a moment.

"I gather you laid down the law?"

She nodded. "And as you can see, it didn't go particularly well."

"He'll come around. He's not a bad kid, he's just a little screwed up right now."

"I hope so." Her mouth twisted. "But I don't like hearing him talk about taking off like that."

"It's natural for a kid to want to see the world."

"Globe-trotting," she said grimly.

"We don't all have horns and a pitchfork," he said mildly.

Embarrassed, Paige quickly apologized. "I'm sorry. I'm just a little touchy. Having your son declare he hates you and always will at every opportunity isn't the easiest thing to live with."

"I imagine not." He looked at her consideringly for a moment. Then very evenly he said, "He seems to still have a great love for his father."

Paige sighed. "Yes, he does."

"You don't sound particularly happy about that."

Paige looked at him then, seeing in his eyes the same gentle warmth that had been there the night he'd shown up on her doorstep. And suddenly the past was alive and beating at her, as strong as it had been the day of Phil's funeral, when the farce had been revealed.

"Paige?"

She didn't know what must have shown in her face. She only knew she had to let out the emotion that was boiling up inside.

"I'm sorry," she said again, "but Phil's endless traveling was a real sore spot. We argued about it constantly."

She half expected him to defend Phil. He was a globetrotter himself, after all. But he said nothing. After a moment she went on.

"It wasn't even the frequency, it was that he never made an effort to come home in between. If he had less than two weeks between jaunts, he just stayed away. Kyle really didn't know his father at all."

Noah shook his head. "Shouldn't be that way. You have a kid, you make some changes."

She gave him a sideways look. "Would you have made changes?"

He didn't toss off a glib answer, which she appreciated. After a moment he said, "Yes. There are ways to work around it. No matter if you're in the Aviation Division, or Tech, or resorts, Redstone's always willing to schedule so you have time to come home in between trips. It's tougher, but it can be done."

"Not according to Phil. The only thing he did was be gone more."

"Did you ever travel with him? Before Kyle?"

"No. I was working then, and I couldn't get away for those lengths of time." Her mouth twisted. "Besides, he never asked."

"His loss," Noah said softly.

Something in his tone broke the barrier she'd managed to keep in place until now. The words, words she'd never spoken to anyone, came out in a rush.

"He didn't think so. And when he got on that plane that last time? He had no intention of ever coming back."

Noah went very still. She kept going, needing to share this with somebody, needing to vent the pain she'd kept bottled up for five years. At the same time, she couldn't quite believe she was telling him what she had told no one, speaking the words she had never, ever said to another human being.

"He had finally decided he no longer wanted either of us. He didn't want to be my husband and certainly not a father. He wanted his complete freedom, and he was leaving the country to be sure he got it."

"Paige—"

"You know how I found out?"

Her voice was sharp, abrupt, but she couldn't help it. She'd spent five years being grateful no one else knew, five years telling herself that at least her humiliation was private, that Phil had died before it became known that he didn't love her or even his son enough to stay, and now she was blurting it out to this man, of all people.

"Go ahead," Noah said, not really answering her question but sounding as if her pain was somehow stabbing at him.

"I got served with divorce papers. Certified mail, delivered the day of his funeral, can you believe that?" He visibly winced. "Lovely, huh? And with them was a letter saying he'd left us the house and would provide child support for Kyle from a trust he'd set up, but we were never to try and find him. That he never wanted to see me, or even his son, again."

"Paige, he was an idiot."

"No, he was cruel," she countered. "Why else would he spend a page of that letter telling me about the wonderful new woman he'd found in London, how much smarter, prettier and more sophisticated she was than me, and how he couldn't wait to be free to start his new life with her? Me, I was so pitiful I went back through his records to try to find out how long it had been going on.''

"Did it matter?"

She met his gaze then, aware of something niggling away at the edge of her consciousness, but not sure what it was. She answered him. "To me it did. At least, it did then. Later I started wondering if she was the only one, if there had been more. A girl in every port, as they say.''

"What was the use?"

"Maybe I wanted to know just how big a fool I'd been.''

"Because you trusted? Because you expected the man you'd married to be honest, and worthy of that trust? You had a right to that expectation, Paige. It wasn't your fault he couldn't live up to it.''

"According to Phil it was.''

"Some men just don't deserve a woman like you, or a family. Phil was one of them.''

There it was again, something she should be noticing, something she should see.

"You know what's really crazy? After I found out, after I got over the first hurt, I wondered about her.'' She shook her head. "Can you believe I actually felt bad for her?''

"Yes,'' Noah said, his voice so soft she could barely hear him. "I can believe that of you.''

"I wondered if she was sitting alone somewhere, waiting for this man who'd promised to leave his wife for her. Maybe she even thought he was just one of those married men who always made the promise but never kept it. Maybe she never knew he was really coming for her.''

"She knew.''

"You think so? Do you think she was waiting at the airport for him, for the plane that would never come?''

"No.''

He was sounding hoarse now, as if each word was being ripped out of him.

"Noah?"

"She knew," he said in that awful voice, "because she was on that plane with him."

Paige stared at him. She opened her mouth to say "What?" but the word never came out. It hit her then, with the force of a blow, what had been bothering her during her outpouring. There had been many things in Noah's eyes: sympathy, support, reassurance, even anger.

What there hadn't been was surprise.

She couldn't seem to breathe. She also couldn't deny what was now so clear. His last words proved it.

He knew. He'd sat here listening to her sad story, her pitiful secret, and the whole time he'd already known.

## Chapter 6

"**P**aige—"

"You knew," she said, her eyes wide with shock as she stared at him.

Rider shifted uncomfortably. "Yes."

"You knew about the woman, about the divorce? Both?"

"It came out during the Redstone post-crash investigation," he said, hating the way she was looking at him, as if he'd just shattered her world all over again. "And he had copies of the papers in his desk. We found them three days after the crash."

She went even paler, so pale he thought she might faint, and he wondered what he'd said now. But Paige didn't faint. She simply sat there, reminding him too painfully of how she had looked the first time he'd gone to her house after Redstone had confirmed her husband had been on that plane.

"We? You mean all of Redstone knew? And—" she

stopped for a gasping breath ''—you all knew even before I did?''

He realized then what he'd done. The funeral, the day she said she'd gotten the papers, had been five days after the crash. ''Paige, I'm sorry—''

''Sorry?''

She leaped to her feet. She swayed slightly, but steadied herself before he could reach out to do it. He stood up slowly, wishing now he'd just kept his mouth shut. But the image of her, freshly widowed and newly betrayed, still having the compassion to worry about the other woman, had been too much for him.

''You're sorry? You knew, days before, and you didn't warn me? That I was about to be served divorce papers from beyond the grave?''

''We tried to stop it altogether. Or at least delay it on the grounds of changed circumstances.'' He rubbed at his eyes; the tropical sun suddenly seemed painfully bright. ''But his lawyer was out of town, and by the time we tracked him down, it was too late. They'd already been sent.''

When he looked at her again, there was no doubting that the betrayal shadowing her eyes this time was aimed at him. ''Why didn't you tell me? You were supposedly there to help.''

''I didn't know. I didn't find out they'd already been sent until I checked with the office that night. I didn't realize you'd gotten the papers that day, or...I never would have left you alone to deal with it. I was planning to delay my trip and stay until they did arrive, but then...''

He let his voice trail off and saw by the tightening of her lips that she realized what had changed his plans.

''It was all just rotten timing, that's all,'' he said, rubbing at the back of his neck where a nasty tightness had settled in.

A flicker of realization showed in her face. ''That's why

somebody from Redstone kept calling, and checking on me, after you left, isn't it? Because they knew.''

He nodded. ''I had to be in Tokyo, so they followed up.''

''You could have told me. You knew about the papers—you could have at least told me that much.''

''I was hoping they could stop it, that you'd never have to know at all.''

She shivered visibly. ''All this time I thought my humiliation was at least private. And now…''

''Paige, everybody at Redstone felt awful about the whole situation. And most of them were really mad at Phil.''

''And you, what did you feel? Sympathy? Pity?''

He reached out and put a hand on her arm. ''Paige, please, don't do this. You have no reason to feel humiliated.''

She yanked free of him and stood there trembling. ''You don't get it, do you? I have every reason to feel humiliated! Because if I hadn't gotten those damned papers, on *that* day, do you think I'd have thrown myself at you like the proverbial love-starved widow?''

Rider gaped at her, suddenly realizing that she wasn't on the verge of tears, she was on the verge of exploding. With anger. ''What?'' he said, wondering if it sounded half as stupid as he felt just now.

''If it hadn't been for those papers, on that day, I never would have made such a fool of myself. I never would have taken your…help as something else.'' She stood there, her quickened breathing audible, the eyes he'd always thought so warm, icy now with rage. ''You should have told me. You could have saved yourself the embarrassment of getting mauled, and me five years of sleepless nights.''

She turned on her heel and walked away, each step rigid with a control that bit into him as deeply as her words had. He started after her, then stopped himself. He was probably the last person she wanted to see right now. And he wasn't sure he could blame her. He'd been trying to help, but it had well and truly backfired on him. And, more important, on Paige. So he stood there, feeling helpless and hating the feeling, staring after her.

A few minutes later he realized he was supposed to be in a meeting, and he snapped at Barry Rutherford's young assistant, who had hunted him down to remind him.

Great. What the hell else can go wrong? he muttered to himself as he turned and hurried toward the main building. And then, wary of the way things had been going today, he added, Don't answer that!

Paige shut the door behind her and leaned against it. She was gasping as if she'd run the length of the island and shivering as if that island were Iceland.

Kyle, thankfully, was shut in his room; she could see the door closed against her from here. She made her way to the lanai and dropped down into one of the lounges facing the water.

She hadn't thought it was possible for the situation around Phil's death to be any worse. Obviously, she'd been as big a fool about that as she had been about everything else.

Everything surrounding that time was now even uglier. She couldn't bear to wonder what Noah must have thought then. And now that she knew all of Redstone had known the truth, she wondered if he'd really been chosen to come because he'd just been in Portugal.

More likely, he got the short straw, she thought. And got jumped by the widow for his trouble.

In a convulsive movement she curled up on the lounge, drawing her knees up as if she could somehow save herself from damage already done. She felt the tears begin, fought them helplessly, uselessly. She hadn't allowed herself to cry for a very long time, but now she couldn't stop.

She wished she could just stay here, lock the door and

hide until Noah left the island. Never have to face him again. But she couldn't. She had children to teach, children she'd made a commitment to—including the stubborn boy in the next room—and she had to honor that commitment. And she would. The best she could do was try to avoid running into Noah.

She lay there, trying uselessly not to think for a long time. The tears slowed and finally stopped. Gradually her shaking stopped, as well, but the sick feeling in the pit of her stomach lingered on and on. She tried taking long, deep breaths, and it helped a little. And after a while her body began to return to normal. Her mind, however, continued to churn.

The breeze picked up, as it always did in the evenings. It brought her the scent of the flowers, frangipani and a variety of ginger, the head gardener had told her.

She'd been moved by all the flowers Redstone had sent to Phil's funeral. And by the Redstone people who had shown up. Now all she could think of was that they'd all known, all been there because they felt sorry for the poor, cheated-on wife. How many of them had known what Phil was doing? Had some of them even met the woman?

She shivered anew and wrapped her arms tighter around herself. Even Joshua Redstone had come, and the tall, lanky, unassuming man had graciously—and she would have sworn sincerely—offered his condolences and any help that he or his company could give her.

Maybe he hadn't known. Maybe it hadn't filtered up that far.

You're not that lucky, she told herself bitterly.

And then, spiking through her like an unexpected shaft of light, came the thought, But you're luckier than she was.

That cooled her anger a little. In those days, five years ago, she had been devastated by the discovery that the husband she had loved hadn't loved her at all. But the thought of the nameless and thankfully faceless woman who had literally died for Phil's brand of love gave her back a little perspective.

She sat up, wiping at her burning eyes. She retreated to her bedroom, where she tried to mask the ravages of her outburst as best she could. Not that Kyle would notice or care in his current mood, but she didn't want to have to explain. Or lie. There'd been enough lies. Too many lies.

She got through the next day fairly well, she thought. If Kyle noticed anything wrong, he didn't want to talk to her enough to find out what. Even when she told him he was released from the house—with the same rules in effect— he'd barely spoken.

She didn't see Noah, which helped. She wondered if he were avoiding her, too, considering rarely had a day gone by that she hadn't seen him at least two or three times. In fact, she only realized now a day hadn't gone by since he'd been here that they hadn't talked. Not just said hello in passing, but actually talked. She didn't realize until now how much she'd looked forward to those moments, even with all the baggage they had between them.

Which was nothing compared to the baggage between them now.

"You're whining," she said aloud that night when she felt tears threaten again. "What difference does it make if the whole world knew before you did? It doesn't change the facts."

That made her feel better, so she added, "And it wasn't Noah's fault. It was none of his business really, and you should be thankful he even tried."

That said, she turned out the light and got the first decent sleep she'd had in two days.

By the next morning she had her equilibrium and her composure back. She managed to be cheerful enough during the early session to annoy Kyle, who then stayed at school for lunch period. Although she suspected that the fact Lani was usually there, as well, had something to do with that.

She had to admit not dealing with her cranky son made her own lunch break much sunnier. She even left early to go back to the school, feeling like someone going outside for the first time after an illness; everything seemed a bit clearer, more vivid, in sharper focus.

She was startled when she glimpsed a young man in what looked like camouflage pants back in the trees above the resort, but guessed he must be an employee she hadn't met yet or a son of one of the locals. Even Kyle had a pair of those pants, but she was surprised the trend had spread this far.

Wondering if she would find Kyle and Lani in another esoteric discussion, she headed toward the schoolhouse.

Shoving his hands in the pockets of his khaki pants Rider leaned back against the wall of the pool house, where the recreation director was giving him the final inventory count on towels, chairs, bottles of suntan lotion and all the other equipment that came with the territory. He'd been paying attention, too. At least, he had been until he'd caught a glimpse of sunlight on coppery hair.

He watched Paige walk across the courtyard, heading, he guessed, for the schoolhouse. He'd made sure to be scarce yesterday, trying to give her the distance he guessed she needed since he'd so clumsily betrayed that her husband's desertion had been, if not common knowledge, then at least hardly a secret.

But it hadn't been easy. He'd had to fight the urge to go to her, to try and make her understand he'd never meant to hurt her or make things worse than they already were. He'd hated leaving that night. He'd meant it when he'd told her he had planned to dump his scheduled departure for Tokyo and stay until the divorce papers had arrived. He'd even had some idea about intercepting them. But he'd been tied up with the funeral arrangements most of the day, never guessing that of all days that would be the one when they arrived.

And then, after that unexpected, passionately hot embrace and kiss, she had virtually ordered him to leave. She'd been embarrassed, he knew, but until now he'd had no idea what else she'd been feeling.

...*five years of sleepless nights.*

In the midst of the emotional turmoil he took some small comfort in that. He'd thought himself alone in those restless nights.

A movement in the distant trees caught his eye. He straightened up, pulling off his sunglasses as he narrowed his eyes. It was a man, no one he'd seen before, and it took Rider a moment to figure out why he was so hard to see. And then, as the man headed in the same general direction Paige had, he stepped into a brighter spot among the trees. Rider saw that he was dressed in the traditional green camouflage, doing what it was supposed to in the thick greenery around the resort. He looked young and seemed to know where he was going.

Or he was following somebody who knew where they were going, he thought suddenly.

Paige?

He considered that as he pulled a pen out of the pocket of the Hawaiian shirt he'd resorted to again today—it had become clear to him why they were popular in tropical climes—and signed off on the clipboard the recreation director handed him. He considered the possibility that the man was here to meet her. The thought that she might be seeing someone here hadn't occurred to him. Besides, she'd told him there was no one.

His mouth twisted. Maybe she'd decided it was time. Maybe he'd somehow driven her to it with his own idiocy.

Maybe, he thought, he should quit dealing in maybes and just find out. He didn't like the fact that this guy seemed to be skulking through the trees, anyway. As Redstone's highest-ranking representative on-site, he should go find out what the guy was doing. It was his job, after all.

"Thanks, Mario," he said.

"We're all ready for the weekend, Mr. Rider. No problems here."

"I can see that. Good job."

The man turned to lock up. Rider checked his cell phone for messages, and when for once he found none, he headed up toward the trees. But the man in green was nowhere in sight now, and Rider wondered if he was just some local come to see the resort that had grown on this end of his island.

He pondered his next move for a moment, then started toward the schoolhouse. It couldn't hurt.

The little building, painted a traditional white, looked absolutely picturesque, he thought as he reached the clearing. There was still no sign of the man, but there were several children milling around outside, some playing, some finishing lunches they'd apparently brought with them. And there was Paige. She must have stopped to talk to someone—the man in the camouflage pants?—for she was just now going up the steps, amid cheerful waves from many of the children.

And off to one side Rider saw Paige's son, looking miserable. Things must still be strained between him and his mother, Rider thought. But then he saw that Kyle was intently, almost hungrily watching an exotically lovely young girl who was talking to another boy, and he realized there was more than just his home situation making the boy unhappy.

He stood watching for a moment, but then turned his attention to the schoolhouse. He'd worked on the plans, and Paige had told him how it had turned out, but he hadn't made it over there to see it yet in person. He did need to check it out, he told himself. It was on his list, waiting to be signed off. And besides, he was curious to see how the changes he'd made worked in actual use.

And it would be a chance to see if Paige was still furious at him.

He headed toward the stairs. A few of the kids he'd met already recognized him and waved, although not with the obvious affection they'd shown Paige. Kyle glanced his way, seemed surprised to see him there but didn't wave. He supposed the boy was still mad at him, too, for siding with his mother over his attitude.

He still didn't understand it. How could that kid be so downright nasty to his mother, who not only far from deserved it but was also the only parent he had left? How could he still glorify a father who had died in the act of abandoning him for life, who had cared so little for his own son that he hadn't even said goodbye?

It made no sense to him. He'd loved his mother dearly, but he still remembered how angry he'd been when she'd died, even knowing she certainly hadn't chosen to leave him. If she had instead done what Kyle's father had done, he doubted he ever would have forgiven her.

And Paige had clearly tried so hard to make it easier on the boy. She—

He stopped in his tracks.

She *had* tried hard to make it easier on her son. Of course she had; what else would a woman who was capable of feeling compassion for the woman who had broken up her marriage do? And a woman who could do that…

She hadn't told him.

# Chapter 7

The minute the thought formed in his head, Rider knew it was the truth. Paige had never told her son the real truth behind his father's death. Had never told him they were being abandoned, deserted, tossed aside for something newer, flashier, less complicated. And so Kyle had developed this idealized image of a man who could never do anything to tarnish it. It was the only explanation for the way the boy still idolized his father.

And it would be like her to keep that knowledge buried in her, carrying the burden alone so that her son wouldn't have to. And there was a decent chance Kyle would never encounter anyone who would know, or even if they did, would ever tell him his father had had every intention of never seeing him again.

The depth and strength of that kind of love amazed him. He wasn't sure he—or any man—was capable of it. But then he realized he had living proof of a man who did, in his own way. His father. He'd brought Rider's mom home to die, and he'd nursed her, cared for her until the very end, never complaining, treasuring each minute with the woman he loved stolen from the grim reaper. And he himself had given the old man some tough times in those years after his mother's death, but his dad never gave up.

He wondered if he had that kind of strength in him somewhere. If that kind of thing could be hereditary. He could only hope.

He started moving again, taking the four steps to the raised porch two at a time. It was an old-fashioned, one-room schoolhouse, built the way many buildings in the tropics were—raised off the ground to let air circulate beneath and to help avoid water damage in case of storm surge. But it was completely modern, with the indoor plumbing he'd joked to Paige about and the computer center she had been so excited about. It even smelled new. He thought he caught a whiff of fresh paint as he came through the small vestibule where students apparently stowed backpacks and other gear not immediately needed.

He paused in the doorway to the big room itself, looking. It was oriented so the double doors were at the rear. The large space was loosely divided into a half-dozen sections—one the computer center on the raised platform in the front corner, another where he saw small mats rolled up on shelves, he guessed for the younger ones to take naps or have a quiet time during the day.

The rest of the sections, separated only by office cubicle-type walls festooned with pictures and artwork of various types, seemed to be divided by age levels. At the front of the room were several rows of chairs with half desktops, smaller ones in the front, enough for all the students to sit at one time. A good setup, he thought; Paige couldn't be everywhere, but with the low walls, she could see if a problem arose anywhere in the room.

Right now she was seated at the front of the room on a brightly-covered sofa. There was a large desk behind it, flanked by two tall filing cabinets. Behind the desk, sofa and file arrangement was the other way into and out of the school, a single, solid mahogany door. In front of Paige was a long, low table, and she had papers spread out over it, studying them intently.

Her hair today wasn't in the usual braid, but pulled back into a jaunty ponytail at the back of her head. It hung halfway down her back, giving him the answer to one of the things he'd always wondered about, how long that red mane would be if let loose.

Heat jolted through him, and he took a moment to fight it down before he actually stepped into the room. An odd sort of tension stayed with him, as if he were wondering if the teacher would throw him out of class.

He only took a couple of steps before he noticed the floor. He stopped, staring, bemused. Teak wood had been used, because of the threat of water from severe storms and the rare hurricane that hit this island. It was beautiful and one of the few woods that wasn't a termite attractant in this climate. But now it had been decorated. Five sets of whimsical, cartoonish bare footprints had been painted in a path from the back of the room up to where Paige sat. In red, blue, green, orange and black, they wound their way crookedly around the different sections, then split into four separate paths as they approached her sofa and desk.

He found himself smiling as he followed the chubby little feet through the room. But when he got to where they split, he stopped and looked up again.

She was watching him, her expression unreadable. She was dressed simply in a pair of navy-blue cotton slacks with a navy trimmed white blouse and a pair of white canvas shoes. He thought she'd never looked lovelier.

Forcing himself to stop staring at her, he gestured down at the floor. "I don't know which path to take."

She smiled then, and he felt a little of the tension leave him. And she seemed quite calm, even friendly as she explained. "Red is for if you're angry about something. Blue if you're sad, no reason required. Black is for excuses, good or bad. Orange is if you're sorry about something. Green is for good news to share."

Well, that makes it easy, Rider thought. With a quirk of his mouth he stepped out along the orange path. When he got to the end, she was standing. Everything he'd planned to say escaped him, and he just stood there for a moment. As if the silence made her uncomfortable, she explained even further.

"I used the sofa to make this place seem like home rather than school, to make me more approachable to the little ones. And I painted those paths—in water-soluble paint, by the way—to make it clear that it was okay to talk about all those things," she said, and added with the slightest emphasis, "and that I'm always willing to listen."

He stood there for a moment, struggling for words. Finally he said simply, "I'm sorry."

There were so many other things he wanted to say, to explain, but right now that "I'm sorry" was all he could manage.

After a moment of silence Paige nodded.

"All right." When he said nothing more, she left it at that and asked if he wanted to look around. "You should see how your work paid off."

He followed her around the room, listening as she pointed out the ways she was using the changes he'd made in the plans, from the audio/visual corner to the small library to the computer center.

"It must be difficult, teaching all different ages."

"It can be. And there will be times when I have to call in someone for things I'm not as versed in, for the older kids."

"Then you get time off, I hope?"

She smiled. "Maybe. Or I'll stay and hope I learn, too."

That didn't surprise him, he thought. "How about your personal quarters? Everything all right?"

She nodded. "Who could ask for more than the Redstone pay scale plus meals and lodging?"

"Sounds cushy," Rider agreed, then gestured at the room. "*Until* you think about being the only teacher for the whole range of students from kindergarten to high school."

She gave him a smile that seemed to be thanking him for understanding. It warmed him.

"It's working, though, even with the addition of the island's resident children."

"It must be rough having them all in the same room," he said as she showed him how she'd divided up the big space.

"It gets hectic sometimes," she admitted. "There's nothing to stop the noise between the groups. But kids have a great capacity for tuning out what they don't want to hear."

"Honed on their parents, no doubt," Rider said dryly.

She smiled, but the fact that it didn't quite reach her eyes warned him things were still not going well at home.

"Is Kyle still angry?"

"Very. But he's still sticking to the rules, so far. Of course, the silent treatment goes with it."

Rider gave her a sympathetic half smile. "Me, I fought. Loud, every time my dad tightened his hold. We raised the roof more than once. I'm surprised the neighbors didn't call the cops."

She smiled back. "By the way, I should thank you for what you did."

He blinked. "For what?"

"For sharing that story with me. I knew I had to do something about Kyle, before I lost all his respect, but I was afraid to. You showed me a different perspective, one that was just what I needed to help me decide."

"But he's still mad."

"Yes. But he's still obeying, however reluctantly. I haven't lost him completely."

Rider nodded in understanding. "I don't think that will ever happen."

"I hope you're right. But," she said with a shake of her head that sent the ponytail bouncing, "one of these days he's going to realize I don't really have any control over him. He's already bigger and taller than I am."

Rider shook his head in turn. "That's physical control. That means little. It's the emotional sway you hold that counts, and you'll never lose that. You're his mother, and however angry he may be with you now, he'll come around."

"I just have to live that long," she said wryly.

Rider hesitated, then decided he needed to know, although he wasn't sure why.

"You never told him, did you? About the divorce and why Phil was on that plane?"

Her head snapped around to face him as she faltered midstride, then stopped where she was.

"How did you know that?"

"It's the only thing that makes sense. The only explanation for why he so obviously still loves and misses his dad, under the circumstances."

"Oh." She seemed somehow relieved by his answer.

"Why?" he asked.

"Why? What earthly good would it have done?"

"It might have made things easier on you."

"At the cost of destroying my son? What was I supposed to do, let a ten-year-old child help me carry my burden? He was already the only reason I went on, it would have been hideously unfair to ask that of him, too."

He wondered if she knew how incredible she was. He doubted it; she'd probably laugh at him if he told her so.

"He tried so hard to win his father's approval," she said. "No matter how much Phil ignored Kyle, that boy never gave up trying. How could I tell him it never would have happened no matter how long his father had lived?''

"Maybe," Rider said slowly, "maybe someday he'll *need* to know that it never would have happened. That he didn't fall short, because no amount of time would have made a difference. He didn't fail, because there had never been any chance of succeeding. Maybe he'll need that to finally let go.''

He could tell by her expression that she'd never thought of it that way before. He hoped she would think about it, because he knew the strain between her and her son was wearing on her.

"Paige? Why did you marry him?''

Her mouth curled into a wry half smile. "If you only know the hours I've spent trying to answer that. I guess because he talked a good game.''

"Salesman.''

She nodded. "My parents had a very happy marriage, up until the day my father died. I thought I'd have that with Phil. He promised me I would, and fool that I was I believed him.''

"Maybe he meant it at the time," Rider said grudgingly.

"Maybe." She didn't sound convinced. But then, neither was he.

She continued showing him around, and he could see from the colorful, imaginative and in some cases very well-executed drawings that adorned the walls, and from glancing at the essays that were posted, that she was a teacher who got through to her students. Just as he would have suspected. He listened quietly, liking the pride he heard in her voice. He knew from the files that when Josh hired her she hadn't taught for several years, but she clearly had never lost her love for it.

"Is there anything else you need?''

"Need? No.''

He smiled at the careful way she phrased it. "Okay, want, then."

She smiled back then. "Other than having all the computers online instead of one, no."

"That's going to take more wiring than we could get done in time, but it's still on the list."

"Fine. We can make do with one for now."

Paige went on to discuss other school-related matters, and he lapsed into silence. By the time she'd finished, his mind was bursting with everything he wanted to say, to explain to her. Finally, guessing he had a limited amount of time before class started, he stopped at the foot of the barefoot trails.

"Can we go back up the orange path?"

She studied him for a moment, nodded, and led the way back to the sofa. He sat down beside her, trying to sort out where to begin. And then she surprised him by speaking first.

"Look, Noah, I'm sure you and everybody else at Redstone meant well. I only reacted as I did the other day out of remembered pain. I'm sorry, too. And I don't blame you for not telling me."

With those simple, honest and direct words she disarmed him completely. And as if her honesty were catching, he found himself blurting out the rest of the truth about that week choreographed in hell. He'd thought he would just never tell her, that there was no point, but now…he still wasn't sure there was a point, but he knew it had to come out.

"It wasn't just that I hoped you wouldn't ever have to know," he admitted. "I couldn't tell you. I couldn't tell you what a jerk he was when his body wasn't even home yet. Not when I was…"

"Was what?"

He let out a compressed breath, wishing yet again he'd kept his mouth shut, and wondering what it was about this woman that loosened his usually reticent tongue. But it was too late now to take it back.

"Not when I was so attracted to you myself," he admitted, his voice tight. Her eyes widened, and she drew back slightly, but he kept on. Now that he'd started, he was going to finish. "It just didn't seem fair. Like fighting somebody who couldn't fight back. He was dead, he couldn't compete, couldn't defend himself."

Paige was staring at him. He wondered what she was thinking, what was going on in that agile mind. Then he wondered if maybe he was better off not knowing.

Would he have been better off if he hadn't admitted any of this? But that didn't seem any fairer than bad-mouthing her newly deceased husband.

Paige cut directly to the heart of the matter.

"Then why didn't you come back?" she asked.

He sighed heavily. "Because I felt so damned guilty after that night. When you told me to leave, I figured you would never want to lay eyes on me again."

She lapsed into silence again. She was still watching him. He wanted to look away, to dodge the intensity of her steady gaze. But the fact that she appeared almost stunned kept him right where he was, waiting. Hoping.

Then a loud buzzer sounded, and he knew his chance was gone. For now.

Paige heard the sound of the electronically controlled buzzer announcing the start of school, but for a long moment she didn't—couldn't—move. What Noah had said put an entirely different spin on what he'd done five years ago. And put an entirely different spin on her own actions as well. Had she somehow picked up on some signal, had she really not misinterpreted his intentions at all?

Had he—she barely dared wonder—felt the same heat and power and churning response that she had?

She heard the clatter and chatter of the children coming

in, and that did rouse her out of her stunned state. She got to her feet.

"Mind if I watch?" he asked.

She did mind, because his presence unsettled her. But she could hardly say so, especially now, in front of the kids who were already scrambling into their seats.

"Fine. Have a seat, anywhere you want."

He resumed his place on the sofa, and after a moment of watching the kids come in, spot him and get suddenly quiet, he leaned back and propped his feet up on the table, as if sending a silent signal they should relax. She appreciated his understanding and was pleasantly surprised that he'd picked up on the mood so quickly and done something about it.

The kids still settled down rather more quickly than usual, and she knew it was Noah's presence. The ones whose parents worked for Redstone knew who he was, of course, and she wouldn't be surprised if some of the others did, too. Lani in particular, she thought as she saw the girl sliding Rider sideways glances. She wondered what Kyle had told her.

She introduced him briefly, telling them that he had ten days to do the equivalent of what they had to do in an entire semester. Noah laughed at that and told the kids it wasn't nearly as much fun, though, since he didn't have a smart and pretty teacher to help him go the right way.

Paige tried not to blush. But what he'd said to her was glowing in her mind, seared into her memory. She desperately wanted some time alone to absorb his revelation and decide how she felt about it, but she knew she wasn't going to get that now. Especially not if Noah stayed. As, it seemed, he was content to do.

She went through each grade's assignments for the afternoon, and he seemed perfectly content to loll on the sofa, feet up, watching and listening as if he had absolutely nothing better to do. She knew that wasn't true, not two days before the first high-rolling guests were due to arrive.

When the general announcements were done, she ushered the youngest group, consisting of eleven children ages five to seven, up-front. It was their turn on the computers. The next group was ages eight to twelve, and she set them to work drawing pictures to illustrate the story she'd read to them yesterday. The next group skipped to fourteen and up. That group was Kyle's and Lani's, and she got them set up to work on the debate they were putting together. She'd given them the circumstances of a situation and asked each of them to write it based on how they personally would deal with it. Later they would argue all the points of view they'd come up with. That the circumstances were those of a famous event, she would tell them later, when they compared their results to the actual history.

Rider seemed fascinated by it all, and Paige began to wonder if he was going to spend all afternoon with them. When she had everyone started on their work, she debated whether to join him, but decided she couldn't disrupt her teaching routine because he'd dropped in, and started her usual rounds. She managed to give each group individual attention and made sure to talk to each child alone for at least a few minutes each day; if there were any problems, she wanted to know about them now, not get blindsided later.

When she moved over to the computer center, Noah got up and joined her. "Something I at least know something about," he explained.

"Do you work in that big building we saw?" one of the boys asked.

Noah looked at Paige questioningly. "I showed them Redstone headquarters online," she said.

"Oh. Yes, sometimes. I have an office there."

"Are you way up high?" Hannah, the girl nearest him, asked.

"Sort of. I'm on the twelfth floor."

Her eyes widened, and Paige wondered if he realized that if the girl had spent her entire life here, she well might have never seen a building that tall.

"That's three times as tall as the tallest building here at the resort," he said, and her eyes got even bigger.

And then the questions started coming fast and furious, from all of the kids, but mostly from Hannah. He slid up to sit on one of the tables and for a moment glanced at Paige. She smiled at his expression. He looked as if he knew this was what kept teachers going. Just watching those young minds soak things in, and seeing them coming up with the most unexpected and fascinating questions, was somehow invigorating.

Even if you do look like you've been put in the hot seat, she told him silently.

He glanced at Paige again, and she knew he saw the grin she was trying to keep under wraps. He grinned back, and she thought she saw traces of relief in his eyes, and she wondered if he hadn't been sure until this moment that he was really forgiven.

What happened now—where they would go from here— she had no idea. She had every reason to be wary of a man who traveled as her husband had. She had every reason to—

The crash at the back of the room spun every head around. A man in camouflage leaped into the room. The same man she'd seen in the trees.

Rider slid from the table back to his feet. For a split second he glanced at Paige, almost as if he thought she might know this man.

The smaller door behind her desk burst open, slamming hard against the wall. The clock above it bounced, then crashed to the floor. Another man. In camouflage.

A child somewhere in the back began to scream. Another began to cry.

With reason, Paige thought, as she stared at the two men who had invaded this peaceful place. Both of them were carrying automatic weapons.

# Chapter 8

More children were screaming and crying now. Paige moved toward the smallest ones. Rider tensed. One of the men yelled and waved his weapon at her. It looked like the photographs he'd seen of Russian AK-47s, and Rider's mind went immediately to their relative proximity to Cuba. Whatever the weapon was, the sight of it stopped Paige in her tracks.

One of the youngest children, tears streaming down his face, broke and ran toward Paige. The man at the small door swung his weapon around and aimed it at the child.

"Stevie, no!" Paige screamed, and before Rider could stop her she was moving toward the little boy.

For a frozen instant of time, Rider saw it all happening. Saw in his mind a bloody, ugly vision of spraying gunfire and falling children. And Paige. Paige who never thought about what she was risking, only that there was a terrified child who needed her. He knew how one wrong move in a situation like this could bring on disaster and tragedy. But that move had already been made. The only thing he could do was try to keep the aftermath from turning into that bloody vision.

He snapped back to real time. He spun on his heel. He took two steps toward the man aiming at the child.

"Hold your fire!" the older man who had come in the big door shouted.

The younger man stopped. Rider stopped. Paige swept down on the child like a guardian angel. She picked him up and put her body between him and the itchy gunman. The initial threat of a massacre seemed to subside.

The older man—although he still didn't look much over thirty, Rider thought—moved toward the children at the back of the room. He started with the group of the littlest, from which the boy who had come within seconds of dying had broken loose.

"Move! All of you. Up front."

He gestured with one hand rather than the weapon. Rider wondered if that was to lessen the fear that could immobilize the kids, or if he just didn't want the thing to go off by accident.

Rider heard a smothered sob and glanced over to see Hannah, the little girl who had been so wide-eyed and enthused, now fighting tears. He edged back toward her. The itchy one's head snapped around, along with his weapon, and Rider held up his hands. But he kept moving until he was next to the girl. The younger man apparently decided his superior's order still held and lowered the deadly rifle.

Rider reached for Hannah, and she buried her face against him. He put his arm around her, squeezing gently, trying to give her what reassurance he could.

The older man moved toward the next cubicle and did the same as before, herding the kids toward them. Even the oldest ones were clearly terrified. Rider saw a very pale Kyle swipe quickly at his eyes. The lovely girl he'd noticed earlier, however, while obviously frightened, was dry-eyed, watching the armed men with a steady expression.

When all the children were gathered in the front of the schoolroom, the first man jerked his head toward the younger man, who quickly ran back to the door he'd come in. He leaned outside, picked up a duffel bag and set it inside the door, then took up a guarding stance. The older man then took a small, rather battered-looking walkie-talkie from his belt and spoke into it.

"The school is secured."

The radio crackled back something, but from where he was Rider couldn't hear it. Not that he needed to: the presence alone of the radio told him enough for the moment. These men were organized, there were more of them and they were equipped well enough to have radio communication.

They obviously had some kind of objective, Rider thought. Although right at the moment it seemed to be simply terrifying everyone. Successfully, he noted. Everybody in this room—including himself—was afraid.

He watched with jaw clenched as the younger man searched Paige, running his hands over her with thinly disguised glee. Paige stood in stony silence, her face completely still. The older man did a cursory search of Rider, clearly interested only in weapons, however unlikely it might be that there would be any here in the small school. But, as a result, the man missed the cell phone that was virtually invisible in the loose shirt pocket.

"Now," the older man commanded. "You will all stay quiet and behave. No one moves without clearance from me. We will be here until we get what we want, so be smart and don't do anything foolish."

The tension in the room ratcheted up a notch. Some huddled together, some clung to each other, some simply stared in detached shock. But the fear was uppermost in every face.

Every face except one.

He'd meant only to glance at Paige, to make sure she

was holding together, not that he doubted her. But what he saw stopped his gaze dead. He knew the look too well, since it had so recently been directed at him.

Paige Cooper wasn't afraid.

She was furious.

Seated on her sofa, Paige cuddled little Stevie, who had calmed down enough to breathe between sobs. She tried to be gentle, but the anger that was boiling in her made it a difficult task.

She knew who these men were. Oh, not specifically, but the specifics didn't matter, not with soulless brutes like this. No matter what their cause, they were all alike in one critical way: they didn't care who they hurt or killed or how many lives they destroyed in their single-minded fanaticism. She squeezed Stevie tighter. Like the cowards they were, they preyed on the innocent—people who had nothing to do with whatever their ultimate goal was—rather than face their enemy openly. Men like these had murdered her husband, and regardless of their problems, Phil had been the father of her son, and Kyle had been devastated at the loss.

Her anger burned hotter. She had left everything behind to come to this remote place for peace, and now the ugliness had invaded even here.

The older of the two invaders walked over to where Paige was huddled on the sofa with the little boy.

"Keep them all quiet," he ordered her. "I do not like noisy children."

Paige looked up at him, letting every bit of contempt she was feeling show in her face and echo in her voice. "You've already bought your ticket to hell with your actions. Go use it."

The man frowned. She could see him working it out, and by the time he realized exactly what she'd just told him to do, she had turned back to the boy and refused to look at him again.

"I think you fail to realize who is in charge here," he said to her. Paige ignored him. After a moment he said, "No matter. You will know soon enough."

Then he walked away and took up a position at the door he'd come in. His younger counterpart was at the other door. Only then did Paige risk a look around. The children had calmed a bit, what crying there was was mostly silent or at least hushed. She felt a little jolt of pride as she realized the oldest ones, even Kyle, were helping the youngest, hugging them, holding on.

Even Noah was doing his part: Hannah, the girl who'd been asking him questions, was clinging to him like a lifeline. But Paige realized he wasn't looking at Hannah but at her, with an expression of both apprehension and something warmer, almost like admiration.

She didn't know what he could be admiring. She felt on the verge of completely losing control, whether to her own fear or anger she wasn't sure. But she knew neither would do the children any good, so she tried desperately to regain some equilibrium.

She looked over at Kyle again. He had a couple of the smallest children beside him, and on the other side he had Lani. She could tell he was trying to act protectively, but she saw in his face he was as scared as they all were. He looked up then, as if he'd felt her gaze, and in that moment she was looking at the child she remembered. Whatever problems they'd been having weren't between them now.

Kyle opened his mouth to speak. In the instant before he got out "Mom," Noah suddenly coughed, loud enough to draw the boy's attention. Paige saw Noah give a slight, sharp shake of his head. Kyle looked puzzled—no more than she herself felt—but lapsed back into silence.

Noah looked at her then, and caught her frown. His gaze

flicked to the man back at the doors, then to Kyle and back to her, again with that little shake of his head.

Her frown deepened, as did her puzzlement. She didn't know what Noah was trying to communicate. She also wondered why nothing was happening, why the armed men seemed only to be waiting.

Noah leaned over and whispered something to Hannah, who wiped at her eyes and nodded. He patted her on the back, then started to walk toward Paige. Instantly the younger man, the one who seemed to want to shoot first and not bother with questions after, had his weapon trained on Noah.

"I said not to move without permission!" the older one snapped from the main doors.

"Look, it's my back," Noah said, sounding meek and almost whiny. "I can't stand up for too long."

Paige frowned; she'd never noticed him having a problem before. Of course, she hadn't seen him on his feet at length, either, except for the welcome speech he'd given the first day. And given her state of mind when she'd realized it was him, she didn't think she could trust her memories of that. She'd never heard this tone of voice from him, either, but then she'd obviously never seen him in a situation like this.

"Sit, then," the apparent leader said, with an expression that said he had little patience for such minor complaints. He went back to digging into his duffel bag for whatever he'd been after when Noah had moved. God knew what terrorists carted around with them, Paige thought.

Noah walked to the sofa and sat down close to her, but not close enough to draw their captors' attention. He reached out and tweaked Stevie's cheek and gave the child a reassuring smile. Then, still looking down at the boy, he spoke in a low voice clearly meant only for her.

"It's better if they don't know he's yours."

It took her a second, but then she got it. He didn't want

Kyle to betray that he was her son. She thought about that and then realized his point. If they knew he was her son, and if she didn't do exactly what they wanted, they might try to use Kyle to force her to comply. She never would have thought of it herself, but she knew he was right.

She peeked up at Noah, saw he was now looking at her, and she quickly, barely nodded to indicate she understood.

She glanced at the two men. "Why here?" she muttered under her breath, not really expecting an answer.

"Probably because the island's containable," Noah said, still keeping his voice low. "And there's just the staff here now, with no real security yet. They won't be coming in until the guests do. And as long as they hold the children, the parents will cooperate."

His calm assessment, at odds with the near whine she'd heard moments ago, surprised her.

"But what could they want here?" she asked.

He shrugged. "Maybe it's just about Redstone. Josh is always a target for any disgruntled group who wants to strike out at wealth or power. They don't care that he came up the hard way, from a worse start than most of them ever had."

"In my experience," Paige said tightly, "they don't care about anyone."

Still, she was surprised at his astute assessment. She supposed he had to know about such things, the way he gallivanted around the world. But that he was calm enough to think about it when they were almost literally looking down the barrel of a gun was unexpected.

For a long time nothing happened. They all just sat still. The children were afraid to move, and Paige was growing angrier by the moment. Terrorizing children was beyond cowardice, it was evil. This was the second time in her life she'd confronted this kind of malignancy, and she found it even more repugnant now than she had before. No matter what they were after, no matter what injustice they felt had been done them, nothing justified this. Nothing.

"I wonder what they're waiting for," Noah said softly, his voice so quiet she doubted anybody more than two feet away could have heard him.

Paige felt something jump then tighten inside her. Yes, she'd wondered why nothing was happening, but somehow Noah's phrasing, that they were waiting for something specific, made the lack of activity now even more ominous. She hadn't thought they might be simply waiting for something, some sign or order. and she didn't want to think of what the result of that sign or order might be.

She looked at the younger man, the one who made her most nervous because of his apparent desire to shoot when anything at all happened. He was lounging against the doorjamb behind her desk, the powerful, threatening-looking rifle cradled in his arms like a baby. She wondered what sort of twisted mind could come so close to murdering a child, yet would take such loving care of a lethal weapon. She believed guns had their place, but that place was most certainly not in the hands of a man who apparently saw nothing wrong with that dichotomy.

The older man at the main doors, however, seemed much more restless. She didn't know if his constant glances outside were merely wariness, watchfulness or if he was actually expecting something. And if he was expecting something, she wondered what.

Maybe, she thought, they were afraid someone would be coming to rescue them. That idea cheered her until she realized the catastrophe it could turn into, with the children caught in the middle.

She looked over at Kyle. He was sitting with his arm around Lani, who for once wasn't lecturing him on his attitude. Kyle was clearly trying to comfort her, and she was proud of him for that. Her son, the boy she remembered, the generous, smiling boy who had loved her, was still in there somewhere. And she would reach him. Somehow. She would—

The sudden movement of the older man stopped her thoughts. He leaned partially out the door, as if peering at something in the distance. Then he came back and shouted urgently to his companion.

"Filipo! He is coming!"

The younger man, the swaggering, trigger-happy one, snapped to attention. He stood up straight, rifle at the ready. His expression, which had until now consisted of an arrogance-tinged smirk, became impassive, even stern.

Paige glanced at Noah. He lifted a brow and his mouth twisted at one corner, indicating he, too, realized that this was what they'd been waiting for. Whoever the "he" was, he was obviously the leader of these two, and possibly this entire operation. Whatever this operation was.

She had a feeling they were about to find out.

She heard the footsteps on the stairs, then a heavy, measured tread across the small porch. This was followed by other footsteps, more than one set, she thought.

She realized she was holding her breath, but couldn't seem to make herself let it out. A man stepped inside. He was wearing regular green fatigues, not camouflage. He carried no rifle, but had a sidearm in a covered holster at his hip. She had a chance to study him as he paused to speak to the man at the doors.

He was taller than both of the men who had taken over the school but not quite as tall as Noah. He was older than both, as well, judging by the faint touch of silver at the temples in his otherwise brown hair. Although, not much older, perhaps mid to late thirties, with clean-cut, pleasant features.

Apparently finished with their discussion, the newcomer looked over his shoulder toward the outside and made a summoning gesture. Two other men, near duplicates of the first two, down to the rifles and camouflage, stepped into the schoolroom. They took up positions, one in front and one behind the man who was clearly a leader of some sort. Then the entourage of three headed toward the front of the schoolroom.

The children stirred restlessly, made nervous all over again by this new threat.

"Shhh," Paige said, trying to soothe them.

The two escorts split and went to each side of the area where the children were sitting. The leader came toward the sofa. He glanced at Noah assessingly. Noah seemed to sink down into the cushions, as if trying to disappear, and after a moment the man shifted his gaze to Paige.

He waited, as if expecting her to rise to her feet. *Not likely,* she told him silently.

She couldn't help noticing he had ridiculously long and thick eyelashes. In fact, if you set aside who he was and what he was doing, he might be considered a rather handsome man...if you also set aside the unnatural brightness in his eyes that made Paige think of drugs or madness.

Paige knew she could never set any of that aside, knew that to her he could only be ugly.

And after a moment he seemed to think better of waiting for her to rise and spoke.

"You are Mrs. Cooper? I am called Ares."

His English was slightly accented, but rather formal. That he knew her name bothered her. "I wondered what silly name you would pick to make yourself feel like a man," she muttered.

A pair of dark, almost femininely arched eyebrows shot upward in surprise. She knew he'd heard her, but he apparently decided to pretend he hadn't.

"I am the leader of the People's Freedom Cell of Arethusa."

She glanced at the two escorts. "Such a brave leader that you must have four armed men with you to face a room of schoolchildren?"

The man called Ares tensed.

"Paige, stop," Noah urged. "Don't antagonize him."

"And who are you?" Ares asked, frowning at Noah.

"Me? I'm just a fellow teacher."

Ares didn't look convinced.

"He's a supervisor," Paige said quickly, much more calmly. "He's here to monitor my class."

Unimpressed, Ares turned back to her. "In any case, he is right. Do not antagonize me."

As quickly as that her calm deserted her again. "I've lived through the worst your kind can do. You don't scare me."

To her surprise the man laughed suddenly. "I was told you were a special woman. I can see that is correct."

He spoke it as a compliment, but the laughing words stabbed fear through Paige like a bayonet. *He was told?*

All of a sudden this went from a random, impossible-to-understand bit of terrorist insanity to something much more personal. Something, at least in some way, aimed at her. She fought to regain some semblance of composure, knowing she didn't dare lose it now, not when the children were in jeopardy.

"First," Ares said, with every evidence of cheer, "let me warn you not to expect any help. My men hold the entire premises, and have secured everyone on the hotel grounds. We also control all communications apparatus. No call can be made without our knowledge. There will be no rescue."

Paige looked quickly at the children, but either the man's words hadn't gotten through their shock or they didn't realize he'd just told many of them their parents were now also hostages. She hoped it stayed that way; they were already scared enough without adding fear for their parents into the mix.

With a suppressed shiver she looked back at their captor. "I have heard," the man said, "that you are a fair woman. That you teach your students to see both sides of a situation.''

She wanted to look away, but the man called Ares never took his eyes off her, and she wouldn't let herself look away until he did, no matter how frightened she was by the fact that someone had apparently talked to this man about her.

''That makes you a lucky woman,'' Ares told her. ''You will be moved to the hotel. Your things will be brought to you, and you will be treated well.''

''I can't leave these children!'' The words burst from her.

''My men will stay with them.''

''That does *not* make me feel any better,'' she said, her tone sarcastic as her fear ebbed a little in the face of his absurd effort at reassuring her.

''Then your superior can stay, as well,'' he said, jerking a thumb at Noah, ''if you like.''

''And who do I have to betray for these thirty pieces of silver?''

''Betray?'' Was he mocking her with that tone of utter innocence? ''Why, no one. In fact, the opposite. You will be in a position to save many lives.''

With a great effort Paige hid the shiver that rippled through her at his indirect admission that lives might be lost before this was over. In an inane flash she remembered her journal entry, and suddenly knew exactly how the woman in that book had felt, as if she'd brought all this down upon herself with her silly musings.

''You will be,'' Ares said grandly, ''the spokesperson.''

Her fear faded, replaced by bewilderment. ''Spokesperson? For whom?''

''Why, the hostages, of course.''

Her breath caught. She glanced toward the children, toward Kyle, but Ares shook his head. ''Not them,'' he said impatiently. ''They are merely insurance. I'm speaking of the true hostages. The ones to come, who can get the attention of the world.''

She heard Noah suck in a breath. And it hit her then: Ares was talking about the wealthy, high-profile guests who would be arriving in two days.

''Ah, I see you understand. Very good. So you comprehend the honor I have given you.''

''Honor?'' Her voice was tight.

''Indeed. You will become a celebrity of sorts, when the media arrive.''

She blinked. ''The media?''

''Of course. As soon as everything is secure, they will be notified of our takeover. And you will be the voice of the hostages. You are a woman, a teacher, the world will believe you. You will tell the world they are being treated well, that we are reasonable men and that we should be given what we ask for.''

Paige did rise then. She stood because she could no longer sit still in the face of this insanity.

''People held against their will have no voice,'' she said icily, matching his formality of speech. ''Nor do reasonable men do such abhorrent things. I truly hope that you are given *exactly* what you are asking for.''

Her words slowed him for a moment, but she saw the anger flash in his eyes when he understood what she had meant.

She barely saw his hand move. In the next instant pain slammed through her head as he backhanded her on the side of the head. She heard Kyle yell ''No!'' heard someone else swear, realized it was Noah only when he leaped to his feet. She fell back on the sofa, her ears ringing, tears welling up, tears she would *not* let Ares see. And despite the pain she felt a sense of triumph that enabled her to fight back the tears before they spilled over. She'd gotten to him. She'd stuck him right in his ego.

''Sit down!'' Ares ordered Noah.

*Do it,* Paige pled silently.

"Go to hell," Noah spat out. "And if you touch her again I'll send you there myself."

Paige, startled by his fervent defense, looked up just in time to see Ares make the slightest of motions with one finger toward the trigger-happy guard. The man gleefully raised his rifle, aimed it toward Noah and fired.

# Chapter 9

Paige knew she'd let out a little scream at the shot, but it was nothing compared to the wailing that now arose from several of the children. If she hadn't been looking right at Noah, if she couldn't see that he was still standing, unhurt, she'd have done worse than scream.

Slowly Noah turned his head. She saw where he was looking, saw the hole that had appeared in the wall of the room, directly behind where he was standing. Grimacing, Noah sank slowly back down onto the sofa. The sound of the children's sobbing ebbed slightly, as again the older students hushed them.

"The next time," Ares warned, "I will not tell him to miss."

Noah stared at his knees and swallowed visibly.

"And you," Ares said, glaring down at Paige, "you will stay here, along with these children, until you change your mind. And you *will* change your mind. Or you will pay dearly, I promise you that."

He looked up and called orders to the first two men, the

ones who had taken over the school. "Tarak, Filipo, you will guard both doors of the building. Be watchful and careful. I want no one hurt. Yet. I'm trusting you."

Paige barely heard; his words were echoing in her head. *Pay dearly.*

Paige surreptitiously peeked at Noah from the corner of her eye, grateful that he had had the foresight to see that keeping Kyle's relationship to her a secret would be wise. He didn't seem to notice her glance. Now he was staring at his hands, which were knotted in his lap.

As Ares snapped at his two escorts to follow him and strode angrily out of the school, something else occurred to her. Instead of striking her across the face, as she might have expected, the man had instead hit the side of her head. She'd thought he was just striking out wildly, but what if it had been intentional? What if he'd hit her where he could be sure it wouldn't show when he was trying to convince the world his captives were being treated well?

Somehow, the idea that he could think so clearly, never losing sight of his plan even in anger, chilled her more than a bout of uncontrolled rage would have.

When they were again alone with the original two men, Paige risked looking at Noah. He hadn't moved. In fact, he seemed utterly, totally chastened by his near-fatal encounter with the man.

She couldn't blame him for being rattled, not after coming that close to death. And he'd done it for her, after all, leaping to her defense after Ares had struck her, so she should give him a lot of credit for that. Still, she was surprised he'd so completely collapsed. It was such a change from the dynamic, take-charge man she'd always seen.

But then, he'd probably never been shot at before, either, she admitted. It probably wasn't a common risk in his job. In fact, ironically and sadly, it was probably less of a risk for him than it was for most teachers these days. And he had stood up in the face of five armed men when Ares had hit her.

She'd be doing the same thing, in his place. In fact, she felt like doing it right now, just sitting down and giving in to the tremors that were so hard to quell. But she couldn't. She had a roomful of kids counting on her.

She glanced at Noah once more and then turned back to the children.


Rider watched the two guards as best he could without betraying himself, his mind racing. In the wake of their leader's visit, they acted as if they'd been honored by what was clearly simple guard duty. If this was a sign of Ares's power over his troops, they were dealing with the worst kind of charisma-blinded zealots.

They both seemed quite enamored of their roles. And now he had to choose what his role was going to be. The closest he'd ever come to actual combat was reading Sun-Tzu. And while the millennia-old treatise on the art of war was concise and educational, he'd been reading it as a businessman, not a warrior. Had the situation not been so grim, he would have laughed aloud at the idea of himself as a warrior of any kind. He'd never even been in the service. What could he possibly do?

But somebody had to do something—that was clear. And he was, theoretically, the person in charge while he was here. There was no way around it, it was up to him.

Still, the circumstances limited him greatly. Surprise and his wits were the only weapons he had, and he could only think of one possibility of how to best use them. It was a twisted path, but hadn't Sun-Tzu said that he who perceives the circuitous route as direct would be victorious? Something like that, anyway.

It wasn't going to be easy. Paige was already looking at him in an odd way, with a touch of near disappointment. Even the guards were looking at him with scorn. And it would only get worse if this worked. He'd just have to live with that. He sat silently, thinking, turning over options, until he had a loose sort of a plan. He didn't like it, but he couldn't think of anything better. And he couldn't just sit here and wait.

Still, because he knew what her reaction would be, it took him a moment to work up to looking at Paige as she comforted the children and saying, loudly enough for the hothead at the closest door to hear, "Maybe you should reconsider."

She turned and stared at him, dumfounded, and it was worse than he'd expected. "What?"

"Maybe you should work with them. It might make it easier on all of us."

"You want me to become a mouthpiece for this...this scum?" she exclaimed.

That did it, he thought, seeing both the guards suddenly start paying attention.

"It's better than getting beaten up and shot at," he said, coming as close as he thought he could to a whine without going over the top.

The look in her eyes went from shocked to bewildered to, he was very much afraid, disgust. "You'd really have me cooperate with them? They're a disease on the planet, and you want me to *help* them?"

Damn, he was proud of her! He wanted to kiss her, but he schooled his voice to a wheedling tone now. "What can it hurt? They can't want anything very important. Probably only money, that's all their kind care about, really."

"Shut up!" shouted the hotheaded Filipo. "You know nothing!"

Bingo, thought Rider. He was about to open his mouth when Paige spoke, following his lead as perfectly as if she had a script before her.

"I suppose," she said to Filipo, in a voice that chilled even Rider, "you're going to tell me you have some kind of noble cause, that you're above such things as hostage taking for mere money.''

She'd played into his plans perfectly, but Noah still wished she would take it a little easier. Although, perhaps she'd realized that when Ares had said he wanted no one hurt—yet—he'd particularly meant her. Still, she wasn't doing herself any favors by provoking these two.

''We fight injustice!'' Filipo cried. ''We fight for the release of our brothers, rotting in an Arethusan prison. Money means nothing to us.''

''Especially,'' Rider said almost conversationally to Paige, ''since they probably have no shortage of it. Most terrorist groups in this region are also drug smugglers.''

Filipo swore and took a step toward them. Only a shout from Tarak across the room stopped him. ''Do not let them play you like a flute,'' he warned.

''Take it easy,'' Noah put in, holding up his hands in meek surrender. ''I'm sorry, I was just mouthing off.''

Filipo fell back, grumbling. But he resumed his post at the door.

He probably should have kept his mouth shut, Rider thought. But the outraged loftiness of the man had grated. He knew from the in-depth studies Redstone had done before starting the resort that what he'd said was accurate. And coupled with his quick, sniveling backpedaling, it might just make what he had to do more believable. He had only to look at Paige's face to see that he'd been convincing.

The sickened feeling he had when he saw her looking at him with such hurt bewilderment was trying to tell him something, but he didn't have time to sort it out now. Now he had to concentrate on the job at hand. Whether he liked it or not.

To Paige the afternoon seemed endless. The only thing that seemed to happen was that about every half hour, one of their two guards—they seemed to trade off—would close his door and walk away, apparently to check the area surrounding the school. After these regular patrols they would return and take up their posts again.

Despite their initial fear, the younger children soon became restless. And the more restless they became, the edgier Tarak, the older guard, became. He had apparently been telling the truth when he'd said he didn't like noisy children. And when she had reluctantly been allowed to escort a couple of the younger ones to the bathroom in the back, off the vestibule, things had only gotten worse while she was out of sight.

Finally Tarak left his post and strode down the center aisle, treading heedlessly down the barefoot paths, until he stopped in front of Paige.

"Make them be quiet," he ordered her.

"They're children," she retorted sharply. "They're children and you've frightened them. They should have gone home long ago, and you're making them stay here, away from their parents. What do you expect?"

"I expect them to be quiet! And if you do not make them, I will tie them all up and tape their mouths shut!"

That threat got through to several of the children, and the noise level grew instantly, wails joining with children scrambling to cling to Paige.

"Well, that helped a lot," Paige told the man sourly.

Tarak glared at her. "You are far too disrespectful, for a woman. When this is over and we have gotten what we wanted, I will let Filipo teach you not to be."

"When this is over, you'll have no one to teach but your cell mate," Paige returned.

Rider winced inwardly, yet at the same time he wanted to cheer her. Tarak opened his mouth, then shut it again. Was he seeing the futility of carrying on a battle of wits when he was unarmed and his opponent had a howitzer? Rider thought with a grin he had to stifle.

"Just keep them quiet," Tarak ordered, and stalked back to his post.

"And just how," Paige muttered, "am I supposed to do that?"

How was she supposed to keep restless kids quiet? Rider had no answer. She was the teacher, not him. The only thing he knew about it was old memories of his own school days, longer ago than he cared to remember. Back then, the only thing—

He looked at Paige. "Read to them."

She blinked. "What?"

"Read to them. Isn't that what teachers do for quiet times?"

She waved a hand toward the gathered kids. "I've got twenty-six kids here, of all ages. What on earth am I going to read that will keep them all quiet? There's not a book around that…"

Her voice trailed off. He could almost see her thinking. She turned to look at the kids, specifically at the girl Rider had seen Kyle mooning after.

"Lani? Do you still have the book I gave you? The wizard book?"

The girl looked up, startled. "Yes, I do."

"May I borrow it back for a while?"

The girl nodded. "Of course. But it's in my bag. In the back."

Paige stood up. Without a glance at the guard behind them she started walking toward the main doors. Tarak shifted his weapon. Paige kept going.

The woman wasn't afraid of anything, Rider thought. And he wondered how much of that quiet courage she'd found since Phil's desertion and death.

"What are you doing?" Tarak asked sharply as she came up to him.

"If you want them to be quiet, then you'd better let me do this."

After a moment he let her pass, but he kept his eyes and his rifle trained on her as she disappeared into the vestibule. Rider held his breath. Less than two minutes later she was back in the doorway, a thick hardcover book in her hands. Tarak looked at it as if to inspect it. Rider saw Paige say something, saw the guard glare at her yet again, then waved her on with an annoyed gesture.

She'd probably made some crack about smuggling a weapon in the book, Rider thought, wondering if she would ever be able to pass up a chance to needle their captors. Then again, as long as they were under a mandate not to hurt her, she could do the rest of them nothing but good by keeping the men focused on her, while he sat back meekly cowering.

When she returned to the front of the room, she pulled up a seat he hadn't noticed before, a director's-style folding chair the height of a bar stool. She settled into it, the book on her lap. By then most of the kids were watching her.

"If we're going to be stuck here awhile," Paige told them, "we might as well escape in a different way." She opened the book to the first page and began the story of a young boy about to learn he was a wizard.

It took a while, but after a few pages the kids had settled down and were listening. Even the older ones, Rider noted. He couldn't blame them, not only was the story engrossing, but Paige read it well, like a storyteller herself. Once he even thought he caught Filipo tuning in, although he turned away quickly when he realized Rider had seen him.

Paige read and read, until her voice started to sound scratchy. Rider found himself getting as wrapped up in the story of the mistreated young boy who discovered he was a wizard as the kids were. But he also noticed the time passing, and wondered what Tarak and Filipo were going to do when they had a bunch of hungry, tired kids on their hands.

As if she'd had the same thought at the same moment,

when she reached the end of the next chapter, Paige looked up from the pages. "You're going to have to feed these children," she told Tarak in an almost belligerent tone that told Rider she'd fight if she had to.

"Food will come," Tarak said shortly.

She went back to her reading until the light began to fade. Then she slid off the chair and started toward the wall. Filipo moved immediately to stop her.

"I need light to continue," she explained.

"No lights," Tarak said from the back.

She turned to him. "No lights? You want tired, hungry children to stay quiet in the dark?"

"They will not be hungry. The food is on the way. And they will be quiet, because they will be sleeping."

Rider thought the man was being a bit optimistic. He himself might not know much about kids, but he didn't think any of them over the age of ten were real keen on going to sleep the instant it was dark. But he understood the no-lights order: it was like going hunting and, when it got dark, staring into the fire. You destroyed your night vision, and by the time you got it back, you could be dead. Besides, the moon was nearly full and cast more light than most people realized, at least for eyes adjusted to the night.

The man had told the truth about the food. The sound of footsteps came shortly after his words, accompanied by the clatter of dishes. Two more armed men came in, loaded down with food on banquet-style, covered plates stacked on huge trays. Different men than before, a lower rung than the bodyguards, Rider guessed. Elected for this detail because Ares wouldn't allow any of the hotel personnel outside, especially not to see their children.

The men set the trays down on Paige's desk while making a couple of jokes about baby-sitting that made Filipo bristle and Tarak retort unkindly about their respective mothers. Laughing, the food carriers left.

"You will each get a fork, nothing else," Tarak instructed. "And they will all be accounted for when you are done, or no one will eat the next time. You have one half hour."

The two guards retreated to eat their own meal, although they took turns so one was always watching. Paige ignored her own food and set about coaxing the younger ones, upset all over again at the sight of yet more armed men, to eat. The guards seemed to regard this as unthreatening and didn't challenge her. Rider gulped down what he could of the meal he barely tasted, knowing he was going to need the fuel. Then he went to Paige.

"Go eat. I'll do this now."

"I don't know," she began.

Unsure what else to do, Rider appealed to the little ones. "You don't mind, do you? If I sit with you, so Mrs. Cooper can eat? She's hungry, too."

The kids looked doubtfully at him, but their regard for Paige won out, as he'd hoped. She still hesitated, but when he insisted, she did as he asked and sat down at her desk to hastily eat, all the while watching the children. Redstone Resorts had a reputation for fine cuisine, but Rider somehow doubted whether he or Paige could tell anybody what they'd just eaten.

By the time the half hour was up and their guards began to collect and count the forks, it was past twilight and growing dark. "Get them ready to sleep," Tarak instructed.

Paige laughed in his face. Tarak tensed. Rider winced yet again. "You don't have kids, do you?" she asked the man.

"I do," Tarak retorted. "But *my* children are properly obedient!"

"And terrified of their father?"

"Respectful," Tarak said. "Now do it!"

Rider feared he was losing patience with his troublesome hostage.

"Why does he always yell at her?" little Hannah asked him as he knelt beside her chair.

"She's angry about what he's doing, keeping you all here," Rider explained, "so he gets angry back."

"I don't like it," Hannah said firmly.

"I don't, either," Rider told her. "So we've got to do what she wants us to, so she's not so angry, okay?"

He gave her a squeeze and got to his feet. When Paige rejoined him, he pitched his voice low to speak to her.

"You've got to back off, Paige. You might push him too far and somebody could get hurt."

"Including you?" she snapped, although no louder than he had spoken; she might be angry, but she was still thinking. And he'd had that coming, from her point of view.

"Including me, you and the children. Give it a rest, at least for a while. Let's get them settled. It's going to be a long night."

She said nothing more, but began to do as he said. She had a couple of the older kids go to the little ones' cubicle—warily watching Tarak every step of the way—to gather up the mats that were there. They brought them back and then moved the chairs out of the way and laid them out. There were extras, but not enough for all the older kids. Kyle took it upon himself to volunteer the boys to rough it. Lani quickly vetoed that idea.

"Girls can be just as tough as boys," she said firmly.

"Tougher," Kyle said easily. "You have to have the babies."

Rider smothered a grin but gave Kyle an approving wink. Kyle in turn gave him a sideways look that Rider couldn't quite read, although it clearly meant something.

Paige then began the lengthy process of taking the little ones to the bathroom. The older ones she merely escorted, so they wouldn't have to go past the guard alone. Once that was done, and she had the littlest ones settled on the mats, the older ones at least sitting on the floor, Rider casually moved toward her, putting himself between her and Filipo so that he could turn his back to the young guard.

"Let's move the sofa up here," he said, loud enough for both guards to hear, gesturing toward the raised computer center. "If we put it up there on the platform then you can see everyone and anybody who might need something."

For a moment she looked puzzled; there wasn't really anything to be gained by moving it, she could see everybody anyway and he knew she knew that. But when he mouthed "Say yes," at her, after a moment she just nodded.

"All right," she said, loud enough for the guard to hear.

It took them a couple of minutes to lever the sofa up onto the computer platform and get it exactly where he wanted it. Paige clearly didn't understand why it needed to be exactly there, and there was barely room for it, but she helped him, anyway. So, he thought, there was at least some small amount of trust left.

Or she was just withholding final judgment, waiting a bit longer before she wrote him off entirely.

By the time they were done with everything, it was completely dark, although not as dark as it could have been, thanks to the moon. Paige went from child to child, reassuring them with encouraging words that Rider wasn't sure she believed herself. But they seemed to believe her and began to settle down for a night she'd told them to think of as camping out. And if she lingered a tiny bit longer with Kyle, Rider didn't think anyone had noticed. Finally she retreated to the sofa they'd moved, and sank down onto it wearily.

Their two guards had taken chairs to their respective doors and appeared to be settling in for the night, their attention divided between their prisoners and the outside, and broken only by their regular rounds. Time spun out. When at last he was certain neither of them was looking, he walked to the back of the sofa to once more make sure it was in the right place. Then he went to stand behind Paige, leaned over and put his hands on her shoulders. He felt how incredibly tight her muscles were, just before she instinctively tensed. He rubbed gently and leaned over farther.

"It's going to be okay," he told her. "I promise."

He doubted that she believed him. He didn't blame her at all, since he had no idea himself if he'd be able to keep that promise.

# Chapter 10

She didn't understand. The terrorists, with their scare tactics, disgusting methods and pseudo-noble demands, seemed downright simple to understand next to Noah Rider. One minute he was acting afraid of his own shadow, next he was calming the kids. He'd been so good with them, even though he insisted he knew next to nothing about dealing with children. And now he was rubbing the tenseness out of her shoulders and telling her it was going to be okay in a voice she almost believed.

Barely aware of what she was doing, she leaned back into his hands, only realizing how knotted her muscles were by the feel of strong yet gentle fingers working them, easing them. She closed her eyes. Just for a minute, she thought. Just for a minute she could stop thinking and just feel the warmth spreading beneath his hands. Just for a minute, and then she'd get back to worrying about their situation.

She felt him move and opened her eyes. She realized he was now kneeling behind the sofa. She started to turn her head, but stopped when he whispered, "There's nothing more you can do right now."

She nearly shivered at the feel of his breath against her ear. And then his fingers brushed the skin at the back of her neck and she did shiver. How could he do this to her with just a touch, and in the middle of chaos?

She made herself concentrate on his words. "I can't just sit here," she said, speaking as quietly as he had, hoping that in the darkness nothing would draw the guard's attention.

"That's all you can do for now. You have the kids to think about. If anything happened to you, think what it would do to them. Look how upset they got when that bastard hit you."

And you almost got shot, she thought, shivering anew at the memory. She didn't flinch at all at his epithet. It fit in most senses of the word.

But he had a point. She hadn't thought of that. She knew the kids liked her, as well as they could like any teacher they'd only been with a few weeks. And the little ones especially had taken to her. And it would be the little ones who would be affected most if something happened to her.

"Just wait until morning. Things may change by then."

"You mean they may go away? Get what they want and leave?"

Noah sighed. "Not likely. Not if they want somebody out of jail in Arethusa. The government won't negotiate. I've worked with them when we were making the deal for Redstone Bay, and they're pretty hard-nosed."

"What could change, then?"

"Maybe Ares will have other things to think about besides a spokesperson and leave you alone for the moment."

"Like how to terrorize everyone into being too afraid to resist?" It was all she could do to maintain a whisper.

"That is the usual MO, I believe," Noah agreed.

How could he sound so cool, almost casual, when she

knew he was as frightened as she was? She'd seen it in his face, in his body language. Did the darkness, and the fact that their captors couldn't see them make that much difference?

Another little shiver rippled through her as she realized the tiny tug she was feeling on her hair was Noah. It felt as if he were running her ponytail through his hands, as if he liked the feel of it.

"Why don't you try to rest?" he asked softly. "You'll need to be on your toes tomorrow."

"How can I rest with those two ready to shoot anything that moves?"

"They're not going to shoot you. Not when their leader wants to use you."

She'd already reached that conclusion, but it didn't alleviate her concern very much. "What about the children?"

"I doubt they'll chance shooting one of them, either. They may need them later, for leverage."

Paige tried to smother the exclamation of hatred that wanted to break free at the thought of these evil men using children as bargaining chips, with no more feeling than if they were the palm trees that abounded on the island.

Noah came around the couch and sat down next to her. "Try not to think about it right now," he urged. "They're just getting set up. Nothing's likely to happen tonight."

She wished she could be sure of that. Noah put his arm around her shoulders and pulled her to him. She hadn't the energy to resist and didn't want to. It just felt too good to have somebody to lean on. Maybe Noah wasn't Arnold Schwarzenegger, but this would have been so much worse if she'd been alone.

She listened to his steady breathing, to the occasional rustle as a child shifted on one of the mats. Noah generated a wonderful warmth, and after a while it was all she could do not to snuggle even closer and drift off.

"Just doze," he told her softly. "You know you'll wake up if one of them needs you."

She supposed he was right. When Kyle had been younger, he couldn't make a sound, even down the hall, without her coming awake to check on him.

She stifled a yawn. Those had been precious days. Days when all was right with her world, when her child trusted her implicitly and when she'd believed her husband had loved her. Then terrorists had destroyed that world, just as they had now.

No, she told herself as she stifled another yawn, Phil had already destroyed it. All the terrorists had done was destroy the facade, tear the lid off Phil's secret life, when they had taken down that plane. Even if they hadn't killed him, he would have been gone. The only difference was that it would have done even more damage to Kyle.

She'd saved him that, at least, she thought sleepily....

Paige came awake with a start, with no idea of how long she'd been asleep. A little confused and groggy, she listened, wondering if one of the children had stirred, awakening her. But she heard nothing from them. And the guards had not moved. They were still in their chairs, angled so they could see outside but still hear anything above a whisper in the schoolroom.

In that instant she thought of Noah and realized that he and his comforting warmth were gone. But he was there, moving more quietly than she ever would have thought possible for a man of his size. He was behind the sofa, which puzzled her, since the only place he could have been coming from was the bathroom, yet that was the other direction. His rising must have been what had begun to rouse her, although she hadn't really awakened until his return.

Then he was beside her again, and she felt the urge to curl up against him. At first she fought it but then wondered why. These could hardly be called normal conditions, so she couldn't be blamed for what she wanted, could she?

And he certainly didn't seem to mind. In fact, he shifted to make more room for her, gently urged her to pull her feet up and lie back against him. Before she really realized it, they were lying on the sofa, her back to his chest, and it felt so good she didn't make the slightest protest. Not that she wanted to.

He was even warmer than before, and his breathing seemed a bit quicker, as if that short trip to the bathroom had been an exertion.

She hadn't found it too pleasant a trip herself, under guard, she reminded herself.

She tried to think, but it was difficult when she was so close to Noah, in such an intimate position. And she was still tired, she guessed, as she tried to figure the time. Then she gave up and whispered a question to the man who would know better than anyone.

"When are the first guests scheduled?"

"The day after tomorrow," he said. Then she felt him shift, saw him lift his arm to look at his watch. "Make that tomorrow," he corrected, "it's nearly one."

That startled her. She hadn't expected to sleep at all, yet she'd slept more than two hours. But then, she'd done the same thing when Phil had been killed, slept as if it had been the way to avoid the reality that had suddenly crashed in on her. That was, until she got served those papers the day she'd buried him. After that she was beyond the healing power of sleep for a very long time.

But now, even amid this horror, she felt oddly soothed with Noah so close. And after a few minutes she drifted off once more.

"Ms. Cooper?"

The tiny voice brought her bolt upright. She glanced around. The nearest door was closed. Filipo must be on his patrol. Then she saw that Noah was gone again, but she didn't dwell on it, because the voice had belonged to little

Stevie. He'd been too scared to risk going near the guard earlier, so she'd half expected to see him when the need to go to the bathroom grew urgent.

"I'm sorry, I gotta go."

"It's okay, Stevie," she said. "I'll take you."

Perhaps Noah was already there, she thought, as she led the child through the maze of other children, some sleeping, some afraid to, she was sure. When they got close to the door, she picked up the terrified little boy and carried him past Tarak, wondering if the man never slept.

The door to the bathroom was open and the room stood empty. Puzzled now, wondering where Noah could be, she waited while Stevie took care of his business. Then she took the boy back and got him settled. She did her best to reassure him, gave him a kiss on one tear-stained cheek and patted his shoulder. She checked on the others. More were asleep than she'd expected. But she suspected from the too-tightly closed eyes of some that the demeanor of sleep was only a pretense. Not that she could blame them.

She knelt beside Kyle. His eyes came open instantly. She reached out and cupped her son's face, unable to stop the tears that welled up. Even in the faint light Kyle looked scared. He began to speak, but she hushed him with a quick shake of her head.

"They can't know who you are," she whispered to him. "They'd try to use you to get me to do what they want."

Kyle's eyes widened in realization. Paige longed to embrace him, but knew she didn't dare treat him any differently than the others just in case the guards were watching. Hugging the little ones was one thing, but if she hugged Kyle she'd make him stand out far too much. Possibly enough to make them curious, although they seemed to be more focused on the outdoors now, as if the relative calm inside didn't need their attention anymore.

They think they have us beaten, she thought as she moved on. The thought infuriated her. They might be captives, they might be helpless for the moment, but they were not beaten. She wouldn't allow them to be beaten.

She returned to the sofa, still not knowing where Noah was. The children settled back into silence. She glanced at the guards, who seemed intent only on watching the exterior. Neither of them seemed to be aware one of their prisoners was unaccounted for.

*Unless they did know.*

Her breath caught in her throat as the possibility sliced through her mind. What if they weren't looking for him because they knew where he was? What if they'd done something with him?

What if they'd killed him?

She tried to fight down her wild speculations. Surely she would have heard something. They might be deadly assassins, for all she knew, but surely they couldn't just slip in and kill a man and drag him away without making a sound.

But maybe they had lured him outside somehow and done it there. Maybe even now Noah was lying dead in the moonlight in this tropical paradise turned to hell.

She shivered, even though it was a typically balmy night. She wrapped her arms around herself and curled her legs up under her on the sofa. She missed his solid warmth more than she ever could have imagined, much more than she should have, given she'd only experienced it for such a short while. The thought that now she might never solve the mystery that was Noah Rider made her feel even colder.

*...I was so attracted to you myself.*

His words echoed in her head, the words she'd never expected to hear, words that explained so much, words that validated all her own tangled feelings of the past five years. She'd thought she'd been hideously out of line, throwing herself at a man who had been too kind to crush the fragile spirit of a grieving woman. The knowledge that she hadn't been alone, that maybe, just maybe, she'd acted at least in part on some subtle signal he might have given her, did more to ease her mind about what had happened back then than any amount of trying to rationalize it because of her emotional state.

And it also made her suspicions all the more agonizing. If he was really dead...

She fought off the images that assailed her. She tried not to think at all as the night stretched on and on. She didn't allow herself to lie down, afraid it would happen again, that while she slept another of their number would disappear.

The barest whisper of sound from behind her made her go still, holding her breath. She flicked her gaze to both guards; neither had moved. The sound again, this time punctuated by a slight rubbing noise. She checked the guards again, then risked a quick peek over her shoulder.

What she saw stunned her. A square of the custom flooring of the computer platform had been pushed aside, leaving a darkened gap. And up out of the darkness beneath the school, rising like some sort of night creature, came Noah Rider.

A gasp escaped her, and he spun around in the act of quietly replacing the square. In the instant she opened her mouth to speak he was there. He swooped down on her like that night creature he'd brought to mind and did what she never would have expected.

He kissed her.

Sudden and fierce and hot, he kissed her. He cupped her face in his hands and took her mouth with his inexorably. For an instant she simply sat there, unable to react, to think, even to breathe. And then a burgeoning heat welled up, billowing through her with a speed that shocked her.

What had been fierce suddenly gentled. His lips went from demanding to coaxing, and when he silently pled his case she responded, opening to the gentle probe of his tongue. He tasted her, slowly, the barest swipe of his tongue over the ridge of her teeth. She responded, unable not to, with a tiny flick of her own tongue to the tip of his, and heat rocketed through her again when she heard him make a low, harsh sound.

He broke the kiss then, and for a moment they just stared at each other. She could hear his breathing, even quicker than when she'd noticed it before. Or maybe it was her own. She didn't know.

He came around the end of the sofa, just as he had the last time she'd awakened. He hadn't been coming back from the bathroom at all, she thought. He'd come up through the floor then, too.

Realizations tumbled through her mind. He'd known about the flooring, known some of the two-foot-square tiles had been left unbolted to allow for repair of the complex wiring. Of course he'd known—he'd practically designed it. And this was the reason behind his sudden urge to move the sofa; it was giving him some small screen for his actions. Except for that quick move when he'd kissed her.

When he'd kissed her...

If she'd spoken out of shock when she'd first seen him, it might well have been loud enough to alert the guards. Was that why he'd done it?

He sat down next to her again, close, where he'd been before.

"I've been wanting that for days," he whispered, with a husky timbre to his voice that sent heat through her yet again.

She wanted to say that she had, too, wanted to believe that keeping her quiet hadn't been his only reason. And she realized with a little jolt that even if he had kissed her just to keep her quiet, it didn't matter. It had been as hot and consuming as their first kiss had been five years ago, and why he'd done it didn't change that one bit.

So where did that leave them? Without the baggage of Phil's desertion and death between them, where did they go from here?

Nowhere, she realized, unless they got out of this alive. And there was a very real possibility they might not.

"What were you doing?" she whispered.

"Trusting they didn't know there's another way out than the doors they're guarding," he said with a wry twist of his mouth.

"But—"

He put a finger to her lips. "Let's not push our luck any further. There's still an hour or so before dawn. Try to get some more sleep."

"I thought they'd killed you." Her whisper sounded shaky, but she couldn't help it.

For a long moment he just looked at her, as if he very much wanted to ask if she'd care. But all he said was, "They may yet. I'm not cut out for this kind of thing."

"Then why—"

He hushed her again, nodding toward Tarak, who was looking their way.

"Lie down again," he whispered. "So he won't think it odd he couldn't see me earlier, either."

That made sense, she told herself. And no matter the reason, she liked the feeling of him being so very close. Liked the sound of his breathing in her ear, liked the feel of his arm around her, pulling her to him. For a moment she let herself wonder what it would be like if they weren't in this situation, let herself fantasize about being with him like this under normal conditions—free to explore whatever this was that exploded to life so quickly between them.

She was allowed a little fantasy, she thought. Especially since it might be all she ever got.

She woke to the faint light of early morning and a lovely feeling of safety. Noah was holding her tight, and she was snuggled up against the curve of his body so nicely. Sleepily she wiggled, wanting to be closer. Noah gave a low, smothered exhalation, as if she'd hurt him somehow.

She came awake with a little start. He was holding her close. Very close. And if his state of arousal, obvious as he pressed against her, was any indication, pain hadn't been what he'd expressed.

She wanted to move closer but made herself try to edge away instead. He tightened his arms around her. "Stay," he whispered.

"But you...you're..." She stammered to a halt, very aware that there were twenty-six children close at hand.

"Yes. I'll live. Don't go."

She couldn't say no to the barely disguised plea in his voice. She settled back down, at least until the first child started to stir.

That came sooner than she'd hoped, with the sudden sound of excited voices at the back of the schoolroom. She sat up then, watching the children as they awoke to the noise, listening as well to the rapid conversation between the two guards and another man, the jokester who had helped bring the food last night. Filipo had closed his door and left his post to join them, so she knew it must be important. She got up and walked amid the children, until she got close enough to hear.

"—half the power at the hotel is out. Lights, elevators, everything but the kitchens."

"They are supposed to open tomorrow night! How can they not have electricity for those rich pigs?

"There's more. Two of our boats were sunk last night, and the third damaged."

"What about Sabaya? Wasn't he watching the boats? Did he not see or hear something?"

"He saw someone, a man he thinks. He tried to chase him, but he lost him in the brush on the north side."

"Sabaya is an idiot," Tarak exclaimed. "He can't do the simplest of jobs, guarding the stupid boats. Now we will have to repair them. What more can go wrong?"

"Ares thinks the boats may be sabotaged."

"Sabotaged? By who? Isn't all the staff accounted for?"

The joker nodded. "He doesn't know who. But he is suspicious."

"Mrs. Cooper, can we get up now?"

Paige tore her attention away from the incredible conversation. It was all she could do not to turn and stare at Noah.

Could it be? He'd seemed so cowed, so subdued since Filipo had shot at him. But she couldn't deny what she'd seen, either—Noah had slipped out twice during the night. Could he really be responsible? Noah Rider, Redstone executive who claimed not to be cut out for heroics, who had seemed so timid after that near escape, out on midnight sabotage missions?

Finally she could no longer resist and looked at him. In the morning light she noticed for the first time that he had a long scratch on the side of his neck.

*...he lost him in the brush.*

Most of her doubt faded. Unlikely as it seemed, impossible as it sounded, it looked as though it had to be true.

Noah was the stealthy saboteur.

# Chapter 11

Uh-oh, Rider thought.

If he was judging Paige's expression right, she'd just put enough jigsaw pieces together to see the picture. She didn't look positive yet, but it wouldn't take much. He could only hope she was uncertain, or was at least able to hide the knowledge. The last thing he needed was to have Tarak or Filipo guess that they had their midnight skulker right under their guns.

He dodged her gaze then, and got up to help with the kids. He hadn't been kidding, he really didn't know much about them or how to deal with them, but the image of a nurturing, softhearted soul was exactly what he wanted to project to their captors. He didn't know how much the concept of machismo came into play in this part of the world, but if acting like a fussy mother hen would divert their attention from him, he'd play it to the hilt.

Not that these kids didn't deserve some fussing, he thought as Hannah lifted her arms to him with a faith he found oddly throat tightening. He picked her up, and she cuddled against him and let out a little sigh. She hadn't cried since it had first happened, and seemed to have accepted waking up to find herself still in what she must have hoped was just a bad dream.

In fact, he'd been surprised at how well they'd all held up. Even the little ones seemed to have realized that, while they couldn't go home, they were safe for the moment, and the outbreaks of wailing and tears had lessened. As for the older ones, they'd surprised him with their willingness to help the younger ones, although he suspected Lani had a bit to do with that. She'd quickly started to direct the others of her own age group, and they'd let her, glad, apparently, to have someone take charge. And to be doing something, anything, Rider guessed.

Right now she and Kyle had their heads together, and there was something about the intensity of their whispered conversation that made him nervous. Before he could edge close enough to hear anything, Kyle had gotten to his feet. After a quick glance to be sure his mother was occupied, the boy shoved his hands in his pockets and started to walk around, as if aimlessly. But Rider sensed there was purpose in Kyle's actions, and that made him even more nervous.

When he saw the boy was working his way toward the small door Filipo had left closed but unguarded when he'd rushed to hear the damage report, Rider went very still. Surely Kyle wasn't stupid enough to try and escape? They'd mow him down without a second thought; they needed Paige, but one kid more or less wasn't going to make that much difference.

Rider flicked a glance at Paige, but she was thankfully busy with little Stevie. He didn't want to think how she'd react if she saw what her son was doing.

He was almost to the door, and Rider was about to put Hannah down and do something—although he wasn't at all sure what—when Lani got up, walked over to one of the cubicles on the opposite side of the room from the doorway.

Kyle had halted six feet short of the door. Rider watched as Lani hesitated, glancing cautiously at the three men who were still agitatedly discussing the night's events. Then, with a movement he couldn't mistake for anything but intentional, she hit a stack of what appeared to be computer software CD boxes, sending them flying with a clatter that drew every eye in the place.

Except Kyle's.

Rider shifted Hannah so that he could look back at the door without the guards seeing him, sure he was going to see the boy making a dash out the door. Kyle was right next to the door now, but instead of running, he was straightening up from a crouch and casually walking back toward the group, unnoticed by the men at the doors.

"I'm sorry, Mrs. Cooper," Lani said as she threw an apologetic look to Paige, who had turned at the noise as they all had. "I'm just so scared by those men."

Paige smiled encouragingly at the girl, who then busied herself picking up the jewel cases, as if she had simply knocked them over by accident.

Girl, you're my kind of scared, Rider thought in silent salute to the nervy teenager.

However, the commotion had drawn their captors' attention back to them, and Filipo quickly returned to his post. Whatever Kyle had been doing, the man didn't seem to notice anything amiss. He opened his door once more, but this time didn't sit down; the possibility that their plans had been sabotaged had clearly raised their attention level.

Rider guessed from Filipo's disgruntled expression that he felt left out of the real action, stuck here guarding a bunch of school kids and their teacher...

And, Rider added with an inward smile, that teacher's wimpy, Milquetoast supervisor, no more threat than any of the six-year-olds.

Not that he felt like a threat. In fact, he'd rarely felt more out of his depth in his life. Yes, he knew how to move silently, knew how to stalk prey, had enough familiarity with guns and hunting to know how and where to hide, but he was unarmed and flying blind. Except that, unlike their uninvited guests, he knew every inch of Redstone Bay. And most of the rest of the island, too. It was all he had going for him. He could only hope it would be enough.

He'd accomplished what he'd wanted to last night. He'd inconvenienced them with the electrical power and hopefully the damage he'd inflicted on the boats. Making their escape a bit more complicated would make them think about their own skins.

But he'd also drawn their attention. Ares hadn't taken long to figure out they had an enemy on the loose, and judging by the heightened alertness of their own guards, he'd made his own job much more difficult.

And I wasn't all that good at it to begin with, he thought wryly.

Then he remembered Paige's look of speculation and couldn't help feeling a little glad that she'd guessed. He hadn't much liked the idea of her thinking he would just sit back and let these fanatics take over without even a token fight. It would have been better if she hadn't figured it out—what she didn't know she couldn't let slip, even unintentionally—but now that she had...

"Breakfast is coming. Get ready," Tarak called out in Paige's general direction.

Figuring this would be the time when their guards would get any new information, he took Hannah to the bathroom under the guise of washing up. He didn't like using the child, but she'd already said she needed to go, anyway, so he figured all he'd done was arrange the timing.

Breakfast arrived in the same manner dinner had the night before. However, this time it was minus the joking deliverymen. Everyone was deadly serious now, and from what he could hear of their hushed talk from inside the bathroom, Ares wasn't making the connection between the power problems and the damage to their boats.

"—thinks some local did it."

"Some local? What fool would go up against us?" Tarak scoffed.

Hannah finished and asked him to lift her up so she could wash her hands. Rider noted there was a small footstool handy, but if she wanted him to lift her, lift her he would. While he listened.

"Ares doesn't think anyone on the outside even knows we are here yet. It's possible that some poor islander scuttled the boats, hoping they'd be abandoned, and then he could repair and sell them," the deliveryman said.

There was a moment of silence as Tarak apparently pondered this, then Rider heard the deliveryman say, "I have to get back."

In the same moment Hannah said, "All done." Rider moved to put the child down, but she clung to him, shaking her head adamantly. "No. Please. Not by those nasty men."

He pulled her up and settled her comfortably against his chest. "You," he said, reaching out to tap her nose, "are a very discerning young lady."

She scrunched up her forehead. "Is that good?"

"It's very, very good," he promised her, and she gave him a smile that made him feel ridiculously gooey inside, while at the same time solidified his determination that someone was going to pay for terrifying this little girl.

Paige saw Noah bringing Hannah back from the bathroom. Despite everything, she couldn't help but smile at the picture they made—the tall, strong man with the wide-eyed little girl, her arms entwined so tightly around his neck, his arms holding her so safely. She wondered if there was a woman in the world who wouldn't be moved by such a sight. There was something about a strong man with a child...

A strong man. She'd always thought of him that way, an image from when he'd been there for her, so solidly, when she'd needed someone. And even though he'd been sent by his company, she'd been certain he'd gone above and beyond the call for her; she doubted holding her as she wept was part of the deal.

Then this had happened, and she'd had her image of him rattled. She had thought him a man only strong in his own world, in the halls of business, not the jungles of battle. And she'd not been happy with herself for judging him on that basis. How was a businessman supposed to face heavily armed men? He'd be a fool to even try.

So he hadn't faced them. He'd gone behind them, around them and apparently right under their noses.

It was possible, she thought, that it was somebody else, but she didn't think so. And now the guards were paying less attention to them and a lot more to the outside threat, never guessing it was right here.

She didn't think she could completely smother her smile, so even though they weren't watching their prisoners as closely, she turned away. She went back to counting up the utensils. She didn't want them to be accused of hiding any when it came time to present them to Tarak for the return count. It seemed so silly. What did they think, that someone would ignore the fact of their automatic weapons and attack them with a fork?

When she was sure there were the right number, she handed half to Lani to pass out, the other half to Kyle, while she began to hand plates of scrambled eggs and sausage to the children. She wondered if Rudy had fixed them. He was Stevie's father, and Paige could only imagine what hell he must be going through, knowing his little boy was held captive just as he was.

She set first Lani's, then Kyle's plates on their chairs

until they were done with the silverware. Kyle returned just as she finished and leaned over to pick up his plate. In that instant Paige took the chance to look at her son without being seen by the guards. She opened her mouth to say how proud she was of how he was behaving in this awful situation when, as he leaned over, she caught a glimpse of something beneath his shirt, shoved into his waistband at the small of his back. Her heart, her breath, even her vision seemed to short-circuit for an instant.

Kyle had a gun.

Her fingers clenched, white-knuckle tight, around the two remaining forks, hers and Noah's.

She knew nothing about guns. Well, next to nothing; she knew what those men were carrying were the powerful automatic rifles she'd heard so much about. Beyond that she knew there was a difference between an automatic pistol and a revolver and that they all came in different calibers. That was about the extent of her knowledge.

But there was one thing about guns that she was absolutely sure of: she did not want her son to have one. Most especially now.

He was sitting down now, paying more attention to Lani than to his food. Paige tried to think. She was vaguely aware that Noah was with Hannah and was settling her down with her breakfast, but only vaguely aware. Her mind just keep running that image over and over, like an endless loop of videotape, that dark-gray, unmistakable handle of a gun. What on earth did he think he was going to do? He didn't even know how to shoot a gun.

At least, she thought—hoped—he didn't. She'd lost control of him in the weeks before they'd left L.A., but could it have been that bad? Could those boys he'd been hanging out with have been that bad?

Of course they could, you fool, she chided herself. Wasn't it on the news every night?

She tried to get a grip. What had happened in L.A. didn't

matter now. What mattered was that her son had a gun, and whatever he had in mind, he would likely be the one who ended up getting shot.

She knew if she asked him for it he'd argue with her, and that could have lethal consequences if their guards were drawn by the commotion. She had to do something, and she had to do it now. She made a quick decision. It would have to be fast and smooth and over before he realized it.

She took the two steps over to Kyle's chair and dropped one of the forks she held.

"I'm sorry," she said, sounding brittle even to herself, "would you get that for me?"

Kyle bent to pick up the utensil. His shirt rode up again. Paige's hand darted forward. She had the gun in her hand almost before she realized it.

Kyle let out a yelp and jumped.

"Be quiet," she ordered through clenched teeth, hiding the gun behind her, hating the heavy, deadly weight of it.

Her son glared up at her. Anger glinted in his eyes. But when he spoke, he kept it down to a fierce whisper. "Give it back."

"Don't even ask."

"Somebody has to *do* something!" Kyle's fists were clenched as tightly as her teeth.

"Not you."

"Nobody else will!"

Don't be so sure, Paige thought, but she didn't say it. Something stopped her, something that made her think Noah had good reason for not wanting anyone to know.

And then Noah was there, at her side. He glanced at the guards to be sure they were still occupied, this time both eating at their posts between visual scans of the perimeter. Then he reached down and took the weapon from her unprotesting fingers. When he had it, he pulled up a chair left empty by a child who'd chosen to sit on the floor, and sat down at an angle that put his back to the guards.

"So," he said in a low but calm, nonconfrontational voice, "that's what you were up to. Swiped it out of his duffel, did you?"

"Yeah," Kyle said proudly. "Lani helped, and I—"

"So you risked her life as well as your own?"

"We didn't get caught," Kyle protested.

"True enough," Noah agreed. "But did you even wonder what he might do when he found it missing? Did it occur to you that he might start shooting people as punishment? Maybe starting with Lani?"

Kyle paled. Obviously, he hadn't thought that far at all. And frankly, neither had Paige, and now that Noah brought it up she was even more upset.

Noah glanced at both guards again. Then he swiftly and smoothly pushed something on the handle and the little rack of bullets slid out. He pulled back the top part of the gun, leaving what she guessed was the barrel oddly exposed. He looked into an empty chamber on the top, then did something that let the gun slide back into its original position. All the while Kyle stared, wide-eyed.

She didn't know what any of the parts were called, but it was clear even to her that he was no stranger to handling this kind of weapon. And if she'd had any remaining doubts about the identity of the person who'd caused their captors so much trouble, they vanished now.

And as he handled the gun with the ease of long experience, she realized his cowed facade was just that, a facade.

"You just wanted them to think you were too frightened to do anything, didn't you?" she whispered.

Noah gave her a sideways glance. "The less attention they paid to me, the better," was all he said.

"You mean, it was all an act?" Kyle asked, wide-eyed. "That acting like you were a coward and afraid and all that?"

"I *am* afraid," Noah said. "And anybody who isn't afraid with terrorists around is a fool."

"What are you, a cop?"

Noah slid the weapon under his own loose, Hawaiian-style shirt, then looked at the boy. "No. I'm just a businessman, stuck in this situation like we all are. I've got a bit of knowledge of how outfits like this operate, but only from reading."

"But the gun, you handle it like—"

"I grew up around guns. My father taught me how to stalk and track, and I'm a good shot, but that's all."

"How good a shot?" Kyle asked, clearly entranced.

"Very," Noah said. He glanced at their guards. "But I'm out of my league here."

"But the gun will help, won't it?" Kyle said eagerly.

"At least now it won't get you killed," Paige said sharply.

The old rage flashed in her son's eyes. "It's better than just sitting here and letting *them* win," he said in a harsh whisper.

Paige shivered. She hadn't realized how much of her own rage at these kind of men Kyle had absorbed. She lowered her voice, adding quietly yet earnestly, "I couldn't bear to lose you, too, Kyle. I just couldn't bear it."

The anger slowly ebbed, and Kyle looked away.

Later, as the children gathered up their dishes and put them on the trays, and Lani began to gather the utensils for counting again, Paige took Noah aside.

"Thank you," she said. "It scared me to death when I saw he had that gun."

Noah shrugged. "It was pretty clever of him. And Lani, diverting their attention like that."

"That's what that was?" Paige asked. "That bit with her knocking over the CD-ROM cases?"

He nodded. "While Kyle was over snagging it out of Filipo's bag."

"I wondered. She's just never clumsy."

"She's a beautiful girl."

"And smarter than she is beautiful."

Noah looked at her consideringly. "You do know that Kyle's really got a thing for her, don't you?"

"Oh, I hope so," Paige said. "She could do him a world of good."

"No motherly desire to keep him a little boy forever?"

"He quit being a little boy five years ago," Paige said. "Right now I'm for anything and anyone who can reach him."

"He'll be all right," Noah told her. "You just stick to your guns—"

He broke off with a wry grimace, as if realizing the irony of the expression. Paige gave him a quick smile to show she hadn't taken offense.

"What will you do with it?"

"For the moment keep it and hope Filipo doesn't notice it's gone before I get a chance to try and put it back."

"You won't...it won't help?"

"One handgun against their weapons? It'd help get me killed, maybe."

"But if you were caught by just one of them?"

"Not worth the risk. It might stop that one, but it would put the rest of them even more on guard. And so far they haven't really been trigger happy. I'd just as soon not give them reason."

Paige nodded. He made sense. But she couldn't help thinking most men would have kept the gun, wouldn't have been able to make such a rational, cool decision when the risk was their own life.

"Are you sure you've never done this before?"

He grimaced, rolling his eyes. "Very. And I know I'm going to wish I'd never tried to do it this time." Then, clearly changing the subject, he asked her, "What about the kids today?"

"I can kill a certain amount of time making sure they all get washed up and as clean as possible, but after that, there's still a long day ahead. They're going to be going stir-crazy, all cooped up like this."

"What would you normally be doing when they're all together like this?"

"Reading to them, some of the time, and I can do that, but not all day. They won't sit still for it."

"What else?"

"Well, sometimes we just talk about things."

"Then do that," he suggested. "Just like you normally would."

She thought about that for a moment. "It might help if they could talk about how scared they are."

And then an idea struck her, and she began to plan.

"Do you all know what terrorism is?" Paige asked from her seat in the high director's chair in front of her class. Rider sat on the sofa, watching her, curious about where she was going with this. She'd said it rather loudly, and it sounded odd after all the whispering they'd all been doing.

She lifted the large book she held and opened it on her lap. "The dictionary says it is 'the systematic use of terror, especially as a means of coercion.'" She looked back at the kids. "Let's talk about that. Terror means being very afraid." Noah realized she was being careful to say things so they wouldn't go over the heads of the younger kids. "Systematic means there's a plan to it, that they know exactly what they're doing, that it's intentional, and that they do it often. Do you understand that?"

She got a chorus of nods.

"All right, then, who knows what coercion means?"

Lani politely raised her hand. Some traditions held, even in the face of chaos, Rider thought in amazement.

"Lani?"

"It means being forced to do something you don't want to."

"Exactly. Now how many of you have been terrorized by, oh, maybe a brother or sister?"

A couple of hands went up, but many of the younger ones just looked puzzled. Paige tried again.

"How many of you have had a brother or sister try to scare you into doing something you didn't want to? Like maybe telling you they'd beat you up if you didn't do their chores for them, or take the blame for something they did?"

At least a half dozen more little hands shot up.

"Okay, that's a form of terrorism. But there's a big difference here. First, these men don't want anything from you except for you to be scared. They want to use you to force someone else to do something."

"Why us?" a tiny voice asked from the back.

When Paige answered, her voice was even louder. "Why innocent, defenseless children? Because terrorists are cowards—heartless, cold, cruel cowards."

Noah leaned forward. What was she trying to do? He glanced at the guards. For the first time since they'd gotten the report on possible sabotage, their attention was fully on the inside of this schoolroom.

"And," Paige went on, "they don't care who they hurt as long as they get their way."

"Bullies," Kyle said suddenly.

"Yes, they are. Can anyone think of any other names for them?"

"Criminals?" Lani suggested.

"Yes, terrorists are definitely criminals."

"Stop this!" Filipo called from his post. Paige ignored him.

"How about villains?" she said.

"Chickens?" somebody else offered.

"That's true, too," Paige agreed.

"I said stop!" Filipo shouted again, on his feet now. "We are not terrorists!"

"Sit down, you're interrupting my class," Paige said as if he were no more than a rowdy student. The kids took their cue from her and continued.

"Tyrants!" another girl exclaimed.

"Gangsters!" A boy this time, shouting gleefully.

The kids were getting into it now, and Noah realized this was exactly what Paige had wanted.

"Nasty!" little Hannah called out. The entire group laughed, Noah included. Until he realized that being laughed at could well be the one thing guaranteed to provoke their guards beyond control.

"Yes, sweetie, they are very, very nasty," Paige said with a wide smile at the little girl.

Filipo broke then and started toward Paige. He waved his rifle at her. "Stop this. Now."

Paige flicked him a disdainful glance, then turned back to her class. "Something else about terrorists. They often deny, even to themselves, what they really are. They try to hide it by saying they're fighting for a noble cause, or that they're after something important, like justice. But underneath they're just scared little bullies, who aren't smart enough to think of any other way to get what they want."

"You will stop this instantly!"

"All right," Paige said, suddenly agreeable. "Let's talk about something else, kids. Remember how that other terrorist, the one who thinks he's a leader, said he was called Ares?"

Some of the kids nodded, most just sat still, looking from Paige to the man she was taunting, their eyes wide.

"Does anyone know who the real Ares is?"

"A mythological god," Lani said when no one else spoke up.

"Yes," Paige said. "The son of Zeus and Hera."

Filipo seemed to relax slightly, although he didn't return

to his post. This line of instruction was clearly preferable to him. Rider had a feeling his mood wasn't going to last, not if Paige had anything to say about it.

"Ares was the god of war. And he was a bully—nasty and bloodthirsty. Nobody much liked him, gods or humans. He was particularly fond of looting and butchery, and was cowardly besides. Sounds like the perfect name for that man, doesn't it?"

That did it, Rider thought as Filipo shouted again. This time he snapped his rifle to his shoulder, aimed at Paige. Noah leaped to his feet. So did Kyle.

Tarak started walking toward them. Paige never looked at the older man, just turned to face Filipo. And his rifle. Noah could see that she was scared, but her head came up and her shoulders went back.

"Go ahead," she said, her voice tight, "prove me right. Show them all that you're nothing but a coward who thinks shooting an unarmed woman or child proves he's a man."

Tarak called out then. "Filipo!"

Filipo looked over at the older man, but didn't lower his weapon. "You heard what she was doing! She was insulting us, calling us names!"

Tarak's gaze slid to Paige. He looked at her intently for a moment before saying, "Only if you admit she is right, that we are terrorists."

Filipo's brow creased in puzzlement. Tarak, Rider thought, was brighter than he'd given him credit for.

"Go back to your post," Tarak ordered.

Filipo hesitated. But finally, after a glare that promised Paige would pay for the insults, he went back to his doorway. And after a long look of his own at Paige, Tarak turned and went back to his own post.

Rider covered the six feet between himself and Paige in a step and a half. He saw her sway slightly in the instant before he put an arm around her.

"Point made," he said.

She leaned against him, and he felt a shiver go through her.

"You are," he whispered, "the smartest, gutsiest, most totally *insane* woman I have ever met."

She looked up at him. He saw her swallow, as if she wasn't certain her voice would work anymore. He saw traces of the fear that lingered but also a flicker of triumph glinting in her cinnamon eyes.

"Should I take that as a compliment?" she finally asked.

"Absolutely," he said.

He'd meant every word of it. He'd never in his life met a woman like Paige Cooper. A woman who could be scared down to her bones and yet stand up to the source of her fear. A woman who would risk her life to ease the load on a bunch of terrified kids. A woman who would wave a red flag in front of terrorists just on general principle.

And that night, when they settled down on the sofa, he found himself thinking that here was a woman worth staying home for. Hell, you'd have to stay home, just to keep up with her.

And when she let him pull her close in the darkness once more, when he felt her in his arms, felt the lovely curves of her body as she snuggled closer, he thought it no less than a miracle that somehow that fearless fighter and this warm, soft woman were all wrapped up in one person.

Too bad he'd never earned a miracle.

# Chapter 12

This time Paige was awake when he left. In fact, neither of them had slept much. There was a new, humming sort of tension between them, and it had been all he could do not to kiss her again, long and deep.

"You're going out again now?" she whispered when he began to move slowly, intending to roll up over the top of the sofa without ever standing up, as he had last night.

"If I stay any longer," he said into her ear, "with you this close, I'll go stark raving crazy."

He heard a tiny catch in her breath and chose to take that as proof she was as wound up as he was.

"Someday," he said, his voice even lower, his mouth even closer to her ear, "I want to be in that same position with you. In private. Naked."

This time he was sure she gasped. But this was not the time or the place to pursue this fire that sparked between them. He wondered if they would ever be in the right time or the right place.

"Don't go," she said. "Not alone."

"No choice."

"I'll go with you."

He hugged her then. "Lady, I'd tackle anything, with you to watch my back. But you can't. The kids need you. You're all they've got."

He felt it when she gave in, letting out a little sigh that was an acknowledgment of his point. "Be careful, Noah," she whispered.

He went over the sofa and inched toward the trap door. Funny, he didn't hate his name when she said it. In fact, it made him feel kind of funny inside, warm and welcome and a few other things he was better off not thinking about just now.

He froze when the trap door made more sound than he'd intended as it fell shut. Then he heard another sound, foot steps, and held his breath. But they were light steps, not the heavy tread of a soldier. And then the direction of the steps, back and forth in the area where the children were told him Paige was up and moving, no doubt covering for his noise with her own footsteps as she gave the appearance of checking on the children once more.

Definitely the smartest, gutsiest, most totally insane woman he'd ever met, he thought as he belly crawled toward the back of the building, to where he was out of sight of both guards and could make it into the trees.

He had only one goal tonight. He knew the most important things to any attacking force were weapons, transportation and communication. He couldn't do much about the weapons—they didn't appear to have an arsenal, only the weapons they carried—and he'd already damaged their transportation. So that left communications.

The handheld radios he'd seen looked old, battered and bulky. He thought that in sets that old, there had to be a base station somewhere, with some sort of antenna that allowed signals to be transmitted from one handheld unit to another. If he could just find it....

He searched all the buildings he could get to. Then every acre of the grounds. He hurried as best he could while maintaining some kind of quiet, but it still took a very long time. And every hour that passed made it more likely his absence would be discovered.

Finally he drew back into the shelter of the trees and sat down to think. He'd been going about this all wrong, he decided, by just searching randomly. He needed to think. If he had an antiquated radio system that required some kind of base station, where would he put it?

High ground, obviously. But the hill just above the resort had been deserted. And from there he'd been able to see the top of all the buildings, and there was no sign of anything unusual. He drew his knees up and tried to keep thinking, tried to ignore that little voice in his head that was shouting "Who do you think you are, James Bond?"

The only other really high ground was the mountain—if you could call the eight-hundred-foot bump a mountain—where the microwave towers were. And while there were doubtless men there to guard those towers, he thought that was too distant for those antiquated radios.

But where else could it be? Where else would they set up to get a clear signal over the whole resort area?

A clear signal…

If you had clear view of the whole resort, you'd have a clear signal, wouldn't you? And there was one other place that had an unbroken line of sight on the whole resort.

In an instant he was on his feet and moving. In a few minutes he was peering through the trees to the lookout deck. And there was a man with a large, boxy piece of equipment. He wasn't certain until the man moved and he saw a pair of earphones over his head.

"Bada-bing," he muttered. And he settled in to wait for his moment.

It was getting perilously close to dawn when it finally came. The operator rose, yawned, stretched and walked off the cantilevered deck. At the bottom of the stairway he made a right turn, and Rider guessed he was heading for the bathroom farther down toward the beach. He searched the ground around him, and a few feet away spotted a soft-ball-sized rock. He grabbed it and then returned to his spot, still watching.

He edged closer, then closer still, waiting…and then the man disappeared inside the small cabana-type building. Rider ran for the deck.

The thing was even older than he'd thought, army surplus from somewhere gone astray. There was no time for finesse or hiding his handiwork, and he couldn't assume they didn't have a replacement battery pack, so he simply pried the thing open and yanked out what guts he could, and smashed the rest with the rock. For good measure he broke off what looked to be two antennae.

The noise had brought the still-unzipped operator running back, but Rider was already over the side of the deck—that drop was a lot longer than he'd realized—and into the trees before the man looked beyond his ruined equipment.

"…don't think it can be repaired. We're going to have to use the cell phones we confiscated from the prisoners for communication," today's breakfast man said.

Rider smothered a smile of satisfaction and went on cheerfully eating his toast.

The men were clustered at the back door this time, where they'd been since Tarak had realized his radio wasn't working and had come back to try Filipo's. When it, too, had proven useless, there had been a lively discussion on what they should do next, ended only by the arrival of a messenger sent by their leader with the news that the radio had been destroyed.

"But cell phones are easily monitored," Tarak was saying. Rider could only see his back, but by the man's tone he would be willing to bet he was frowning.

"Since we have control of all the equipment, we will be the ones monitoring," the other man pointed out. "The only problem is not having enough. Ares has one, of course, and his aide and the three lieutenants, but they have to use runners to talk to their men."

Rider managed not to pat his shirt pocket, holding his own cell. He'd thought about using it when they'd missed it in their first search of him, to notify Redstone Security. But he'd also known they probably had secured the microwave towers immediately. And Ares had wasted no time in letting them know they'd done just that, so while his decision had been right, his phone was indeed useless for calling for help.

But now they had to use the openly monitorable means of communication themselves, and somebody might be listening in and get suspicious.

"We'll have more, of course, when the others start to arrive. You know all those rich pigs will have them. But until then, we must be extra cautious and watchful."

They didn't seem to care that they could be overheard by anyone in the schoolroom. Rider hoped it was because they saw no threat coming from this direction, that they thought it didn't matter if he or Paige or the kids heard because they couldn't do anything, anyway.

Rider finished his toast and was reaching for the small can of orange juice they'd provided when Paige said from behind him, "Nice work."

She sat down beside him, nibbling delicately at a piece of bacon. He watched in fascination as she licked a crumb from her fingers. Then he made himself look away.

"You've got them in quite an uproar," she said.

"All I did was make their lives a little harder," Noah said. "I don't have the skills for an all-out guerilla war."

"I'll bet they don't think so," Paige said pointedly. "Not anymore."

"You? It was you?"

Kyle's voice was too loud to be missed. Neither of them had realized he was within earshot. And his astonishment was so extreme, Rider had the vague thought he should be insulted. But right now he had to cover this—Filipo was looking his way and had probably heard the boy's exclamation.

"Yes," he said, looking at Kyle, and loudly enough for Filipo to hear. "I did write that textbook. You found it boring?"

To his credit Kyle caught on quickly. "Oh. Sorry, but yeah, it really was."

The guard turned his attention back to the other conversation, as Rider had hoped.

But Kyle clearly had no intention of leaving. He sat down, his gaze never leaving Rider. But this time when he spoke his voice was low enough not to draw attention.

"You're the one who...did all that?"

Rider shrugged.

"If you're not a cop you gotta be, like, CIA or something," Kyle said, sounding utterly convinced of his own theory.

"Easy," Rider said. "Don't be tossing around those initials. Not only am I not nor have I ever been, but I'd as soon nobody planted that idea. It's hard to get it out of their heads once it's in."

"But you have to be—"

"You think only people who get paid for it try to stand up to slime like this?"

"No, but that kind of stuff, that stealth stuff..." His voice trailed off as something occurred to him. "Hey, how'd you get out past—"

Rider cut him off as the meeting at the back door ended and their two guards returned to their posts. At least Tarak did. Filipo came toward them instead. He looked at Paige, his jaw clenched and near hatred gleaming in his eyes.

"You do again what you did yesterday, and I will decrease your class by one." He flicked a calculating glance at Rider. "And I will start with—" he spun around, and aimed right at Hannah "—her!"

Rider leaped to his feet. The child wailed, terrified. Filipo laughed.

"You son of a—" Rider spat out, breaking off when he remembered the children.

Filipo kept laughing as he returned to the door.

Rider practically ran to Hannah and swept her up into his arms. He carried her back to his seat, the terrified wail ripping at his gut. Paige crouched beside them, awkwardly patting the child's hand. Kyle just stood there, looking paler than ever, as if he were only now realizing the true lethalness of their captors.

"It's okay, baby, I won't let the nasty men hurt you," Rider said. He'd always thought adults who talked like children to children were idiots, but it suddenly seemed the only way.

"The other kids are upset, too," Paige said as Hannah's screams changed gradually to slightly quieter sobs. "He scared them all over again. I don't know how much longer we can keep them calm."

Rider cuddled little Hannah, and rage blossomed in him anew as the girl shuddered in his arms. He had to do something. He couldn't just stand by and let these bastards destroy these children.

"What can we do, Noah?" Paige asked. "There must be something."

"I don't know." He didn't tell her he was on the verge of taking out the pistol and using it on Filipo, then Tarak if necessary, and damn the consequences. At least they could get the children out.

Well, some of them, he realized grimly. Shots would

bring reinforcements on the run, and that could result in any number of children being hurt or worse. There just wouldn't be enough time. They had to assume the other troops would hear and respond instantly.

Too bad there's not a silencer on the damn gun Kyle snagged, he thought. If this had been a movie, there would have been one. And they would have called it that, a silencer, not a suppresser or muffler, as was technically correct. The kind of thing that drove his dad crazy. But in a movie the hero would have rid the entire island of this plague by now. And here he sat, helpless, useless...

God, he was rambling now. But the sight and feel of this delicate little girl weeping, her face buried against his shirt as she clung to him, was tearing him apart. And the lowlife who'd done this to her didn't give a damn, he just sat there, ignoring her as he ignored all the children he'd helped terrify. As if they weren't even worth watching over, weren't worth guarding.

Rider went very still. Hannah was still weeping, but more quietly now. And his mind was racing.

*What can we do, Noah? There must be something.*

Well, maybe there was. Maybe, just maybe, they could take a few levers out of the hands of the terrorists.

"Paige," he whispered. She had stepped past him to try and calm the other children as best she could. She turned back toward him, took one look at his face and quickly returned and sat beside him.

"Who's the smartest, coolest, local kid here?"

"Lani," she answered without hesitation.

He frowned. "None of the boys?"

"The oldest local boy is fourteen."

"I can do it," Kyle said.

"Do what?" Paige asked.

"Whatever it is," Kyle answered. "I can hot-wire a car or make a Molotov cocktail or shoot a gun, whatever."

Rider saw Paige gaping at her son. Saw the boy shrug

and give her an annoyed look. "Hey, you want me to pretend I can't do all that, or try to help?"

"Maybe you can help," Rider said. If Paige wanted to chew out her son, she'd have to do it later. Although later he, too, was going to have a word with Kyle, about the tone he used with his mother all too often.

"Can you get her over here?" he asked Paige.

She nodded, lifting her head. "Lani? Could you give us a hand with Hannah, please? That awful man scared her so, and she trusts you."

The girl quickly got up and came to them, muttering a few choice words of her own under her breath, words Rider could only guess were aimed at Filipo.

"Lani," Rider said when she had knelt down beside the chair, "how scared are you?"

The girl gave him a startled glance. "I'm afraid," she admitted. "But I'm even more angry. No one has the right to do this."

"You're right," Rider said. "Lani, I need you to be very, very honest now. Do you think you can stay more angry than scared? Can you think straight and help watch out for the little ones?"

She didn't give him an answer instantly, which Rider knew meant she was taking him seriously. "You're going to try something?" she asked.

He nodded.

She thought another minute. Then slowly but firmly she nodded. "I can help."

"It could be dangerous."

"It already is."

He couldn't argue with that, so he quickly told them his plan. To his surprise no one, not even Paige, told him he was crazy. In fact, they all seemed more than ready to try.

"I even know where to hide," Lani said.

"Where?" Paige asked.

"There is a big lava cave, straight east from here. It is

a venerated place and kept secret by our people. Because it's on the cliff side, you can't get there by car, but it's easy on foot if you know your way. I've done it many times. Even the little ones will be able to do it.''

Rider grinned at the girl's quick solution to the one part of his plan he hadn't been able to figure out.

"Good girl," he said, and she smiled. "All right," he said. "Kyle will help. Listen up."

He began to explain. Lani's eyes widened, and Kyle gave a low whistle. But they were both nodding eagerly by the time he was done.

"We won't have much time," he cautioned.

"We'll do it," Kyle said determinedly.

"All right. You've probably got an hour before Filipo makes his next perimeter check. Can you be ready by then?"

"We will be," Lani promised.

The two were anxious to get started, Rider could feel it radiating from them, but they reined it in without a warning from him and drifted away toward the other children as casually as if nothing of any import had been said.

Rider felt a tug on his shirt. He looked down to see Hannah, who had been miraculously quiet during the entire plan, staring up at him.

"We're going away? From the nasty men?"

He couldn't help himself; he hugged her. "You bet you are," he promised her. "But you have to go back to your chair and be very quiet from now on, so the nasty men don't hear."

Wide-eyed but closemouthed, she nodded. She scrambled out of his lap and ran back to her chair, climbed into it and sat, quietly waiting.

"They're tougher than you think they are," Paige said softly.

Rider met her gaze. "Yes, they are," he said, pointedly

glancing at Kyle. "They tend to be as tough as they have to be, it seems."

Paige glanced at her son herself, then back to Rider. Her forehead creased slightly, as if she didn't understand what he meant.

"You protected him when he needed it, but he can take the truth now, Paige. And you deserve it."

She lowered her eyes. "I don't know. Maybe…after this is over."

He left it at that, because he had something else to tell her. He reached into his shirt pocket and pulled out his cell phone. He palmed it and passed it to Paige.

"If anything happens," he said, "if it falls apart and they start shooting at the kids, hit Recall on that and explain the situation to whoever answers."

"Who will answer?"

"It'll be Josh Redstone's private line. He or his assistant, St. John, should pick up."

She nodded but looked troubled. She glanced at the phone, then back at him. "But Ares said they controlled all communications."

"I know. But if you have to use it, it won't matter anymore."

# Chapter 13

It was all Paige could do not to pace the floor.

They had been held here for two days, and yet the past hour had seemed longer than the entire time. She could see that Kyle and Lani were tense, as well. Noah was the only one who appeared calm, and Paige wondered if he really was, or if he'd somehow perfected a facade. It would be helpful in his work to be able to present that calm, steady image, as if he were certain it would turn out all right, especially during the turmoil of final preparations for the opening of a new resort.

She was far from certain this would turn out all right. They'd gone from child to child, explaining to each what was going to happen and how quiet they absolutely had to be. But it was asking a great deal from too-young and already frightened children. She was glad the wait wouldn't be much longer; Noah had said it would be too risky to wait until dark, too easy for them to be heard in the quiet of night, that it was better now, with all the usual daytime noises for cover.

Thankfully, the guards were paying them little attention. They had other things to think about since Noah's night-time raids had begun. But neither were they sticking to the routine they'd established before, of one man leaving his post every half hour to scout around the perimeter of the building. Once, Tarak had gotten up and walked a ways into the trees, but Noah had insisted they had to wait until Filipo, the guard closest to them, took his turn on patrol.

Paige swore she could hear every tick of the clock, as if the small schoolroom had become some kind of echo chamber. The children grew ever more restless, until finally she resorted to her ace in the hole, the book that had kept them all so enthralled up till now. She could only hope the story could overcome the strain of waiting, knowing.

She took up her seat once more, called for the children's attention and began to read, and gradually they—except for Lani and Kyle, who knew the most about what they were going to attempt—settled down to listen.

After nearly an hour Noah walked past her as if restless, whispering, "Announce a break." She was puzzled, but did as he said. Noah flicked a glance at Filipo, then back to her. "I think he's listening. That's why he's not moving."

The idea of a terrorist held rapt by a children's book was so incongruous to her she nearly turned to stare at Filipo. He *had* been very still since she'd begun reading. And he'd been that way yesterday, too. Could it really be? It seemed impossible, but then, so did this entire thing.

A few minutes later Filipo gave unexpected credence to Noah's theory. He rose from his seat, stretched, glanced toward them, then called out to Tarak that he was making his patrol. Tarak nodded and promptly went back to his scrutiny of his side of the building. Filipo closed his door and began his own check of the surrounding area.

"Start reading again," Noah told Paige softly. "We'll use it as cover. If Tarak can hear you all the time, maybe he won't bother to look."

She nodded, picked up the book and began reading aloud once more.

Noah went slowly toward the still-guarded main doors, strolling as if he were doing something no more important than taking an afternoon walk. He'd done this several times already, and only now Paige realized he'd been gauging Tarak's comfort zone, the point at which the man switched his attention from outside to inside. And this time Noah stopped just short of that point, a distance from the children, but also still ten feet short of the door. Then he looked back and nodded.

As if they'd rehearsed it countless times—as they had in their minds—they each went to work. As his mother read aloud, Kyle lifted the square of flooring, then went to take his place at the closed door. He nudged it open a fraction of an inch to see if Filipo was where they thought he was, far enough in the right direction. When he spotted him, Kyle gave the "go" signal they'd arranged. Lani lowered herself down through the opening, took a split second to orient herself, then crawled quickly to the back side of the building. Noah had promised if she stuck to the path he'd marked under the building, she would come out at the rear, out of sight, with only a few feet to run before she was in trees thick enough to hide in.

Paige counted to herself, gave the girl an extra five seconds to reach safety. And then the real work began. While still reading, and starting with the youngest, Stevie, she pointed to each child in turn. When selected, they obediently tiptoed to her, each young face scrunched up in an agony of strain as they tried to be so very quiet.

"Follow the arrows, then run to Lani," she whispered between sentences to each one, then sent them on their way to freedom with a kiss on the forehead.

Her heart was pounding so loudly she was surprised it didn't betray them. It took every bit of her concentration to try and follow her reading and make it sound normal, all the while using minute breaks in the story to whisper the directions to the children. But child after child followed instructions to the letter.

Hannah was reluctant to leave Noah, and kept looking back at him as she inched her way to the front of the room. She bumped into a desk, and the sound seemed much louder than it should have.

"Keep going," Paige whispered urgently in the same instant Noah moved. As if casually stretching muscles weary of lack of activity, he turned his back to Tarak, placing his body in the man's line of sight, blocking his view. He gave the little girl a grin and a wink and, reassured, she scuttled out of sight.

The chain began again. As the number of children dwindled, Noah moved gradually closer, as if ready to shield the few remaining again if necessary. They kept going, so smoothly that Paige was almost afraid to breathe. Child after child, escaping from the horror, and a joyous triumph began to sing along her nerves, until she could feel the hum.

*Bless you, Noah Rider! Twenty,* she counted. *Twenty-one. Take that, you bastards! This is for all the innocents who have died at your hands.*

And then it happened. One of the bigger boys misjudged and hit the side of the opening with his shoe, making a loud, resounding thump.

Too loud. Paige knew instantly there was no masking this one. In that same instant Noah gestured to Kyle to take his mother's place helping the last children escape before he got out himself. Then Noah grabbed Paige and pulled her toward the guarded doors.

She had no time to speak, barely enough time to wonder what he was doing before he yanked her hard against him. His mouth came down on hers, fast and fierce. The shock that jolted her was quickly replaced by a swift, searing heat. She was too nervous, too frightened to give in to it totally, and because of that she was oddly able to think, that here it was again, that instant fire she'd felt only with Noah. Even now, beneath the fear, it was still there.

Noah wrested the book she'd somehow clung to out of her hand. She heard a heavy thud as it dropped to the floor. The fear of making noise that had been their life for two days shot through her. What if the guard had heard?

"A little outrage would help," Noah whispered lovingly.

She came totally back to herself with a start. The guard was *supposed* to have heard, she realized belatedly. This whole thing was a diversion.

Once she'd snapped out of her distraction she reacted quickly. She shoved against Noah's chest with both hands. He resisted; she shoved harder. And poured every bit of the embarrassment she was feeling at missing her cue into her voice.

"What do you think you're doing?" she asked, with what she hoped sounded like the outrage he'd asked for, and only now noticed they were at the front doors and that Tarak was watching them with interest.

"Hey, take it easy," Noah said, with a smirking grin she'd never seen before on his face.

"Easy!" She let her voice rise. "You start *pawing* me like that and I'm supposed to take it easy?"

"Hey, now, don't go getting all upset," he said, trying to pull her back into his arms. He bent his head close in the process and whispered, "Better slap me. Hard."

"Leave me alone!" she yelled. She'd never slapped anyone before, but she gave it her best shot. As her hand connected with Noah's face the sound was horrible. And she was afraid she'd given him too good a shot, because he reeled backward. But when he ended up nearly outside, with Tarak starting to laugh out loud, she knew it was intentional.

Quickly she followed the action to the door. Noah backed up and actually stepped outside. All Tarak did was laugh again, making a joke about men who can't control their women. And then he called out to Filipo to come watch the fun.

Yes, do, Paige thought, stepping outside herself.

With what she guessed was his idea of a placating smile, Noah came toward her again.

"Aw, come on, honey, don't be mad." He grabbed her again, at an oddly awkward angle. "Just calm down," he said, patting her on the back as one would an upset child.

She was starting to get genuinely annoyed, and if she hadn't known he was acting, she might have clobbered him again. Especially when Filipo arrived at a run and gave her a look that frightened her, so clearly did it tell her she was lucky it wasn't he who had his hands on her.

And then she realized the reason for the uncomfortable twist of her body Noah was forcing her to; it enabled him to see back into the school without being obvious.

"They made it," he whispered, and it was all Paige could do not to make the hug real. "Your turn. Move fast. They need you."

And in the next moment Noah stumbled back as if she'd pushed him away again.

"Leave me alone," she repeated, figuring she'd better play along.

"Can't handle the little schoolteacher?" Filipo crowed loudly. "I can. Just wait and see."

Noah shrugged. "Okay, okay, just go sit down and cool off," he told her.

His gaze flicked toward the inside of the room, and she knew he meant for her to go now. For an instant as he looked back at her their gazes locked and held. In his eyes she saw determination, encouragement and something that she couldn't name, not in this split second.

She hesitated, not wanting to leave him there. But she knew he was right. Those kids needed her. She couldn't leave Lani and Kyle alone to handle two dozen scared children. She summoned up the demeanor she knew she should be trying to present for their captors.

"Fine," she said icily. "You just stay here and cool off, yourself!"

With all the offended dignity she could muster, she turned on her heel and marched back into the school. She could hear the laughter of the guards, heard Noah saying sheepishly, "Well, can't blame a guy for trying."

Paige hurried to the front of the now empty schoolhouse. God, they hadn't talked about this, had only talked about how to get the kids out. And now that she thought back, Noah had always referred to what she—not they—would do once they got the children to the sanctuary of Lani's cave.

Did he have a plan for his own escape? Should she leave the floor open? She could feel her safety margin ticking away. Finally deciding what puzzlement the closed floor might cause wasn't worth the extra seconds it might cost Noah, she left it open.

He'd shown the way carefully, with thick, white arrows marked on the uprights of the school's foundation with her chalk. She crawled as fast as she could, heedless of the damage to her elbows—the floor over her head was too low for her to crawl normally—and her knees. There was plenty of light, and she could see the break in the outer shell that was her goal.

She hadn't thought the small space had bothered her until she scrambled out into the sunlight and relief swamped her. It seemed like forever since she'd been outside, and she had to resist the urge to simply stop and breathe in the clean air.

She heard a hissing sound, and looked just to her right to see Kyle half-hidden in the trees, gesturing at her to hurry up. She ran toward her son, grateful for the cover of the trees when she got there.

"Consider yourself hugged," she said, knowing they didn't have time nor would Kyle tolerate the real thing.

"You, too," he said, surprising her.

"Where are the kids?"

"I sent them ahead with Lani. They shouldn't be far, though. Where's Mr. Rider?"

"Stalling the guards," she said.

"But how's he going to—"

"I don't know."

Her own unease about the same question made her voice sharp. What would they do when they realized their hostages were gone? The possibilities were many and all of them were ugly. She hesitated, looking back toward the school.

And then they heard Filipo shout. Curses followed, and then another shout from Filipo.

She knew it was too late to do anything but run.

"We better run," Kyle said even as her thought formed.

And run they did. Kyle led the way, unhesitatingly making his way through the thick trees and brush that qualified as jungle in her mind. He clearly knew exactly where he was going, for which Paige was thankful.

When he slowed, she looked at him questioningly.

"We're almost where I left them," he explained. "I told Lani—"

The sound that echoed through the trees cut off his words. Paige froze. Kyle went pale. Denial was impossible. The sound was what it was.

A shot.

# Chapter 14

She'd never been fond of caves, Paige thought as she walked back and forth near the entrance, but she wouldn't trade this one for the Ritz. Even the littlest children seemed to realize that while they were without the comforts of the school, they had gained something so much more precious: the absence of those nasty men, as Hannah put it.

Hannah.

Lord, how would the child deal with it, if her beloved Noah was—

Paige shook her head, trying not to think about it. Trying not to think about how *she* would deal with it. Trying above all not to think about the magnitude of that "if."

An old memory shot through her mind, something she hadn't thought about in years. She'd wondered, back then, if Phil had had time to realize what was happening, that the plane was going down. That he was about to die. If he'd had any last regrets about what he'd thrown away. Of course, he'd never have gotten on that plane if he'd known. Nothing mattered that much to Phil.

Noah had known. He had to have known. And yet he'd gone ahead, had—

"Mrs. Cooper?"

Paige stopped her wretched pacing as Lani hesitantly approached. "Yes, Lani?"

"Is there anything I can do?"

Paige put a hand on the girl's shoulder. "No. You've done so much already. You should be very proud, Lani."

The girl colored. "Thank you."

"We could never have saved these children if not for you," Paige said.

"And Mr. Rider," Lani said, her eyes troubled now.

"Yes." Paige swallowed against the sudden tightness of her throat. "It was all his idea, after all."

And it had been his idea to stay behind, she thought. He had to have known what he was risking, when he'd stayed to distract the guards so she could escape.

"Kyle told me," Lani said, her eyes suspiciously bright.

"Told you? That he planned it all?"

The girl shook her head. "About…the shot you heard."

"Oh."

"Do you think…they shot him? When they found we were gone?"

"I don't know."

"Hannah keeps asking for him. Do you think he's still alive?"

"I don't know that, either."

And that was the truth, as far as it went. She didn't know, because she hadn't been there. Thankfully. But what she was refusing to acknowledge, even to herself, was the very high likelihood that that was exactly what they'd done, that it was exactly what men like that would do. In fact, it would be more unusual if they hadn't shot him the moment they had discovered he'd made a fool of them. Right there, on the spot where he'd staged that reckless diversion, he'd set himself up once more as a weakling to be laughed at, this time so she could escape.

The vision she'd been trying to fight off since that frozen moment in the trees swamped her, a nightmare image grown out of too many film clips, too many still shots of the carnage left behind by terrorists the world over. Noah, forced to his knees, the last seconds of his life ticking away, Filipo aiming at the back of his head. A sacrifice too big to ask of anyone, and he'd given it without hesitation.

A sacrifice...

Dear God, he'd known all along. He'd known all along he would have to stay behind to give them a chance. That was why he'd never referred to himself in their plans after the escape, he'd known from the beginning he wouldn't be with them.

Suddenly the vision shifted, back to the night he'd come back after his first foray. Back to her own shaky voice...

*I thought they'd killed you.*

*They may yet. I'm not cut out for this kind of thing.*

Not cut out to be a hero, he'd meant. And she wondered if he'd ever realized that a man not cut out to be a hero who goes ahead and does it, anyway, is the biggest hero of all.

She nearly whimpered aloud when she recognized that she had thought of him in the past tense.

She tried to hang on to some hope. She tried to come up with at least one feasible reason why they wouldn't have killed him where he stood. The only one she could think of was Ares, that they wouldn't do anything on their own, without a direct order from their charismatic leader.

It was a hope so slim it was barely existent. But it was all she had.

The cave wasn't exactly comfortable, Paige thought, but the view was spectacular. Beneath them, in a small cove, was a little beach of gleaming white sand. Not too much farther out was a reef, marked on the surface by ranks of breaking waves. The result was a small circle of calm, clear water, a natural swimming pool.

And she wasn't about to complain about the cave, not when it was providing the most important thing of all, safety. Bless Lani for knowing about it and thinking of it.

As if her thoughts had drawn the girl, she appeared again and dropped down to sit beside Paige.

"Most of them are napping," she said. "This was all pretty rough on them."

"On all of us," Paige said, with the best smile she could manage for the girl. "Thank you for your help, Lani. We all would have fallen apart without you."

The girl smiled shyly but didn't speak. After a long silence Paige said, "It's a good thing Redstone didn't see this place. I'm sure they'd want to add this to the resort. It's lovely."

"My father says Mr. Redstone did see it. He found it himself, when he was hiking around the island. He asked about it, and Father explained this cave was the spiritual home of our ancestors."

"Joshua Redstone personally hiked this island?"

Lani nodded. "All alone, before he bought the land for the resort."

Paige had a hard time picturing the high-powered executive tramping around like that. But then she remembered the few times she'd met him—tall, lean, with a depth of understanding in his gray eyes that hadn't come from an easy life.

*He came up the hard way, from a worse start than most of us ever had.* Noah's words came back to her, along with the ache that accompanied every thought of him. It didn't seem possible he could be dead, her heart wanted to scream that it wasn't true, but she knew she was kidding herself by clinging to that hope. The sound of that shot was seared into her memory. He'd saved them, saved them all, and he'd known what it was going to cost him. This man who had thought himself anything but a hero had become one, in the hardest possible way.

"My uncle expected him to want the cove," Lani said, thankfully distracting her, "so he was ready to fight. My uncle assured everyone the night before the discussions began that it would never be allowed. He kept waiting for Mr. Redstone to say something about it, but he never did."

"It never even came up?"

Lani smiled. "My uncle finally couldn't stand it, so he asked. Mr. Redstone said he had never considered it because he respected what this place meant to us. He even asked if we wanted him to put up a fence or a hedge to assure no guest found it accidentally. I think that is what decided my father that this was a man we could trust."

"Have they ever regretted it?" Paige asked, curious now.

Lani shook her head. "We were in a bad way. We had no doctor, no medical service at all. There is a visiting doctor who flies to the islands, but we couldn't afford him. There was no school, no teacher for the children. No work for our people."

"How did you survive?"

"Only…" Lani paused, as if searching for words. "Hand to mouth, is how you say it I think. But now we have all those things, even a small clinic with a nurse, thanks to Mr. Redstone. He has kept his word."

No wonder Noah thought so much of his boss, Paige thought. And on that thought the pain returned, tightening her chest until it was all she could do to draw another breath. She stared out at the turquoise sea, the never-changing sea that cared nothing for the foibles of mankind or the cruelties—cruelties that could kill a man without qualm. No matter what happened to Noah, the sea would roll on as if nothing had changed; whereas, Paige knew the world was suddenly a lesser place for the loss of that one man.

And she knew her own life would never be the same.

She watched the waves breaking endlessly on the reef. They would go on, never stopping. And so would she, somehow. But she would always wonder what they could have made of what had flashed so briefly between them—what had been alive even five years ago. It seemed they were destined to meet at the wrong times, always amid upheaval.

And now it was over, before it had even begun, and all she had were the memories of a few kisses and the way her body had leaped to life at his touch. And the image she knew would never fade—of Noah telling her to go, that it was her turn and the children needed her. Of his eyes so full of determination, that nudge of encouragement she'd needed, and something deeper, more intense, that she couldn't bear to think about now, because if she allowed it to surface it would hurt too much.

She knew from painful experience that she would have to deal with it eventually, but she had to think about the kids now. She had to make sure they were kept safe, or Noah's sacrifice would have been for nothing.

"I'm sorry about Mr. Rider," Lani said softly.

Paige looked at the girl, who was watching her with wide, troubled eyes. "Is it that obvious?"

"That you're thinking of him? Yes." Lani hesitated, then said, "You cared for him, didn't you?"

Denying it now seemed somehow a betrayal. And pointless. "Yes. Yes, I did."

"Kyle said you knew him before."

"Briefly, yes. Kyle's father worked for Redstone, and Noah came to help when he was killed."

Lani nodded. "Kyle told me he brought his father home."

"Yes, he did. It could have been very complicated, since there were so many things involved, with him being an American on a foreign airline, downed in a foreign country and because of a terrorist act that required tremendous investigations by so many agencies. Noah cut through all the problems in a way I never could have done.''

''A man who gets things done,'' Lani said.

''Yes.''

''And he died for us. All of us.''

Paige's eyes stung again as moisture welled up anew. ''Yes.''

''I think we should do something. A ceremony or something. Here in this cave of my ancestors, so that they will welcome his spirit.''

Paige was touched by her words. Lani was truly of two worlds: she embraced the modern world, was one of the quickest of her students to learn the computers, yet at the same time she respected customs and beliefs of her people that others would consider primitive.

''I think that would be very nice, Lani,'' Paige said, taking the girl's hand and squeezing it.

''Maybe when Kyle returns. We could—''

''Returns? What do you mean?''

Lani looked puzzled. ''When he comes back, and we're all here, we could—''

Paige scrambled to her feet. She scanned the cave, searching. At first she refused to believe what her eyes were telling her, but at last she had no choice.

Kyle was gone.

She whirled back to face Lani. ''Where is he?'' she demanded, terror making her voice sharp.

Realization crept across the girl's face. ''He didn't tell you? He told me you knew!''

''He lied,'' Paige said flatly, feeling hollowed out inside.

''Why would he do that?'' Lani looked honestly bewildered, and Paige felt a jab of sympathy for her.

''Because he knew I'd never let him leave this cave,'' she told her. ''Where did he go, Lani?''

''Just to my home,'' she said. ''He went to get my father,

who will bring help.'' Guessing at part of Paige's shock, she added, ''You were upset about Mr. Rider, it's no wonder you didn't notice.''

''Oh.''

She wasn't sure what she'd expected, but something that sensible wasn't it. And no matter how upset she'd been, there was no excuse for completely losing track of her own son. She was going to have to go after him. She couldn't believe he'd done something so stupid as to venture out when, for all they knew, there were terrorists all over the island, even in Lani's small village.

''It's not far, really,'' Lani reassured her. ''I was going to go myself, but Kyle didn't want me to go alone, and he wouldn't leave you alone to watch all the children by yourself.''

Surprised at that, Paige managed not to point out that both Lani and Kyle weren't that far removed from childhood themselves. Nor did she say anything about her fears that Kyle might have walked right back into the clutches of the men they'd just escaped. She didn't want the girl worrying about her parents on top of everything else.

''When did he leave?'' she asked, still horrified that she hadn't noticed.

For the first time concern crossed the girl's face. ''More than an hour ago.''

Paige went still. ''And how long should it have taken him to get to your house and back?''

''Half that,'' the girl admitted. ''But he's probably just waiting for my father to gather everyone together.''

That made sense. And if it were anyone but her angry, reckless son, she might agree. But Kyle had been acting abnormally for too long now for her not to fear the worst.

Surely fate wouldn't be that cruel? she thought as she stepped outside the cave and looked up the narrow trail that had brought them here. Surely not Kyle, too?

Her stomach knotted so fiercely she thought she was going to be ill right there. Because she knew life could indeed be that cruel, and just because she'd already suffered great losses didn't mean there weren't more in store for her.

But not Kyle. Please, not Kyle. Especially not now, with this awful anger between them.

She stared up the steep trail, barely able to restrain herself from racing after her son. Only the fact that it would mean leaving Lani alone to deal with twenty-four still-frightened children stopped her. The girl was quick, bright and amazingly fearless, but it wasn't fair to burden her young shoulders with that load.

She retreated to the cave, pacing across the front opening, her arms wrapped around herself as if it were icy-cold instead of tropically warm. The pacing did nothing to alleviate her jitters, but she couldn't hold still.

She'd give him half an hour more, she told herself. Half an hour and then she was going, and Lani would just have to manage. The kids were her responsibility, but so was Kyle. And right now, Kyle might need her just as much. Maybe more.

The time ticked by. Whenever she glanced at Lani, the girl was looking more worried. Finally Paige couldn't stand it any longer. She motioned the girl over to her.

"Lani, I know this isn't fair to you, but I don't have any choice," she began.

"You're going after Kyle?"

She nodded. "I have to."

"I should go," Lani suggested. "I know the way better."

Paige shook her head. "It's too dangerous."

"But not for you?"

"Not for the mother of that foolish son of mine."

Lani hesitated, then said shyly, "I like your foolish son."

Paige reached out and hugged the girl. "I know. And I know he likes you. A lot."

Lani drew back. "Really?"

"Surprised me, too," Paige said with the best smile she could drum up. "I didn't think he had such good taste."

Lani blushed, but it faded as worry returned to her young face. "You will be careful?"

"Very."

"All right," the girl said, and began to give concise and detailed directions to her village.

She nearly changed her mind. What would Lani do if she didn't come back? How would she take care of all these children? But the thought of losing Kyle on the heels of losing Noah was too much.

"We will be all right," Lani said. "If the path is not safe, there is another way, along the beach. It is difficult, but I can do it. We can fish if we must, and there is much to eat out there." She gestured toward the trees. "It will be an adventure."

"Lani, if I ever have a daughter, I hope…" she began, then stopped. "No. There could never be another girl as amazing as you." She gave her another swift hug, then turned to go.

She had only made it halfway up the trail that led to the cave from above when a sound from above made her freeze. She dodged off the trail, crouching behind a sizable bush, glad there was nothing poisonous on the island. The noise got closer. She peeked through the leaves.

A size-eleven athletic shoe appeared, taking the first step down the trail. A hundred-and-twenty-dollar shoe she recognized.

She let out a huge, relieved breath. She stood up and stepped back onto the trail. Kyle was running and didn't look up for a moment. When he did, he skidded and almost fell.

"Mom! What are you doing out here?"

"About to come after you." Kyle Philip Cooper, she added silently, as she tended to when she was upset with him. But now it seemed best to keep as calm as she could. "Did you get to Lani's parents?"

"Yeah," he said warily, as if he still expected her to blow up. "They're coming, with a bunch of others, as soon as he rounds them all up."

"Good." She'd had time to think, too much, in the past half hour. And when she said what she knew she needed to say, she meant it. "You did a good thing, Kyle. Probably the right thing. Just tell me next time, all right?"

Startled, he stared at her. And for a moment she saw in his eyes her real son—the son who loved her. "You meant it, didn't you?" he said wonderingly. "That you'd never give up?"

"You bet I did. And I wasn't about to let some bastard terrorist hurt the person I love more than anything in the world." She almost never swore in front of him, so it had impact when she did. "They've already taken too much from you."

Usually any reference to his father brought on that glumness she'd learned to live with. But this time he looked suddenly excited.

"He's alive, Mom!"

It took her a moment to make the jump, to realize he wasn't talking about his father.

"What—" her breath caught "—Noah?"

"I saw him!" he exclaimed. "That's why it took me so long, I came back by the hotel, and I saw him!"

For once she wasn't possessed by the urge to throttle him for being reckless. Or, if the urge was there, it was surpassed by her shock.

"You saw Noah?"

He nodded urgently. "He was hurt, all bloody, but he was alive, Mom. I saw him move. They were dragging him across the courtyard toward the main building, and he moved his head."

"When?"

"Just now. I came straight here."

Paige sucked in a harsh breath. Noah was alive. Whether that shot had been aimed at him or not, he was alive.

For now.

# Chapter 15

"We have to *do* something!"

Paige could hardly argue with Kyle when she felt the same way. They had to do something. Noah had sacrificed himself to give them time to escape.

"Yes, we must," Lani agreed.

"I know," Paige said, almost to herself, knowing that if she were honest about it, she'd admit that how she'd come to feel about him was the most powerful reason. The emotions Noah Rider stirred in her demanded she do whatever she could.

"We could storm the hotel," Kyle suggested, sounding utterly serious.

"Don't be silly," Lani said, almost sharply, saving Paige the trouble. "They have guns, and hostages. We have nothing."

"Well, then, what can we get that they'd want?" Kyle asked, sounding a little beleaguered.

"What don't they already have?" Lani countered. Yes, Paige thought, she was good for Kyle.

''Maybe we could take one of them hostage,'' Kyle said. ''Then we'd have something to bargain with.''

''If they'd bargain to get him back,'' Paige said.

''I'd be *glad* if someone took Filipo away,'' Lani said dryly.

Paige smiled, but behind the expression her mind was racing. Something to bargain with...

They did have something the terrorists—or rather Ares in particular—wanted. Or, at least, had wanted.

Her.

*...you will be the voice of the hostages.*

Did he still want her as a puppet mouthpiece? Badly enough to bargain for Noah's welfare? And even if he did, what guarantee did she have that he'd keep his word?

Zero. Zilch. Zip. If he was a man with honor enough to keep his word, he wouldn't be a terrorist.

She knew that, knew this was nearly as harebrained as Kyle's desperate idea to storm the hotel. She could be walking into a death trap. In fact, Noah might already be dead. Kyle said he had seen him being taken into the main building, which was no doubt where Ares was. For all she knew, he'd been brought before the leader and promptly executed. What reason did Ares have to keep him alive?

Unless he'd learned who Noah really was....

Kyle and Lani were still talking, trying to come up with something. She tuned them out, trying to think. If Ares had somehow found out that Noah was a top Redstone executive, if he knew what a powerful tool he had in that hostage, surely he wouldn't kill him. He would keep him as an ace in the hole, a lever to use against Redstone if he had to. Wouldn't he?

A lever. It suddenly struck her that if she offered herself as spokesperson in return for Noah's welfare, Ares would know he meant something to her. It would be nearly as bad as the terrorists learning Kyle was her son. But what other reason could she give him for her change of heart? Now that she'd escaped his guards, why would she give up her freedom?

She'd have to lie, she realized that, but could she do it convincingly? Could she put on a front like the one Noah had, so completely that the guards had barely given him a second thought, had counted him out as cowed and cowardly? Could she convince the man she'd done it for all the hostages, not just Noah?

She wrestled with the idea for a while longer, but finally gave up. It didn't matter if she could pull it off, but only that she try. And for the first time she really understood what Noah had meant: she wasn't cut out for this kind of thing, either.

But the least she could do is what he had done. She had to try. She couldn't just sit here and let them kill him, or worse. Not after what he'd done for the children.

Not after what he'd done for her, awakened her to the possibilities of life once more. Even if whatever had begun between them ended when this was over, she had to try. Doing something was better than nothing.

The call of a bird, disconcertingly close and sounding oddly like maniacal laughter, made Paige jump. Kyle turned to look at the cave entrance, along with many of the children. Only Lani acted differently; with a joyous cry she ran toward the entrance.

"It's my father!" she exclaimed. "He does the best laughing gull on the island!"

Paige ran to the cave entrance herself then, and looked up the trail to see the welcome sight of at least a dozen of the village men, armed with various implements ranging from clubs to what appeared to be scythes of some sort. They must have grabbed up anything that could be used as a weapon and marched off to rescue their children.

The moment they entered the cave, the local children echoed Lani's cry with their own. Sobbing reunions began, and Paige couldn't begin to describe the relief she felt.

After a moment Lani led her father over to Paige. She'd met him twice before, when she'd first arrived and again shortly after school had begun, when the man had come to see where his daughter would be every day.

"I'm so glad you're all right. I was afraid they had taken over the entire island," she told him.

"We have not seen them at all on our side. Two of us went to look when the children did not come home. That's when we saw them. We followed, watched them and saw that they do not have enough men to take the whole island."

"Did you count them?"

"As best we could. There are fifteen of them at least, maybe a few more."

It seemed they must be spread rather thin, then. Although now they no longer had to spare two to guard the school, Paige thought with a little rush of triumph. Or run the radio Noah had disabled.

"We were preparing to do what we had to, to free our children when your son came to us," Lani's father said.

"You should be very, very proud of your daughter, Mr. DeSouza. We never could have done this without her."

"She says the same of you," the man said. "I thank you on behalf of all of my village, for the safety of our children."

"I did only what any teacher would do," she said. "But I must ask a favor of you...the other children, not from your village, will you watch over them as well? There is something I have to do."

"Of course," he answered promptly. "It is the least we can do." He studied her for a moment. "You go to help the man?"

Paige flicked a glance at Kyle, who was huddled with Lani once more.

"Yes, the boy told us. He is a good man, this Rider?"

"He is," she said. "He sacrificed himself so the children could escape."

"Is there more we can do?

Paige shook her head. "Not yet. I think I can get in and at least make sure…"

"That he is still alive?" Mr. DeSouza asked gently.

Paige nodded, blinking rapidly. She saw Kyle headed toward them, and wiped at her eyes.

"Going into the den of the monster is a bad thing, and for a woman alone…"

"Alone is the only way I can do this, I'm afraid. The leader has some use for me, but only me."

"You do as you must. But if you need our help, you have it."

She thought quickly. The first of the guests were due to start arriving late tonight. She knew they had to be warned off.

"Do you have a telephone?"

He nodded. "A cell phone. Mr. Redstone arranged it for anyone who wished one."

"Unfortunately that doesn't help. They control the cell towers. If you use it, they'll know you know they're here, and they might come after you."

Kyle, who had been standing quietly and listening, asked, "What about that boat? The one I saw at the dock?"

Mr. DeSouza frowned. "Which boat? We have many."

"The big blue one. With all the nets."

"Ah, Tikina's fishing boat."

"It had an antenna on it," Kyle said. "Does it have a radio?"

A marine radio. Paige couldn't help herself, she reached out and hugged Kyle. "They'd probably never think of that. You're brilliant, Cooper," she teased in the old way. And Kyle responded, grinning at her in the old way that gave her such hope she was almost afraid to acknowledge it.

"Yes," Lani's father said, then cautioned, "but it doesn't work well here, only out at sea."

"But he could go out to sea, couldn't he?" Kyle asked. "And call for help? It would be safe, really. Mr. Rider— he damaged their boats, they can't go after him even if they see him."

"Who should he call? We do not want war brought to our island."

He had a good point, Paige thought. "Take all the children with you on any boats you have. Then call Redstone," she said. "Tell them what has happened. They have to stop the people who are coming in, it will only give these men more hostages."

DeSouza nodded. "It will be done." He looked at her consideringly. "You are going now?"

She nodded.

"Going where?" Kyle asked.

She took a deep breath, then faced her son. "Back to the hotel."

"The hotel?" He got there quickly. "You're going for Mr. Rider!"

"Yes."

"But you said it was crazy to go back there!"

"I said it was crazy to try and storm it with no weapons. I'm going alone."

"Alone! And that's not crazy?"

"Maybe it is, but I have to."

"But they'll kill you!"

He sounded so upset at that possibility that Paige dared to hope perhaps he didn't hate her quite so much anymore.

"I hope not," she said, as calmly as she could manage, given that she was trembling inside.

"I'm going with you."

"No, Kyle. You—"

"Why is it okay for you to go but not me?"

"Remember what you said? About needing something to bargain with?"

"Yeah," he admitted warily.

"Well, I have something. Ares wanted me to speak to the world for him. So I will."

"You mean...you'll help him if he doesn't kill Mr. Rider?"

"Something like that."

"You still shouldn't go alone," Kyle insisted.

"I have to or he'll get suspicious. He may be, anyway."

"But it's too dangerous."

"He won't hurt me, not as long as he needs me," Paige said. She only wished she believed that herself. For that matter Kyle didn't look particularly convinced.

"I still should go with you."

"I need you out here, free, Kyle."

She didn't say that she'd never be able to do what she had to if she didn't know he was safe. She didn't think he'd be too amenable to that argument. So instead she told him something equally true. She pulled out the small cell phone Noah had given her. She gave it to her son and told him what Noah had told her.

"If it all goes wrong, if shooting starts, push these two buttons. And tell whoever answers who and where you are and what's happening, that the time for stealth is over."

"They'll probably think I'm just some kid playing a joke," he said glumly, thankfully not arguing with her.

"Maybe. But tell them you're using Noah's phone because he's in trouble. If Joshua Redstone is who I think he is, that will be enough."

The villagers had been right, Paige thought. The terrorists were stretched thin. There was no other reason she could think of that she'd made it this far without being spotted.

She had delayed her departure a bit longer than she'd

wanted, while she and Lani's father made some further plans for the children's safety. But now she was here. She crouched in the trees, watching the two men in the courtyard. They were armed like the others had been, and as she watched, one took a cigarette from the other, then lit both with an old-fashioned silver lighter. After a moment of what she supposed was the terrorist version of pleasantries exchanged, both turned and walked in opposite directions.

She edged as close as she could get to the main building. There was only one guard that she could see, and it seemed as if he was staring right at her. Or at least at her hiding place. She stayed motionless, barely breathing, holding her position until her muscles ached with the strain. And finally, just when she knew she had to move, something drew his attention toward the water.

She saw it was a pelican, having made his scoop, now landing to let the excess water drain from his bill. A moment later a laughing gull arrived, perched incongruously on the pelican's back, waiting for any small fish that might escape from the bigger bird's pouch. It was a comical act she'd seen a couple of times since she'd arrived, and she could only bless the birds for putting on the show again now.

She stood up and ran for the doorway.

If she hadn't been so cramped from her forced stillness she might have made it. But she stumbled trying to dodge one of the artfully placed benches, and the guard whipped around, hands on his weapon.

He yelled. Paige ran. She made it through the door before he had a chance to fire, but she could hear him running toward her. She ran to the elevator lobby, surprised there was no sign of other guards. It appeared Lani's father had been accurate in his estimate of their strength.

Then she took a deep, steadying breath and sat down on one of the richly upholstered sofas next to the elevators. She tried for an air of unconcern, crossing her legs and leaning back with her arms stretched out along the back of the sofa.

As she'd hoped, the guard rushed in, then came to a skidding stop when he saw her.

Confused, he just gaped at her for a moment.

"You're just in time," she said, proud of how calm she sounded.

The man's confused expression turned to utter puzzlement. "In time?"

"To take me to Ares." She smiled at him, and his eyes widened. "He's expecting me."

Rider wondered if the hum in his left ear would ever go away. It had begun after Filipo had whacked him on the side of the head with his rifle butt. That constant, low-grade buzz was going to drive him crazy.

It was also something else to think about besides the ache in his head, the bloody nose he could barely breathe through anymore and the eye that felt swollen to about the size and consistency of an overripe tomato.

The man who called himself Ares was having a great time. Of course, what was there not to enjoy? He'd taken over a small island of unarmed people, he'd established himself in the most luxurious of the suites—a large, three-bedroom affair that had been decorated with the care lavished on all Redstone resorts, and he had prisoners to serve him at his beck and call. The only glitch in his whole operation had been the escape of the children.

And that, Rider thought, was the only damn thing that kept him going. No matter what else happened, Paige and the kids were out of the clutches of the terrorists.

He doubted if Ares really believed him when he'd insisted he didn't know where the kids had gone, that he'd just helped them get out. But when his story hadn't changed despite the not-very-loving attentions of Ares's two bodyguards, they'd finally stopped, just short of literally knocking his block off. Why Ares hadn't ordered him killed on sight escaped his battered brain.

He couldn't deny that the leader of this force seemed to know what he was doing. And his men seemed ready to march into hell after him, if he ordered them to. In a different world, he'd be a politician, the kind that could blind people to what they were really doing by the sheer force of his personality.

He let his head loll back on the chair. His arms ached from being tied behind him so long and his shoulders were in knots from the strain. His ankles were secured to the legs of the chairs. Ares had already made clear that he may have underestimated Rider once, but he wasn't about to do it again.

So here he sat, helpless in the living room of this spacious suite, watching Ares go over his plans for the arrival of the true prize of this venture: Redstone guests with a net worth in the billions. And he didn't like being here, didn't like what it implied—that Ares didn't care what he saw or heard, because Noah wouldn't be around to tell anyone about it afterward.

It did him no good to think about it. He had a couple of ideas, but nothing he could put into action now. So for the moment he could only sit. And wait.

He closed his eyes. And he summoned up the image of Paige in those seconds before she'd given in to his urging and run for her life. Those seconds when he'd put everything he was feeling into his gaze, those seconds when it almost seemed as if she knew, as if she saw everything he couldn't say.

He had really blown that part of his life, he thought with an almost wistful sadness. Carrie had been a nice person. He couldn't blame her for leaving him because she wanted more from a husband than he'd been able to give. Linda had been a good person, too, only she'd been a bit smarter, smart enough to take off before she was tied to a man who didn't know how to live except out of a suitcase.

And Paige. The woman he'd never been able to forget, even after only one week with her under the worst of circumstances, even after only a single, stolen kiss he never should have taken. And now, just when he'd found her again and was beginning to realize that maybe he had a reason to think about slowing down, enemy troops roll in. If it wasn't so disastrous, if those guns weren't so damned real, it would almost be a farce.

The cell phone Ares had commandeered for himself rang. So far Paige shouldn't have had to use his, Rider thought, because so far Ares had kept his men under control. But now Rider was worried. He should have had her call, anyway, and at least try to get a message through to Redstone to stop the incoming guests. But all he'd been able to think about at the time was her safety and the children's.

That was why Josh left the action stuff to Draven, he thought wearily. John Draven could have saved the kids, the resort employees and everybody else without breaking a sweat.

"Yes, right away," Ares said into the phone after listening for a long moment. "I'm most curious."

Rider pried one eye open, wondering what could make a man like Ares curious. His wondering increased when, for the first time in what seemed like hours, Ares spoke to him.

"It seems we are about to have company," he said.

"And here I am such a mess."

A flicker of something—Rider wasn't sure if it was irritation or admiration—flashed across Ares's face at his sarcasm.

"I'm sure our guest won't mind, since it's someone you know."

Since he knew almost all of Ares's hostages here in the hotel, that didn't narrow it down much. But he did wond. :

which of them would, apparently voluntarily, ask to see the man.

"Perhaps they even wish to check on you?" Ares suggested.

Rider doubted that, but something about the amusement behind the suggestion made him wary. He was fairly sure he didn't want to know what a terrorist would find amusing.

Moments later he was certain. The door to the suite opened. Ares turned. Rider looked.

And in walked Paige Cooper. Not quite smiling, but certainly not looking frightened.

Looking as if she were perfectly happy to be there.

"You've searched her?" Ares asked.

"Of course he did," Paige answered sharply, cutting off the guard's reply. "And enjoyed it, pig that he is."

Rider stared, even though his field of vision was narrowed somewhat by his swollen eye. He stared as Paige walked into the room as if it were any hotel room under normal circumstances. As if Ares were any ordinary man. As if the entire world hadn't gone insane.

And then she spotted him. For an instant her steps faltered, and he thought she paled slightly. He could only imagine how bad he must look. But then she recovered and turned to face the man she'd apparently come to see.

"Really," she said, with a vague gesture toward Rider, "was that necessary?"

Ares seemed a bit taken aback at her casual ease. Rider couldn't blame him. What was she up to? Why on earth was she here? Had Ares recaptured her somehow? And the children? Had it all been for nothing? But he seemed as bemused as Rider was feeling.

"He has caused me much trouble," Ares said. "He is very lucky to be alive at all."

"Well, he must stay that way. I won't have you indiscriminately hurting innocent people."

Ares gaped at her, his cool definitely rattled. "You dare to give me orders?"

"I'm only following your example," she said, and Rider wondered if she could possibly be as calm as she sounded. "I'm setting terms for my cooperation."

"Your cooperation?"

"You wished me to speak for your hostages. I will, but only if no one is hurt or killed." She glanced at Rider, and this time he knew he saw worry in her eyes. "Or hurt more."

It was there, in a faint tightness of her voice. He doubted Ares would see it—she sounded almost casual, as if her concern for him was an afterthought—but he could see in her face that *he* was why she'd done this. Surreptitiously he tested his bonds and found them as tight as ever.

He felt a rush of tangled emotions. Anger that she'd risked herself to come here. And shock over why she'd done it, the reason that was so clear in her eyes and her words. And, he couldn't deny, a selfish bit of warmth, that she would try and bargain for his life, using the only weapon she had.

But most of all he felt despair, because if there was anything he'd learned in the hours he'd been sitting here, a captive audience to Ares's actions, it was that this man, beneath his charismatic exterior, was utterly, totally ruthless. He would only use her concern against her.

Ares shook his head slowly in amazement. "Are you truly so brave? Or are you just stupid?"

"I'm neither," Paige said. "I just don't want anyone else hurt."

"How noble." His voice was full of scorn now.

"No. Just civilized."

It was the wrong thing to say. "And you think I will allow you to dictate terms? To *me?*"

Ares's voice was so incredulous that Rider knew Paige couldn't help but realize she'd misjudged her importance to him. Then he looked at her face and realized she hadn't misjudged, she'd guessed all along that this wouldn't work.

But she'd done it, anyway.

"You," Ares exclaimed, pointing a finger at her in a way that made Rider think he'd prefer to be pointing a gun, "have caused me as much trouble as he has. In fact, I now believe it was probably you who plotted the escape of those children." He gestured toward Rider. "He doesn't have the nerve."

You got that right, Rider thought. I haven't got half the nerve she has.

Paige gave it another try. "You said you wanted me to represent—"

"I've changed my mind. Why should I trust you, when you've already ruined part of my plan? Where are they?"

Paige went silent.

"Where are they?" Ares demanded again.

Her gaze flicked to Rider again, pointedly, and he wondered what she was trying to tell him. It was as if she was trying to reassure him, but about what he couldn't be sure.

"Does it matter?" she asked, looking back at Ares. "You'll have your big hostages soon. Why bother with children whose families have no money, no prestige?"

"You are a naive little fool, aren't you? They are my backup plan, my insurance."

"Insurance?"

"Of course!" It seemed he was losing patience now. "The world may be willing to let some rich pigs die, but they will always cave in for children. I will kill just one, and they will crumple!"

Paige stared at the man. Then she said something, too low for Rider to hear.

Ares backhanded her across the face.

Rider's shoulders screamed with pain as he fought to get free. Paige went down to her knees, one hand to her face. Rider could see her biting her lip, could see the tears of pain welling in her eyes, but she made no sound. He didn't care if Ares shot him here and now, he had to—

"You wish to die for her?" Ares said, looking at Rider.

Rider could see that Ares looked almost hopeful. And he knew that if he betrayed anything more than a normal concern, Ares would realize what Paige meant to him, and he would use it against them both. He knew that no matter what Ares did to him, he would never tell him where the children were. But if he instead did it to Paige…

"She's a woman," he protested, making sure it sounded rather weak as Paige slowly stood up.

"And she has crossed me. Be still, or you will die right here, and she can watch it."

Without even looking at her, Ares hit her again. This time a small cry escaped her, and she staggered back a step and a half. Rider jerked as if he'd been the one struck. Only then did Ares turn to her.

"Where are they?"

She straightened, met Ares's gaze. The tears were spilling over now, but she stood squarely, refusing to speak. Rider's stomach knotted at her courage.

"You will tell me," Ares promised.

"Go straight to hell," Paige said.

He hit her again and again, punctuating each blow with a shouted "Where?"

Rider couldn't stand this. It was ripping him apart inside, causing a pain much worse than the one in his wrists, which were now bloody as he fought his restraints. Only the memory of the children, trying so hard to be brave, kept him from breaking and telling Ares himself where they were. The memory of little Hannah, clinging to him as if he were her only protection in a world suddenly turned ugly and cruel. If he broke now, what they had done—and what Paige was doing now, enduring this pain—would be for nothing.

She was on the floor, trying uselessly to fend off his blows. And then he kicked her.

Ares drew back his heavily booted foot once more. He was going to kill her, Rider thought in anguish. He couldn't take this anymore. In the moment he opened his mouth to speak, Paige cried out. Ares paused.

"Please," Paige said on a broken sob. "No more."

"Where are the children?" Ares asked in a soft tone that was ominous rather than gentle.

"They're…in a cave. On the other side of the island, straight east from the courtyard. There's a path along the cliff and a narrower path down to the cave."

Ares lowered his foot to the floor. Rider let out a long, shuddering breath. His gut had been churning as she gave up the children's location, but there had been nothing else to do. She was hurt and bleeding, and there had truly been no choice. And her own distress at having given in was clear in her face, in her entire body as she lay on the floor, weeping. For the first time in his life Rider truly understood the phrase *blood lust.* Given the chance he would kill Ares with his bare hands and without a second thought.

Ares crossed to the door and summoned his two body-guards.

"Untie his feet and lock them both up in that bedroom," he ordered, gesturing toward the back room Rider had been kept in when he was first brought here. "Then call in Reyes and his platoon. I have a job for them."

It was over.

# Chapter 16

"It's all right, Paige," Rider said.

She lay curled up on the bed. After checking to make sure they were truly alone, that Ares hadn't planted a spy outside the door, Rider had gone to the adjoining bathroom and gotten a damp washcloth to wipe her face. Ares hadn't drawn blood, but Rider knew she was going to have some nasty bruises.

They would be a matched set, he thought: he'd caught a glimpse of himself in the mirror.

She'd controlled her tears fairly quickly once Ares had dumped them into this room and locked the door. She'd untied his hands, even helped him clean his bleeding wrists. Rider had noticed before that they'd reversed the doorknob so the lock was controlled on the outside. He'd even tried to pick it from this side, although he wasn't sure why. It wasn't as if he wanted to rejoin Ares in the living room. But the room was four floors up, and the door the only way out. He thought he should at least see if he could do it.

He'd almost had it, too, when Ares had dragged him out

for some more questioning about the children, questioning that bore a strong resemblance to what Paige had just endured.

He laid the cooling cloth over her forehead, hoping it would help.

"It's all right," he said again. "Paige, you had no choice."

She went very still, and he sensed her sudden tension. He tried again to reassure her.

"You had to tell him. He would have killed you."

She sat up, so abruptly it startled him. Nothing short of fury sparked in her eyes as she glared at him.

"Do you really think I would do that? That I would sell out those kids to save myself?"

He blinked, then winced as his battered eye protested. "I—"

"The children are long gone from that cave."

"What?"

"Lani's father, and every male still in the village, came for them. By now they've taken them off the island in their own boats, so there's no chance they'll be recaptured even if Ares thinks to send men on to the village from the cave."

"Bless them," Rider said fervently.

"And Kyle noticed one of those boats has a marine radio. They're going to try and get a message relayed to Redstone."

Rider breathed easy for the first time since she'd strolled into the suite. "I knew he was smart beneath all that stubbornness."

"Yes. He is. Reckless but smart." As if her own words had reminded her, she eyed him balefully. "*You* didn't give in, or he wouldn't have been asking me. So why did you think I would?"

He hesitated in the face of her anger. "I don't know," he finally said.

She was calmer now, but strong emotions were still clear in her eyes.

"What happened to you?" she asked.

He shrugged, stifling a wince. "I got lucky. They were afraid to just kill me, without Ares's permission." He grimaced. "So Filipo decided to deafen me instead, with that gun Kyle snagged. Fired it two inches from my head."

She studied him for a moment. "Did you know that's what he was doing?"

His mouth twisted. "No. I thought he was going to blow my brains out."

Paige shivered. "I heard the shot. I thought you were dead."

She sounded so upset it shook him. It wasn't the time, he knew that, but he couldn't stop himself. He leaned forward and kissed her, gently. Or he'd meant it to be gentle, but the moment the heat of her lips warmed his, he lost track of his intent. Lost track of nearly everything except the fact that this was Paige and she was kissing him back.

He poured everything he couldn't yet say into that kiss. And Paige responded as if she heard every word, as if she knew just how deep in his soul he felt what he was giving her now. When a tiny sound escaped her, a quiet but eager whimper, his body surged to attention with a fierceness he hadn't known in years.

He wanted more than anything else to take her down on this bed and lose himself in her sweet, giving heat. But he also knew the only thing more insane than thinking that would be doing it.

"Noah," she whispered against his mouth, a husky note in her voice that made his entire body clench around a white-hot shaft of need.

He'd spent his life hating his first name, and had never quite forgiven his parents for leaving him open to innumerable jokes about boats and animals in pairs. But in this instant he wouldn't change it for the world. Not after hearing it in that way, on Paige's lips.

He went down beside her, unable to stop himself. Convulsively he pulled her to him, felt a glorious burst of gratification when she didn't resist, didn't even protest, but instead clung to him as if he were the last solid thing in a dissolving world.

He kissed her again, not quite so fiercely but no less intensely. And this time she met him equally, lifting her hands to cup his face, whispering his name again, as if it were the only word she knew or wanted to know.

When her tongue brushed over his lips, heat stabbed through him. He opened for her, urging her on with a quick, darting probe of his own tongue. She took the invitation, and he groaned low and deep when she tasted him, hesitantly at first, then as if she couldn't get enough.

He felt her shiver and reveled in it. But then she broke the kiss, and even before she spoke he realized the insanity of it all.

"We can't. Not now."

With a wrenching effort he pulled back from her. "I know." And he hung his every hope for the future on those last two words.

For a long moment he simply looked at her. He was aware of a sense of awe at her pure nerve, but even that was swamped by the knowledge of how badly he'd underestimated her. She had endured a painful beating simply to make her eventual confession more believable, and with pure courage she'd misdirected Ares. He'd send men out to that cave after the children, and they would be gone. A wild-goose chase.

A wild-goose chase....

"What are you thinking?" Paige asked, and he realized the thought that had just struck him must have changed his expression.

"He's going to send men to the cave."

"That's what it sounded like," she agreed.

"A platoon...that must be more than just a couple of men, even if it's not as many as a regular military platoon."

He could see realization dawn in her eyes as she got where he was headed. "Which means...there will be fewer men here."

He nodded.

"Lani's father said that when they'd gone to check the school after the children didn't come home, they saw Ares's men."

"But Tarak and Filipo didn't see them?"

She shook her head. "This is their turf, don't forget. But they did some counting. Their best estimate is that there are only about fifteen of them, maybe a few more up at the cell phone towers."

"Fifteen...Ares and his two goons, a low guess of maybe three in this so-called platoon. That would leave nine."

"The one that brought me in was down on the beach."

"And there's probably at least two or three more on the grounds. Which would leave only about five or six here at the hotel itself."

"So...if we're going to do anything, now is the time."

He nodded again. Paige sat up straighter. "So what do we do?"

Rider felt like asking, "How should I know?" He'd rarely felt more out of his depth than he had since this had started. "We can't assume Kyle's going to be able to get through to Redstone quickly," he said finally.

"Or that they'll be able to do anything if he does," Paige said.

Rider's mouth quirked. "Oh, they'll do something. If they don't already know something's up, I'll be surprised."

"Why?"

He shrugged. "They get daily reports from each facility. Missing one is not that crucial. But two—" he glanced at the clock on the nightstand "—no, three, as of a couple of hours ago, that's going to get their attention."

"What would they do then?"

"Probably start out by calling. They—" He stopped abruptly as the logical next step hit him.

"What?"

"I just realized," he said a bit ruefully, "that if they called, they'd probably ask for me."

"You mean Ares may know by now who you are? And that Redstone is suspicious?"

"It might explain why he hasn't just killed me," Rider said. But then something else occurred to him. "On second thought, he may not know anything. If it's just a routine check on why there's been no contact, they'd probably just call my cell number."

Paige's eyes widened. "Kyle has your phone. I knew they'd search me, so I gave it to him and told him the same thing you told me."

"So…if he was still within range of the cell towers, he may have already talked to Redstone directly."

"And Ares would know," Paige said, her voice tense.

"Easy," Rider said, reaching out to take her hand. "He doesn't know where Kyle is. The only way to find out would be with triangulation gear, and if that radio they were using is any sign of the state of their equipment, they don't have anything that sophisticated. And since Kyle's now offshore, there's not a thing Ares can do." He gave her a half smile. "Wish I'd thought of it myself when this started. I could have taken one of their boats out."

"They would have caught you. Or at least seen you, and probably blown you out of the water."

"Maybe."

"Besides, he probably would have just tortured everybody on the island, thinking he could find…"

Her voice trailed off, and Rider knew it was because she

had just realized that that was still a very real possibility, if they had indeed monitored any call to his cell phone.

In the silence they heard some commotion coming from the common room of the suite. Rider got up and quietly made his way to the door. What he could hear was muffled, but he made out enough to guess that Ares was indeed sending men to the cave. He couldn't tell how many different voices he was hearing, just that there were more than two. But Ares's last words, ordering them to hurry because he couldn't afford for them to be gone long, seemed to confirm what they'd suspected; the man was indeed short on manpower.

When he turned back from the door he saw Paige had moved over to the window and was peering down. There was no real lanai on this smallest bedroom in the suite, only a small mock balcony not even large enough to stand on, with a decorative railing. And the window was simply a window, not a doorway.

"If they're really going, they'll have to go that way," she said when he came up beside her.

Less than two minutes later she was proved right as three men went through the hotel courtyard at a run.

"Three. So we're close on our guess."

"For all the good it will do us."

She sounded as if it was all catching up with her finally. And for some reason that spurred him to renew his efforts to figure a way out of this.

"Four floors," he muttered as he looked at the too-distant ground. "A bit much for the old bed-sheet trick to get down."

"The guards would see, anyway, from the courtyard."

"Yeah."

So far he wasn't doing well on the escape planning. As he was thinking, his gaze fell on the bedside phone. One of the guards had yanked out the cord and removed it when they'd put him in here the first time.

"What are you thinking?"

He shrugged. "That it's too bad we don't have a phone. If Kyle's gotten a call then we're half-burned already, so what's a little more? If we worked it right, maybe we could thin them out even a little more."

"What do you mean?"

"Maybe dupe them into thinking help's closer than it is."

Paige looked thoughtful. "You mean a bogus phone call?"

He nodded. "Hopefully he'd send somebody to check out a possible threat first, and worry about who made the call later."

Both ideas were academic, of course, they had no phone and no way to get down from here, on the top floor.

No way to get down. The top floor.

"We can't go down," he murmured, "but..."

"But what?" Paige asked.

"Maybe we can go up."

"Up? But we're on the top floor."

"Exactly."

As usual she caught up with him quickly. "You mean the roof?"

"I don't think there's anybody up there. There were no guards at night when I was out. I don't think he's got enough men."

"And since he's got everyone locked up, he must figure he doesn't need anyone up there now."

Rider nodded. "And if I recall the drawings correctly, there's a stairway at the far end of the building." He looked out the window once more. "I think I can make it if I stand on that railing. I know you're hurting, but if we knot up a sheet, do you think you could climb?"

"I'm fine. I'll climb," she said firmly. "If it would get me out of here, I'd learn to fly."

"I'll just bet you would," he said softly.

Thankfully, the window slid open quietly enough. While Rider removed the screen, Paige quickly and efficiently tied knots in the bedsheets at one-foot intervals. It was going to be long enough. Barely. Rider edged his way out onto the mock balcony, hoping that the builders hadn't stinted on construction quality here just because it was decorative and not meant to hold weight.

He found he could reach the top of the building, but not enough to get a grip and pull himself up. He dropped back down to the tiny balcony, swearing under his breath.

"I'm about two inches too short."

Paige looked up, then at the railing. "Use me," she said.

"What?"

"Stand on my shoulders. That'll give you enough."

"But you're hurt, can you— Never mind. Of course you can."

For the first time since she'd walked into the suite, Paige grinned at him. And Rider suddenly felt as if he could leap to that rooftop in a single bound.

Instead, after another glance down at the courtyard, he climbed back up on the railing. Paige stepped out and braced her hands on the railing, putting her feet apart to give herself better balance.

"I'll be careful," he said.

"Don't worry about hurting me. Just do it. Fast."

He couldn't help worrying—he'd witnessed what Ares had done to her—but he did it. As fast as he could manage it, ignoring his own sore spots. He winced as he felt one sole of his shoe digging into her, but then he was up and over, the sheet he'd tied to his belt trailing after him. Quickly he secured it to a pipe on the roof and then signaled Paige.

She pulled the window closed behind her and replaced the screen—a good idea, he thought, if it slowed them down even a minute or two in figuring out what they'd done—then reached for the makeshift rope. True to her promise she climbed. She wasn't quick or stylish, but, using the knots for hand and footholds, she got it done. Only when she reached the top did she have a problem, and at that point Rider simply leaned over and pulled her the rest of the way. Then he reeled in the sheets until they were out of sight from the ground.

There was no sign of anyone else on the roof. They moved with agonizing slowness and care until they were certain they were no longer on top of Ares's temporary quarters. Then they moved toward the middle of the roof, so no one could see them from below.

He spotted the triangular structure that was the entrance to the stairway, and pointed. Paige nodded, and they veered that way. In moments they were inside the stairwell. Rider felt both less exposed and more threatened: they were back inside, and so was Ares and what men he had left.

Rider had his foot on the second step down, when he came to an abrupt halt.

"What?" Paige whispered.

He dodged back upstairs, looked on the wall just inside the door, and there it was—a small gray metal box. He went to it and pulled the door open, revealing a telephone.

"It's to report problems with equipment or leaks up here," he explained when Paige came back to stand beside him. "But I think it's got outside-line capabilities, too."

He picked up the receiver and dialed seven. There was a click, then a dial tone.

"Yes," he hissed. He'd been afraid Ares might have had somebody savvy enough to sabotage even this latest model phone system. Quickly he began to dial his cell phone number, then stopped, looking at Paige.

"If this works, you can't talk to him. They might not be sure of a male voice, but…"

"That's all right. As long as I know he's okay."

"He may not answer. If they're too far out at sea, he could be out of range."

She nodded in understanding. He finished dialing. For a moment it seemed nothing would happen. Then a voice said hesitantly, "Hello?" He sounded young, but thankfully not too young.

"Kyle?"

"Yes." Excitement colored the boy's voice. Rider hoped it would help disguise his age to any listener. "Is that you—"

"Yes, it is," Rider said, cutting him off before he could give his name. "Are you and your crew safe?"

"Yeah, we're fine. A couple guys are seasick, but—"

"Good. They're probably monitoring this, so I'll have to talk fast." *Get it, Kyle, get it.* "Have you heard from base?"

There was a pause, then Kyle said uncertainly, "Well, there was a call earlier—"

"Good," Rider said, cutting him off. "Everything's in motion, then. Now listen. Head all the boats around to the leeward side, and stand fast off shore. Have weapons at the ready, but wait for my signal."

"Signal?" Kyle sounded confused.

"Yes. None of your men make a move until then, you just wait within sight but out of range of their weapons."

Suddenly Kyle caught on. "Oh! Yes, sir! You want the rocket launchers ready, too?"

Rider almost laughed. "Yes. We might need them." He hesitated for a split second, wondering how to word his next question. "Any ETA on the backup force?"

Kyle was right there with him on that one. "Yes, sir. They're on the way and ready for a fight."

The kid was *enjoying* this, Rider thought. "Good. Sit tight, my friend."

"Yes, sir."

When the connection was broken, he looked at Paige. "He's going to be okay, honey," he said.

She gave him a smile that said either the endearment that

had just slipped out or his actual words had made her very happy. He wished they could wait until he found out which.

"Do you think they heard you?" she asked as he closed the phone box.

"I don't know. If they did, we'll know shortly. If they didn't, then we'll just lie low until that little flotilla comes around the corner and somebody spots them. The reaction should be the same in either case."

They retreated to the roof, moving toward the end that overlooked the courtyard. They took turns watching to the north and the open space on the roof to their backs.

"You know we can't assume any help is coming immediately," he said after a minute. "They might not realize just how much trouble we're in, here."

"I know." She turned her head to meet his gaze. "We're on our own for now, aren't we?"

He nodded, afraid if he spoke he would sound so grim he'd scare her. They went back to watching.

In less than five minutes shouts and men running toward the main building gave them hope.

A few minutes later a small group of men came out of the building at a run and headed north. One of them was even one of Ares's precious bodyguards. But the man himself had stayed behind.

"Four more down," Rider whispered with a grin at Paige.

"Yes, indeed," she answered, grinning back at him.

"That leaves him with two, maybe three at most."

"Now what?"

Rider hadn't really thought that far. "I'm not sure. All I could think about was to scatter his forces."

"You sure did that," she said.

"*We* did that," he corrected.

He looked back out over the courtyard. He knew they needed to do something, that they were wasting precious time. The smart thing would be to just get away, to get as far away as they could until help arrived. But when that help did arrive, even if Ares was outnumbered, he still held the position of power, because he still had dozens of hostages. He still had the entire Redstone staff.

But now Ares was down to himself and two or maybe three men. He had to either give up guarding the hostages or give up his own bodyguard. And since the hostages were his bargaining chips...

Could they do it? They'd gotten the children away, could they possibly do the same here?

"Noah?"

He looked at Paige. Her eyes were bright, and he could see by her expression she'd just thought of something.

"What?"

"Could we...the others, the staff, do you think we could get them out?"

Noah couldn't help the lopsided grin that spread across his face. "You read my mind."

"How can you remember all this?" Paige whispered in awe as he made yet another turn without hesitation.

"A brain quirk," Noah said. "Plans, diagrams, maps. Can't help it."

"Thank goodness," she said in a heartfelt voice.

Using his knowledge, they'd worked their way from one end of the main hotel building to the other by way of back hallways and utility rooms, and hadn't seen another soul. Given the reasonable supposition that Ares had all the hostages in one place, there were only a couple of places big enough to hold them all at once.

The first, the media room, was empty.

"Got to be the dining room," Noah said.

Still moving quietly, they headed toward the room were he had first stepped back into her life. God, that day seemed forever ago, she thought. So much had happened, even before these crazed men had—

She snapped out of her useless thoughts when they had to dodge around a service cart loaded with kitchen equipment that stood in the hallway. And she nearly ran into Noah's back when he came to an abrupt halt at the corner.

He leaned forward, taking a quick glance down the hall. He dodged back so quickly she knew he'd spotted something. Or someone.

"Guard," he mouthed.

So they'd been right. The hostages had to be in this room. A little thrill jolted through her. But now that they'd found them, she wasn't at all sure how they were going to rescue them with an armed guard at the doors.

They moved out of earshot, backing around the corner they'd just turned. Then she asked quietly, "Just one?"

He nodded.

"Are there any other doors?"

He closed his eyes, as if calling up the memory of the hotel plans in his mind. "None accessible from here." Then, "Wait..."

His eyes snapped open. He looked her up and down, studied her assessingly, almost as if he'd never seen her before. "Are you claustrophobic?"

*What on earth?* she wondered. "Not particularly."

He hesitated, then said, "I know you have to be hurting from what he did, but how limber are you?"

She was hurting, but only asked, "How limber do I have to be?"

He gestured to her to follow and began to backtrack even farther. He stopped midway down the hall. He nodded toward a small metal door in the wall that she had assumed covered some kind of electrical panel or equipment. Paige looked at him, even more puzzled than before. He reached out and swung the hinged door open. The first thing she noticed was a gaping hole at the bottom of the opening, lined with some silver metal and vanishing into darkness like a galvanized rabbit hole.

"It's a laundry chute," Noah explained.

Paige leaned over to take a closer look. On the opposite side it looked to be a solid piece of that same metal. The only hinges she could see were at the bottom, and there were angled pieces of the same metal on the sides.

"It's bottom hinged, so it tilts out on the other side. It's easier to dump tablecloths that way. The door's here in case something gets jammed or stuck."

"The other side is in the dining room?"

He nodded. And what he'd meant about being limber was now clear. She looked once more, with a new eye, to what he was asking. The opening was about two and a half feet high and nearly as wide. There was a narrow lip around the edge of the chute. Not even half as wide as her foot, it could be a tricky balancing act.

"I'd never get through it," he said, as if he felt he had to explain why he wasn't volunteering himself.

"Obviously," she said, glancing back at him. His height made squeezing through nearly impossible, and his shoulders alone would never get through the gap. But she might. Not easily or comfortably, but she just might be able to do it.

She knelt down and looked up into the space. It would be tight, but if she could even get partway, and then got some help on the other side...

"I think I can do it," she said.

He gave her a careful hug that was clearly heartfelt, and over far too quickly. And then he dropped a kiss on her lips, also over far too quickly.

"I'll stay here until you're in. Tell them to start raising a fuss, threaten, break the furniture, whatever it takes to make this guy call for help. We want to draw as many of the guards that are left as possible. Just be careful they don't go too far, tell them they need to settle down fast when the backup arrives, so nobody feels the need to start shooting."

"I think I'll tell them their kids are safe first," she said. "After that, I don't think it'll take much."

Noah grinned as he nodded at her. "You do that. Hold on a sec."

He ran back to the service cart they'd passed. Moving carefully, he checked the various trays. She saw him remove a large carving knife and shove it in his belt under his shirt. She supposed she felt better that at least one of them was armed, but she wouldn't have the slightest idea how to handle a knife as a weapon.

He came back, moving as amazingly quietly as he had been the entire time. She knew he had to be hurting, but there was no sign of it.

"Ready?" he asked.

She nodded. He opened the door all the way on their side, then reached in to shove the chute door on the other side open. For a moment he just listened, and for the first time she wondered if they had a second guard inside.

*Great. I would have just charged right in. And gotten shot, no doubt,* she realized ruefully.

After a moment he backed out. "Sounds clear."

She nodded, moved toward the chute, then stopped as something he'd said finally registered. "What did you mean, you'll stay until I get in? Where are you going?"

He shrugged. "Just to look around. You need help?"

"Not on this side."

"Okay." He hesitated, then said, "Look, if it comes down to it, Redstone will hook you up with my dad. Tell him I love him. And my sister, Michelle, too."

She glanced at the knife in his belt, then back at his face. That moment of hesitation, and his words, said it all, and she knew exactly what he was going to do.

He was going after Ares.

# Chapter 17

Once she got over the image of herself plummeting down the laundry chute like a gravy-stained tablecloth, Paige decided she knew pretty much what a jack-in-the-box felt like. When she popped up out of her little box, it was startling. No one seemed to be looking her way, and she didn't dare call out, for fear the guard just outside the door might hear.

They were sitting all over, in chairs and on the floor. She and Noah—God, don't think about him, what he's going to do, not now—had guessed there must be at least fifty being held here, and she thought the number looked about right. And Paige had never seen a more disheartened group. They all looked a bit worse for wear, and there were signs of tears on many faces, and not all of them female. One of them, Mr. Rutherford, sat huddled in a corner on the floor shaking, his eyes rather glassy.

She spotted Miranda. Desperate now, because she didn't think she could climb out of the awkwardly tilted chute without help, she called as loudly as she dared. The woman turned. Her eyes widened, and her mouth opened.

Paige threw a finger up to her lips and shook her head fiercely. Miranda's mouth shut. But she got to her feet and hurried over, drawing the attention of most of the others in the room. Frantic gestures kept the exclamations down, but the buzz in the room still rose.

With Miranda's help, Paige scrambled out of the chute and into the room. She turned back and tapped twice on the metal siding, as arranged. Noah tapped back, and then the light in the hole vanished as he shut the door on the other side.

Paige tried again not to think about what he was going to do now. He'd refused to confirm her guess, probably because he wanted her to focus on what she had to do here, but she knew she was right. Just as she knew that he knew he would quite possibly not survive. The message he'd left with her for his father and sister had made that hideously clear. But she hadn't been able to stop him. And now, the only thing she could do for him was her part.

Everyone in the room was gathered around her now, and Paige spoke quickly and quietly. "Please, you must keep it down, the guard is still right outside." When they nodded, she said, "First and most important—the children are safe."

Despite the warning, the noise level swelled as those parents in the group nearly cried out in relief. But it died quickly as Paige went on in a near whisper. As she'd hoped, their need to hear what she was saying quieted them.

"They're with the people of the village, led by Lani DeSouza's father. And not only are they safe, completely off the island in the village's boats, they've managed to call for help for us all."

"But how?" Miranda asked. "They told us the children were all being held at the school."

"Thank Noah Rider," Paige said. "He got them out.

And he let the terrorists capture him to give us a few extra minutes to get away.''

She saw the shock and awe in their faces and was glad she'd taken a moment to say it. She was fairly certain Noah would never tell them himself. Besides, they needed to know. They'd gone from grimness to relief, from fear to hope, and now she had to spark them to anger.

"And now you can do something for him," she said. "That is, assuming you're tired of being held here like sheep for the slaughter. Tired enough to be really, really mad."

In that single instant the tenor of the entire group changed. "Mad?" Miranda said. "You bet we are. If it hadn't been for the children, we'd have done something a long time ago."

"Well, now there's nothing holding you back. And here's what you need to do."

They all leaned in closer as she explained Noah's plan.


The last time he'd been down this hallway, he'd been half-conscious, bleeding and figuring his life expectancy had been reduced to minutes. Now he was fully alert, sore but not bleeding and figuring that his life expectancy could again be in minutes.

He waited, trying not to look at his watch more often than every minute, thankful that his blackened eye hadn't swollen completely shut. He wasn't sure why he felt so strongly that Ares would still be holed up in that suite; he just was. Something about the man's image of himself as the noble crusader instead of a terrorist. He probably figured he deserved the best, and taking it from the "rich pigs" he was so fixated on just seem to fit. Not to mention he was personally safer there.

Rider crouched in the elevator alcove, his legs starting to cramp. It was at least a distraction from his head, he thought sourly. And his ribs. He'd been fine when they'd been moving, but now that he'd been motionless for several minutes, it was all catching up with him. When he finally had to move, he'd be lucky if he could.

As time passed and nothing happened, he tried not to jump to the conclusion something had gone wrong, that Paige was in trouble. Maybe Ares had more men than they'd thought, and he'd stationed one inside the dining room, as well. Maybe she'd been captured, maybe she was a prisoner again. Or worse...

He shook his head sharply, knowing the pain would intensify and for a moment at least drive out those spinning thoughts. It did. And when the throb finally died away, he heard the sound he'd been waiting for. Elevator number two, headed down from the top floor.

He stood up, stretching out legs that were stiff and protesting. He nudged open the door behind him, and stepped back to the spot he'd chosen, where he was hidden in the shadows but could see the reflection of the elevators in the mirror on the opposite wall.

The bell chimed and the light above elevator number two came on. The doors slid open.

Three men. None of them Ares. And all headed at a run toward the dining room. She'd done it. She'd lured them out. Leaving Ares to him.

With a grin and a mental salute to the woman who never ceased to amaze him, Rider quickly backed into the darkened room behind him. He flipped a switch that shut down power to elevator number one. Then he went to number two, which the men had used, closed the doors, took in a deep breath and punched the button for the top floor.

When the indicator hit four, he backed into a front corner until the door slid open. When nothing happened, he risked a look. The hotel hallway was empty, and the door to the suite Ares had taken over was closed.

With the doors held open, he flicked the run switch on

the elevator off, so it couldn't be summoned from downstairs. Then he went quickly down the hall.

He hesitated for a moment, wishing he had more of a plan. But he'd been playing this whole thing by ear and he was still alive, so he decided to just keep on doing the same.

He closed his eyes, calling up the layout of the suite— oddly, from the floor plan rather than his actual time in the set of rooms, because that's the way his quirky mind worked. Then he walked toward the single door that was just down from the main double doors of the suite. The single door led to the room that adjoined the others, but could be used as a single room, as well, hence the separate door.

The door was locked, of course, but he took the chance that Ares hadn't bothered to set the dead bolts. Rider pulled out the master card-key Barry had given him that first day. He tried it in the lock, and the light flashed green. Slowly, with his fingers clenched as if that could somehow make it quieter, he pushed down on the door lever. And let out a silent breath when it opened smoothly and with only the tiniest of sounds.

The room was empty. He stepped inside, careful to keep the door under control and hang on to the handle until it snicked closed. The door leading into the central living room of the suite was standing open, and for a moment he just stood there, listening.

Someone was there, moving around. He waited, listening for the silence that would indicate whoever it was had stopped or taken a seat. It didn't come. The sound of movement continued, sometimes closer, sometimes fading slightly. It took him a moment to realize that someone was pacing, back and forth.

He edged toward the door, then stopped dead when he heard a voice.

Ares.

He felt a spurt of grim satisfaction at having guessed ight, that Ares would hide out here and send his men to lo the dirty work. But who was he talking to? Taking on ne armed man was one thing, but two, with one of them ikely toting one of those AK-47s, was something else. )raven would do it, Rider was sure, and come out smelling ike a rose. The man never put a foot wrong in situations ike this. But Draven wasn't here, he was. He was the top Redstone person on this island, which made this his prob- em.

Not to mention that he wanted a crack at Ares. The im- ge of the man beating Paige as she lay crumpled on the loor, while he sat there helplessly was not one that would eave him for a very long time. He wanted—

The man was talking to himself.

On some level, while his thoughts had been racing, Rider lad finally registered that he was only hearing one voice.

The guy's giving a flipping speech, he thought as he leard bits and pieces of dogma and justification for terror- sm. His entire operation is in danger of falling apart—I lope—and he's spouting terrorist doctrine.

Rider moved to the door quickly, waited until the voice eemed to fade slightly, risked a quick glance.

Ares was alone and gesturing almost wildly as he paced, s if he were indeed giving a speech. He was armed, but nly with the holstered sidearm he'd seen when the man lad first come to the schoolroom.

Next time you talk like that, I hope it's in a courtroom, ight before they sentence you, Rider thought.

But before that could happen, he was going to have to lo something. And fast, before something went sour down n the dining room. He had no choice.

He counted off the seconds as Ares paced, trying to time vhen he turned his back to the doorway. Once, it was at velve seconds, once at thirteen. He had to assume the man would realize he was there before he got to him. Had to assume his first move would be to grab his weapon.

Rider had to get to him before he could shoot. He'd managed to get through this so far, he just had to hope hi luck would hold a little while longer.

On the next round Rider drew his knife. Waited. Though of Paige, bruised, hurting and going on, anyway. Paige worth so much more than these overarmed cowards.

At thirteen seconds he looked. Saw Ares's back.

*Now.*

He ran. As quietly as he could. But speed was more important now. When he was three strides away, Ares began to turn. His hand flashed toward the holster. Rider closed on him.

He wasn't going to make it. Rider launched himself in a headlong tackle. He grunted—or maybe it was Ares—when he hit. They both went down. He felt a stinging pain or his left bicep. Realized he'd nicked himself with his own blade. Realized Ares had his hand on the gun.

Rider clawed at him with his left hand. Struggled to bring the knife up with his right. Ares pounded at him with a rock-hard fist. Rider wrenched himself around until he could power a kick to Ares's gun arm. The weapon fell barely a foot from the man's outstretched hand.

Ares abandoned his pummeling and rolled toward the gun. In the instant he reached it Rider was on him. From behind he grabbed the man's chin. Forced his head back. He whipped the gleaming blade forward, making sure Ares saw it before it came to rest across his throat.

"Both hands, out in front of you." Ares hesitated, and Rider tightened his grip. "My life would be a lot simpler if you died right here."

To his surprise, for he'd never thought of himself as a particularly bloodthirsty man, he meant it. At least now, in this moment, with that image of Paige in his head, he did

And Ares must have sensed that, because he did as he was told.

"Who *are* you?" Ares demanded.

"Your worst nightmare," Rider said, grinning recklessly even as he borrowed the movie phrase. "Just an ordinary citizen who's had enough of your kind."

He reached over and picked up the blue steel automatic pistol, saw that it was a Beretta, a model 92. His dad had bought one after the army had switched to the M9 version. As Rider competently checked the load—if it was only a ten-round magazine rather than the older, now-banned in the U.S. fifteen, he figured he'd better know now—and released the safety. The frowning look he saw on Ares's face was downright warming.

"And now," Rider said, pressing his knee over the man's kidneys for emphasis, "you and I are going to take a little walk."

Just her luck, Paige thought, that Filipo would be one of the men Ares sent. He'd been furious with her even before they'd humiliated him by escaping. And now he was looking for revenge.

When he'd first spotted her among the hostages, he'd simply stared, clearly dumbfounded. But his expression had quickly changed, to the pleased smile of a child given an unexpected gift.

More like a cruel little boy who's found a fly to pull the wings off, she thought grimly.

As Rider had instructed, she'd helped calm the now rowdy group down when the guards threatened to start shooting. She'd spent the entire time they were following those instructions, causing as much noise and commotion as they could, trying not to think about where Noah was, or what he was doing.

Or if he was still alive.

He'd pulled off some near miracles, and she would be

first in line to pin a medal on him. But he was not a soldier, or even a brawler, and face-to-face with a man like Ares…he *was* in over his head.

But he'd gone, anyway. He'd gone because it had to be done, and he was the only one who could do it. Her heart ached with the sheer courage that had taken. And she prayed that she would get the chance to tell him. As well as the chance to finish what they'd begun.

Heat had flooded her at the memory of those fleeting moments upstairs. For an instant she had been tempted, so very tempted, to ignore the reality of the nightmare they were living and pretend they were free to continue the hot, deep kisses, the tentative-but-so-very-arousing caresses.

And it was at that moment, with her face flushed with an undeniably sexual heat, that she'd seen Filipo. And the heat had turned to an immediate chill.

When the other two men who had come with him began to herd the hostages into a corner of the room, forcing them to pick up the chairs that had been thrown and tables that had been upended as they went, Filipo had zeroed in on her. By the time he reached her his eyes were lit with a dark eagerness that made her shudder inwardly.

"So, little bitch, you have come back to me."

"Only to see them take you away." Something flickered in his eyes, and Paige wanted very much to believe it was fear. "They're on the way, and soon you'll be rotting in prison. I hope they throw away the key."

He swore in some language she didn't understand, but there was little doubt of the crudity of whatever he'd said. It was written all over his face. He yanked his rifle around and dug the barrel into her throat.

"No!" someone cried out, Paige thought it was Miranda.

"Filipo!" one of the other men yelled.

"She is mine," Filipo hissed. "And I will make her wish she was already dead before I kill her."

He lifted the rifle to the right side of her head. Then he

leaned forward, whispering to her, telling her in ugly, lascivious and lurid detail what he was going to do to her and make her do to him before he put a bullet through her brain.

"And they will all watch, all of your friends here, to show them what happens to those who—"

A commotion at the main doors stopped him midtirade. Every head turned to look. And Paige, even with the barrel of an automatic rifle gouging her temple, couldn't help but smile joyously.

Noah was here. And he had Ares. With a gun barrel pressed to *his* head.

"Tell them to drop their weapons," she heard Noah order the terrorist leader.

Ares did it, clearly convinced Noah would shoot if he had to. The men hesitated. Noah moved his thumb to the pistol's hammer, which was already partly back, and levered it back all the way.

"It's off safety now, and I'm real nervous," he said.

Ares shouted the order this time. And the men obeyed. Except for Filipo.

He twisted in place, pulling Paige with him. "I have the teacher," he exclaimed. "If you don't let him go, I will kill her!"

"Then I kill your boss here," Noah said, so coolly that if she hadn't been able to see the tightness of his jaw and the wire-drawn tension of his body, she would have thought this was his everyday business.

"You won't let her die," Filipo insisted.

Paige saw the change in Ares then, as he registered the probable truth in Filipo's words. And as he looked at her, she saw in Noah's eyes that he saw it, too. He had been in control, but now the entire atmosphere in the room seemed to shift.

She glanced for a split second at Filipo. He was watching Ares, as if looking for some sign. She looked back at Noah.

And her son's eager question echoed in her mind now, along with Noah's answer:

*How good a shot?*

*Very.*

She began to lift her right hand, praying Filipo was so intent on his leader that he wouldn't notice.

But Ares noticed. He opened his mouth, Paige was sure to call out a warning. She snapped her hand up and forward, hitting at the rifle barrel, shoving it upward.

The sound of the shots echoed off the walls.

Her last coherent thought as she sank to the floor was that now she knew what automatic rifle fire sounded like.

# Chapter 18

"Girlfriend, I will never forget that as long as I live," Miranda said with a visible shudder as she knelt beside Paige. "I felt sure that man was going to kill you, and the next thing I know there's Mr. Rider, cool as can be, shooting clear across the room without turning a hair."

Paige smiled weakly at her friend. Her ears were still ringing, and her knees weren't steady enough to hold her yet. But she knew that she, too, had an image seared into her brain that she would never, ever forget. Noah, hanging on to a struggling Ares with one arm while he aimed and fired at Filipo, taking him out with a single shot whose sound hadn't even died away before he had Ares back under control.

"A *very* good shot indeed," she whispered.

It was only after the hostages had thoroughly and happily tied up their former captors including Ares—with tablecloths Rudy cheerfully ripped into strips for the cause—that Noah got to her. She was standing by then, albeit not steadily.

"You're all right?" he asked anxiously, looking her over.

"Fine," she said. "At least, I will be as soon as my ears stop ringing."

"That blood—"

"Is his," she assured him. Filipo wouldn't be terrorizing anybody again, for a very long time. Then her eyes narrowed as she spotted a dark stain spreading on his left shirt-sleeve. "What about you?"

He glanced down at his arm as if he'd forgotten. "Oh, that."

"Yes, that! You're hurt."

"Not really. It's just a little nick." He let out a sigh and admitted sheepishly, "I did it to myself, rolling around with our friend Ares."

She didn't think she was up to any more details of that encounter just now. "Let me look at it for you. There must be a first-aid kit or something around here."

"You don't have to do that."

"I'm a teacher, I do it all the time."

"Okay, but later. We need to figure out what to do next."

"Wait for the cavalry?" she suggested.

He chuckled, but the sound faded quickly. "Damn, you scared me," he said, "when I realized what you were going to do."

"You said you were a good shot."

"Not against a man with an assault rifle!"

"Wrong."

"What?"

"You're just as good against a man with an assault rifle as anywhere else. You just proved it."

He blinked. Then slowly he gave her a lopsided smile as he shook his head. "You never cease to amaze me."

"Oh?" she said. "My jaw has dropped a few times over you, too."

"Mr. Rider? I hear people coming," Miranda called almost apologetically from the doorway Noah had shot from.

Noah swore. "One or the other of those platoons must be back. Damn, I thought we'd have longer." He looked at the handgun he held, then at her. "Can you use this?"

She grimaced, but nodded. "If I have to."

He gave it to her. "Safety's off and it's ready to fire. I only had to shoot once, to convince Ares I was serious, so you should have fourteen more rounds."

He turned then, and went to the small pile of weapons the now-free hostages had made on the floor. Paige followed as he picked up one of the automatic rifles and another handgun that he stuck in his belt. He straightened and looked at her.

"If they get past me—"

"You can't go out there alone," Paige exclaimed. "I'm coming with you."

"No, somebody needs to—"

"I'll go, too," Rudy volunteered unexpectedly. "I'm no sharpshooter like you, but I've shot my share of sharks who were after my mahi mahi."

"I've shot a snake or two back home," someone else offered. "Guess I could do it here, too."

"Me, too!"

Noah looked a bit bemused at the sudden wealth of assistance. But before anyone was put to the test, Miranda called out excitedly, "Hey! It's not them, it's somebody who's *got* them!"

Paige and Noah both ran to the door, followed by most of the rest of the staff.

"Keep an eye on them," Noah said, indicating their prisoners.

Then he stepped out into the hallway. It was possible to see into the courtyard from here, through the glass wall at the front of the lobby, but not well. He watched for a minute, and Paige could feel his tension. Then suddenly he seemed to spot something or someone. And a wide smile spread across his face.

"Draven," he breathed, and the world of relief she heard in his voice told Paige this was very good news.

He turned his head to look at her. "It's Redstone. John Draven, the head of security. They must have gotten Kyle's message."

Paige stared at the approaching group. She'd never again expected to be grateful to see armed, uniformed men coming at her. It was easy to separate them out: the newcomers wore all black, while the rest were in the too-familiar green camouflage. She did a quick count and saw that they had apparently rounded up all the unaccounted-for terrorists.

A little stunned at the realization that it was really over, Paige just stood there, watching as the man Noah had indicated spotted him and waved. The man was about Noah's size, but somehow he seemed even bigger. Paige could see that he moved with that same powerful grace, the kind of effortless motion she'd seen Noah exhibit when they were trying to move quietly.

But as Draven got closer, she could see that that was where the resemblance ended. It wasn't just the fact that his hair was longer and darker than Noah's—nearly black—or that he had a wicked-looking scar down the left side of his face, or that this man's eyes were green not Noah's piercing blue. The real difference was that Draven's eyes were shadowed, with more than a touch of cynicism, as if this *was* his everyday business. As she supposed it could well be.

"Hey, Rider," the leader said with a grin, "nice shiner! And thanks for the trip to paradise."

Noah muttered something she couldn't hear, but the two men shook hands heartily. As the rest of the security team herded the last captives into the dining room with the rest, another man stopped beside Draven.

"Where's Sam?" he asked.

"On the way," Draven said.

The second man pulled off a knit cap, revealing thick, nearly platinum-blond hair, and grinned at Noah, revealing a deep dimple that belied the tough, competent demeanor.

"What's with you? It's not like you to stir up all this trouble."

"Quiet, Singleton. I wasn't stirring, I was in the pot with everybody else, just trying to stay afloat."

"Nice try." Paige was startled to hear a feminine voice coming from behind John Draven. When the source of the voice reached them, she was even more surprised to see a tall, long-legged woman with a striking sort of beauty and hair as blond as the man Noah had called Singleton. In fact, there was a definite resemblance between them.

The woman saw Paige's glance flick to the man and back to her, and her nose crinkled. "Yeah, yeah, I know. But we're not related. Hi," she said to Paige, "I'm Sam."

This was Sam? Paige was beginning to feel a bit woozy.

"What did you mean, nice try?" Draven asked the woman called Sam.

"I meant Rider here, trying to be modest." She winked at him. "But the kid who called us told us what you've been up to."

"Kyle?" Paige asked urgently. "Is he all right?"

The woman looked at her. "This is Paige Cooper," Noah said. "Paige, Samantha Beckett and Rand Singleton. Kyle's her son," he explained.

Sam nodded in understanding. "He's fine. They're just waiting for word to come back to shore."

"Which we should give them now, come to think of it," Draven said. He glanced at the blond man, who nodded, said a quick "see you later," and took off at a trot back the way they had come. Someone called out to Sam, and she tossed a salute to Rider and headed toward the hotel.

Draven looked back at Paige.

"Your boy's a pretty sharp kid. When we first got the

call relayed through the marine operator, we weren't sure
how seriously to take it, but after listening to him, we had
darn near all we needed.''

"I didn't expect you this fast," Noah said.

"We were already on the way."

"You were?" Paige said, surprised.

He nodded. "Redstone was already curious about the
sudden lack of reports when things should have been buzz-
ing here. Then we started picking up some odd cellular
traffic. And one of Josh's connections let him know a splin-
ter group of terrorists from Arethusa had suddenly dropped
off the map. That was enough for him to round us up and
start us this way. Then we got the boy's call, so we stepped
it up.''

"Is there anybody Josh doesn't know?"

"Not likely. He's on the way, too, should be here tonight." Draven studied them both for a moment. "You
both look a little worse for wear. Why don't you let us
wrap this up?"

"Gladly," Noah said. "I've never felt more clueless in
my life.''

"Not what I heard from their not-so-mighty leader!"

Paige turned to look at the man coming up from behind
them, this one a lean, wiry Hispanic man with warm brown
eyes and freckles scattered incongruously over his nose.

"This is Javier Santiago," Draven said. "He's a new
hire. So what did you hear?"

The man poured out a quick version of what had happened since Paige had made her way into the dining room,
more than once giving her a curious yet appreciative
glance.

When he was done, Draven looked at Noah. "If you ever
want a transfer," he began.

Noah shook his head. "No way. I'll leave the heroics to
you guys, I'm no good at it."

Draven looked at Noah, then Paige, then around the

room to the captive terrorists. "You know," he said conversationally, "in my experience heroes are mostly people who do what has to be done at the time. You got it done, Rider."

Noah lowered his gaze and let out a long breath. Paige sensed those simple words were the highest of accolades. And from a man like Draven, perhaps they were.

"Redstone does know how to throw a party," Rider said two days later.

It was just an inane observation. That the party was a wild success was evident all around them. But he had to say something to take his mind off other things, now that aspirin had dulled the last of the aches and pains. Paige had dressed for this gathering in a slender wisp of a dress that made her look almost fragile, made what she had done seem impossible except for the bruises that were starting to show. He was sure the first aid she'd been administered had included a painkiller, as well, because she was moving easily. Smoothly. Gracefully.

But worse for him, she'd left her hair down, freed from its usual braid or twist. It flowed down her back in a mass that made even the bonfire they had going look tame. And Noah thought he was going to slowly go insane just looking at her.

Across the crowded patio was the tall, lanky man who had arrived on the jet that had also brought the supplies for this huge luau.

"I can't believe Mr. Redstone himself showed up," Paige said.

"Josh? I'm not surprised." He grinned at her. "He takes that Redstone family thing real serious."

"I know," she said softly.

Rider saw her peer past the small bonfire to where he'd last seen Kyle. The boy had returned with Lani and the rest of the villagers—including Hannah and her parents, who gushed until Rider was embarrassed—all of whom had been invited to the celebration. He had been quite chastened by the experience, even while exhilarated at the part he'd played. He'd solemnly told his mother the real thing wasn't anything like his violent video games, and she'd heard him telling Lani he knew now they were childish.

"It's going to be fine," Rider told her. He knew they hadn't had a chance to really talk yet, but he guessed from the fierce hug the boy had given her when he'd gotten back to the hotel that they were going to be all right.

"I think so," she agreed, for the first time sounding confident about it.

Draven appeared at the edge of the crowd, scanned the area and, after seeming to find everything to his liking, faded back into the shadows.

"He's quite something, isn't he?" Paige said, nodding toward where he'd vanished. "Where did Mr. Redstone find him?"

"He was in the service with Josh's little brother. And, yes, he's something. Tougher than boiled owl, Josh says."

She smiled at that—it sounded like something the man would say. "What about Sam and Rand?"

"Sam worked her way up through the ranks. She started out as security at one of the other resorts, but it wasn't long before Josh realized she was ready for more. I'm not sure where he found Rand."

"They are quite a pair, visually."

"We rag them a lot about being twins separated at birth. They use it, on occasion, when it will help. Go in as brother and sister."

"Go in?" She frowned. "You mean, like undercover?"

"Redstone's got a lot of operations all over the world. You never know what you might need."

"Can I have your attention, everybody?"

Rider knew the voice, and when he saw Josh Redstone

up on one of the benches at the edge of the patio, he felt a sudden qualm.

"What's he going to do?" Paige asked.

"Embarrass us, most likely," Rider muttered. He still didn't feel like the hero they all called him, felt more as if he'd just stumbled through it all and gotten lucky.

"You, most of all, I hope," she said, sounding rather cheerful about it. And when he looked at her, she merely added, "Your Mr. Draven was right, you know. You can say you're not a hero all you want, but that doesn't change the truth."

Between the soft smile that curved her mouth and the glow of something warm and intimate in her eyes, Rider was speechless.

"I won't interrupt for long here," Josh said in the slight drawl that often fooled competitors into thinking he was a bit slow, much to their chagrin later, when they realized he was sharper than a shark's tooth. "I just want to bring some people up here I know you all want to thank. Kyle, Lani, where are you?"

The two teenagers, holding hands openly now, went to stand beside the bench, looking at the crowd rather shyly. Kyle without his earrings, Rider noticed. Kyle paused to smile at Tess Machado, who as usual was only a few feet away from Josh. She shook the boy's hand and then threw him a snappy salute that made the boy grin.

"Rider? Paige?"

With a sigh Rider took her hand and started toward his boss.

"Why does everyone call you Rider?" Paige asked.

He thought about telling her the whole truth, how he hated his first name, but then decided to tell her the new truth he'd learned.

"Because you're the only one I like to hear call me Noah."

He was gratified to see that she nearly missed a step and

that color rose in her cheeks. He took advantage, shamelessly, of the fact that in a moment she wasn't going to be able to talk back to him, and whispered intimately in her ear exactly how he'd like to hear her call his name, and soon.

To his shock she simply looked up at him, and as they stepped up to Josh's bench, said, "Yes."

And just that neatly, she turned the tables on him. He'd begun by teasing her, hoping she would remember the fevered moments they'd shared and might want to explore further. And wound up in a state of severe, painful arousal, barely aware of the praise that was being heaped on his head.

As soon as he thought they could escape without drawing too much attention, he grabbed Paige's hand and led the way back into the hotel.

"Pick a number between one and four," he said. She looked at him blankly. "Just pick one," he said.

"Three, I guess." She sounded confused. Or maybe it was flustered. He voted for the latter.

"Three it is," he said, and headed down the hallway to the elevators. He spared a moment to think of the last time he'd been in an elevator and how things had changed. But only a moment. He hit the button for the third floor and the doors slid closed. Then he turned to face her.

"If you want to change your mind, you've got the length of this ride to do it," he said, his voice taut.

Paige looked at him, wide-eyed, but she shook her head.

"You're sure? I mean, this could be just adrenaline, could be reaction, or...something."

"Then we need to know, don't we?"

"Need," he said, wondering at the hoarseness of his own voice, "is definitely the word."

He reached for her then, but the elevator came politely to a stop and the door slid open. Smothering a grunt of frustration, Rider held the door for her, then followed her into the hall. Moments later he was using his master key-card on the door of room thirty-three, and then they were inside.

He shut the door behind them.

"Three hundred rooms we could be in," he said as some of the tension inside him let go now that they were alone. "They won't find us for hours."

And suddenly Paige wouldn't look at him. He reached out and gently grasped her shoulders, but she still wouldn't raise her eyes.

It cost him, but he said, "You know I didn't mean that, in the elevator. You can change your mind anytime."

She did look up then. "I don't want to change my mind. It's just that since Phil, I haven't..."

Her voice trailed off. And Rider knew his was thick and rough when he told her, "Then I'm even more honored."

Color rose in her cheeks. He cupped her face as memories flooded through him. He swallowed tightly, tamped down his unruly body, because he knew this needed to be said, and before things went any further. He wasn't sure he was ready for this, he only knew he couldn't walk away this time. No matter what, even if it meant an unexpected fatherhood to a stubborn teenager, he couldn't walk way. He was more than a little in awe that this brave, bright, loving woman wanted him, and he wanted to be sure she knew it.

"I never forgot you, Paige. Even though I felt so damned guilty about that night, I never forgot you. When I saw you again here, I thought I knew why no other woman interested me. But in the past three days I found out I haven't even scratched the surface of who you are."

"I hope," she whispered, "that you like what you find."

That was all he needed to hear.

At first it was an odd sort of dance, each of them trying to be careful, aware of cuts and bruises, yet each of them in a hot, urgent rush. The fires they'd banked for so long threatened to blaze out of control at the first touch. And soon the cuts and bruises didn't matter.

Rider knew he was lost the moment she tugged his shirt up and slid her hands underneath, stroking her fingers over his belly, then his chest. He shuddered at the heat her touch generated and vaguely wondered if they'd survive this, when the first touch nearly sent him up in flames.

He reached out and did what he'd been longing to do all evening. Hell, since the first time he'd ever seen her. He threaded his fingers through that silken mane of red hair, letting it slip over his hands, savoring the heavy silk of it.

"Paige," he whispered, just to say it.

"I've waited a very long time for this," she said, and he saw her tremble. That she would tremble now, when she'd faced down death without a quiver, sent a shudder through him. And he reined in his demanding body.

Gently, carefully, he undressed her, pausing whenever the feel of her caresses aroused him beyond moving. And when her hands hesitated at his belt, he urged her on, wanting to be naked with her more than he'd ever wanted anything—even help when he'd thought he was going to die.

And when he finally was naked, when she shyly stood nude before him, stealing glimpses of his body as if she wasn't sure looking at him was her right, he couldn't resist any longer. He pulled her against him, almost roughly in his haste. His ribs protested, but he ignored it. Nothing mattered, not next to this raging need.

He lowered his mouth to hers, knowing this time they would not be interrupted, yet feeling an incredible urgency just the same. His arms tightened convulsively around her. But then he remembered she, too, had taken a battering, and he gentled his embrace.

His hands slid over her back, delighting in the silken feel of her skin, the taut feel of muscle as he traced her rib cage, then slipped upward. She went still when he reached the gentle swell of her breasts, and he stopped. But then she made a little sound and pressed herself closer. He groaned as the soft flesh filled his hands and her nipples became hard against his palms. He moved slightly, shifting so that his thumbs could rub at those taut peaks. She cried out at his touch, her back arching. Her response was so sweetly immediate that he broke the kiss and lowered his head to her breast, taking first one, then the other nipple in his mouth, flicking them with his tongue.

She sagged against him, as if that alone had robbed her of the strength to stand. He wasn't sure how he made it to the bed, only that he must have done it, because they were there now, facing each other where he'd so often dreamed they might be, alone together with an endless night before them.

And then Paige was returning his caresses, running her hands over him as if she wanted to touch every inch as badly as he wanted her to. He soon learned that it took very little from him, a gasp, a groan, a slight arching of his body, to show her what he liked. And she learned quickly. Too quickly. Within minutes he was panting, groaning with nearly every breath as she explored him. Her fingers circled his nipples, startling him with how good that felt. Then his belly, then lower, slowly, teasingly, until he thought he'd die if she didn't go on. And then she did, curling her fingers around him, rubbing her thumb over flesh so sensitive he did cry out then—her name on a breath that seemed wrenched from him.

At last he broke and rolled over, half covering her, raining kisses on her, on any bit of skin he could reach. He returned to her breasts as his hand slid downward, through dark auburn curls until he could feel her wet heat. He probed further as he drew her nipples once more into his mouth, loving the way she moaned and undulated under his touch.

''Noah!''

Her cry as he found that tiny knot of nerve endings he'd

sought convinced him once and for all that there really was nothing wrong with his name. He continued that insistent circular caress, kept tasting and teasing her breasts, until she was twisting against him.

"Now?" he asked her, taking one of her hands and gently drawing it down his body until she was touching him again.

In answer she clasped him in a sweet, coaxing grip, shifting her body until he could feel her heat, opening for him in an invitation he felt he'd been waiting for all his life. She rubbed him against her slick flesh, and it was more than he could stand.

His hips drove forward, and he slid into her with an ease that told him she was as eager as he was. For an instant he couldn't move, so amazing was the feeling of being inside her. Why it was different with this woman, why it was better, hotter, why it transcended anything he'd ever felt before he didn't know right now. He only knew that he would never be the same after this moment.

And then she moved beneath him, lifting to meet him, and he spiraled out of control. He knew she was with him by her frantic cries, by the feel of her as she grabbed at him and hung on. And then his world narrowed to the feel of her body and the pure emotion shining in her eyes. She tightened around him, fiercely, and he heard her call his name once more, that name he now wouldn't trade for anything. Spasms shook her, and pure, raw wonder crept into her voice as tiny cries broke from her.

And then he let go, soaring wildly upward until the light caught him, seared him and sent him floating back down in pieces he wasn't sure he could ever put back together again.

"So they're going to reschedule the opening in three weeks?"

"Pending the result of the meeting Josh has with the minister of Arethusa," Noah said.

Paige brushed at a mark on her dress, realized it was charcoal, probably from the bonfire last night, and gave up. "Do you think everyone will still come, after all this?"

"Most, who can clear their schedule. But I have a feeling Draven and some of the others may be staying awhile, just to be sure."

She fussed with her left shoe, which had torn near the sole. "It's hard to think about just going back to school."

"I know."

She ran her fingers through the tangled mass of her hair, then realized she didn't have a prayer without a brush.

"I think I'll take over Rudy's job," Noah said.

Startled, she whirled around to stare at him. "What?"

"Well, at least you finally looked at me," he said, his mouth twisting into a wry, rueful grimace.

She felt herself flush. She knew she'd been avoiding his gaze, but hadn't realized she'd been so obvious about it.

"What's wrong, Paige?" She saw him swallow before he added, "Second thoughts?"

She wasn't sure how to answer him. The hours they'd spent together had been the most incredible of her life. She'd never known her body could respond like that, but when this man touched her, she was halfway there before they even began. And any doubts she'd had that it was mutual vanished in the moments when he convulsed in her arms, crying out her name as if she were some miracle he'd found.

But now she couldn't help thinking of what had been seared out of her mind by his touch.

Now what?

He was still a Redstone globe-trotter, and she was still a schoolteacher. A schoolteacher who hadn't had much luck with another traveling man. And for a moment she wished, foolishly, that he hadn't been joking. Not that she could see him as a chef, but at least he'd be in one place for more than a week at a time.

He got up and came to her. She went into his arms, wishing...wishing for so many things she didn't know where to start.

"Paige?" He lifted her chin with a gentle finger. "God, Paige, please don't say this was a mistake or we shouldn't have done it or any of those other morning-after regrets."

"It's not morning yet," she answered, burying her face against his chest, hating herself even as she dodged answering.

She heard him let out a long sigh, felt him go a little bit slack. She'd hurt him, and she hadn't meant to. He didn't deserve that, just because she was feeling so unsure just now. She made herself meet his eyes.

"It wasn't a mistake, Noah. And I don't regret it. The opposite, in fact. You made me feel...more than alive, you made me fly."

His arms tightened around her. "But?"

"I just want you to know that I...understand."

"Understand what?"

"That you're who you are, and I'm who I am."

He went very still. "Meaning?"

"That you're here today, somewhere else tomorrow, and I have a son to raise."

"Funny," he said, "I talked to that son. He kind of liked the idea of seeing the world."

She fought down her gut-level reaction to that. "He has to finish school."

"You know what else he said? He said he thought his mother would like to see the world, too, if she could ever get over being mad at his father for traveling so much."

She stared at him. "Kyle said that?"

He nodded. "But you know what else is funny?"

"No."

"I was talking to Josh about my job."

"Your job?"

"Well, my job later. For a while I'm going to be here."

"Here?" Paige was beginning to feel very stupid.

He nodded. "We found out who'd talked to Ares about you. Who told him you should be the spokesperson. Turns out he was just trying to get out of it himself."

Her eyes widened. "Who?"

"Barry Rutherford," he said with a grimace. "As manager, he was Ares's first choice, but he convinced Ares that a pretty, respected woman would be better, and Josh isn't too happy with him selling you out like that. He's going to be back at Redstone explaining himself for a while."

"And you'll be here? Doing his job?"

He nodded. Paige felt as if she'd just gotten a stay of execution. He wasn't leaving. At least, not right away.

"After that, Josh and I are going to redesign my real job."

"Redesign?"

"Cut down on the travel. Or schedule most of it during holidays. Or summer. You know, when kids are out of school."

"But you love your job," she said, unable to quite believe what she was hearing.

"I did. For five years, I loved it. But now..."

"Now?"

"I love you."

He said it so simply, as if it were a given. But the implications took her breath away. He loved her. He loved her, and if he had to change his life to have her, he'd do it. Unlike Phil, who wouldn't have changed anything.

"I mean it, Paige," he said. "I'll do whatever it takes." He gave her a lopsided smile. "I've realized in the past week that life's too short and uncertain to be a workaholic. Josh can find somebody else to be his main point man. Or we'll divide it. Something. Anything."

"I'm sorry," she said, suddenly realizing she owed him

a large apology. "I got the actions confused with the man. I should have known you weren't like Phil, that even if you had to travel for your job, you wouldn't abandon your family."

Noah shrugged. "As long as you know it now." Then he frowned. "Do you think Kyle's ready for a stepfather?"

"Are you ready to be one?"

He seemed to consider that. "Do you suppose it's worse than terrorists?" he asked innocently.

She couldn't help herself. All the tumbled emotions she'd been feeling burst free, and she laughed until tears were rolling down her cheeks.

"Noah Rider," she finally said when she could speak again, "I'd bet on you over terrorists—or a stubborn teenager—anytime."

## *Epilogue*

Paige knew that if Kyle and Lani realized she could hear them, even from their spot on the other side of that hibiscus, they'd never be carrying on this conversation. She supposed she should get up and give them some privacy, but she was feeling too lazy. The grand opening of the hotel had gone off without a hitch. The party had been long and even more convivial than usual after word came that peace had been restored in Arethusa. And after that Noah had kept her up the rest of the night in the most delicious ways, and her body felt luxuriously sated. Besides, he was on the next lounge chair, holding her hand, and she wasn't about to move.

"They're really going to get married?" Lani was asking.

"Yep. As soon as his black eye's all gone, Rider said. Isn't that cool?" Kyle said. "I mean, I still miss my dad and all, but Rider's a cool guy."

"He's a hero," Lani said fervently. "But then, so is your mother."

There was a pause before Kyle's voice came. "Yeah. Yeah, she is."

Paige was grateful for the sunglasses that masked her eyes, and wondered how she'd hide the tears if they started to spill over. Oddly, at that moment Noah's hand tightened around hers, almost as if he'd heard, although she thought sure he was too far away.

"He's going to travel to all the Redstone Resorts in the summer," Kyle said happily. "And if I keep my grades up, I get to go along."

"You're leaving, then?" Lani sounded sad enough that Paige was sure Kyle would be flattered.

"Not for a while," he said quickly. "Mom says she'll fulfill her contract here, which is for two years. She's big on keeping her word."

"I'm glad you'll be staying."

"Me, too," Kyle said.

And less than a month ago, I was the wicked witch for bringing him here and he couldn't wait to get away, Paige thought with a relieved sigh. And again Noah's hand tightened around hers. He must be able to hear.

"Do you think they're sleeping together?" Lani said in a whisper that, in fact, wasn't much softer than her normal voice.

Paige bit her lip. Noah's hand clenched, so she knew he'd heard that, too.

"Must be," Kyle said nonchalantly. "They're always hugging and touching, and they keep disappearing when they think I won't notice."

"Doesn't that bother you?"

"It freaked me out at first—I mean, it's my mom, so it's kind of gross—but I just kind of ignore it now."

Paige felt Noah's hand shake. And she knew he was fighting, as she was, not to burst out laughing.

"Lani?" Kyle said, sounding tentative.

"Yes?"

"Do you think...would you...be my date, for the wedding?"

The girl's smile echoed in her voice. "I'd like that."

Paige felt her eyes brim once more. Her wedding day was going to be complete; Josh had already arranged to fly her mother in, along with Noah's sister and father, and now her son would be there in heart as well as body.

But most important, she was marrying a man she could always trust, when she'd once thought she would never trust again. A man who adored her and showed it every day. A man she adored and gave thanks for every day.

"Psst."

That man was whispering in her ear. She turned to look at him, pulling down her sunglasses. He'd pulled his off, as well, and she saw the glint in his eyes.

"You think they'd miss us if we disappeared right now?"

Instantly heat bubbled up inside her, always at this man's command it seemed. "I think they'll just ignore our absence. Besides," she added, matching him look for look, "I'm the teacher. I can excuse absences if I want to."

"Then I," he said as he rose and then pulled her to her feet, "plan to make sure you want to."

Paige reached up and kissed him. He was the only paradise she needed.

\* \* \* \* \*

# ANN MAJOR
# CHRISTINE RIMMER
# BEVERLY BARTON

cordially invite you to attend the year's most exclusive party at the **LONE STAR COUNTRY CLUB!**

Meet three very different young women who'll discover that wishes *can* come true!

# LONE STAR
# COUNTRY CLUB:
## *The Debutantes*

**Lone Star Country Club: Where Texas society reigns supreme—and appearances are *everything*.**

Available in May at your favorite retail outlet, only from Silhouette.

Silhouette®
*Where love comes alive™*

PSLSCCTD

When California's most talked about dynasty is threatened, only family, privilege and the power of love can protect them!

# THE COLTONS

Coming in May 2002

# THE HOPECHEST BRIDE

by

# Kasey Michaels

Cowboy Josh Atkins is furious at Emily Blair, the woman he thinks is responsible for his brother's death...so *why* is he so darned attracted to her? After dark accusations—and sizzling sparks—start to fly between Emily and Josh, they both realize that they can make peace...and love!

*Available at your favorite retail outlet.*

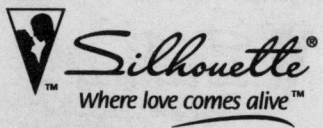

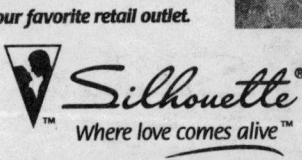

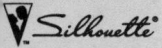
Silhouette®

# INTIMATE MOMENTS™

### presents:

# Romancing the Crown

With the help of their powerful allies,
the royal family of Montebello is
determined to find their missing heir.
But the search for the beloved prince
is not without danger—or passion!

**Available in May 2002:**
**VIRGIN SEDUCTION**
**by Kathleen Creighton (IM #1148)**
Cade Gallagher went to the royal palace of
Tamir for a wedding—and came home with
a bride of his own. The rugged oilman thought he'd married to
gain a business merger, but his innocent bride made him long
to claim his wife in every way....

*This exciting series continues throughout*
*the year with these fabulous titles:*

| | | |
|---|---|---|
| January | (IM #1124) | THE MAN WHO WOULD BE KING by Linda Turner |
| February | (IM #1130) | THE PRINCESS AND THE MERCENARY by Marilyn Pappano |
| March | (IM #1136) | THE DISENCHANTED DUKE by Marie Ferrarella |
| April | (IM #1142) | SECRET-AGENT SHEIK by Linda Winstead Jones |
| May | (IM #1148) | VIRGIN SEDUCTION by Kathleen Creighton |
| June | (IM #1154) | ROYAL SPY by Valerie Parv |
| July | (IM #1160) | HER LORD PROTECTOR by Eileen Wilks |
| August | (IM #1166) | SECRETS OF A PREGNANT PRINCESS by Carla Cassidy |
| September | (IM #1172) | A ROYAL MURDER by Lyn Stone |
| October | (IM #1178) | SARAH'S KNIGHT by Mary McBride |
| November | (IM #1184) | UNDER THE KING'S COMMAND by Ingrid Weaver |
| December | (IM #1190) | THE PRINCE'S WEDDING by Justine Davis |

*Available only from Silhouette Intimate Moments*
*at your favorite retail outlet.*

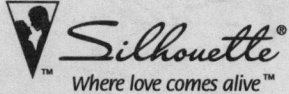
Silhouette®

*Where love comes alive™*

Visit Silhouette at www.eHarlequin.com

SIMRC5

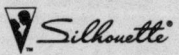

# INTIMATE MOMENTS™

## and *USA TODAY* BESTSELLING AUTHOR

# RUTH LANGAN

### present her new miniseries

Lives—and hearts—are on the line when the Lassiters pledge to uphold the law at any cost.

Available March 2002
**BANNING'S WOMAN (IM #1135)**

When a stalker threatens Congresswoman Mary Brendan Lassiter, the only one who can help is a police captain who's falling for the feisty Lassiter lady!

Available May 2002
**HIS FATHER'S SON (IM #1147)**

Lawyer Cameron Lassiter discovers there's more to life than fun and games when he loses his heart to a beautiful social worker.

And if you missed them,
look for books one and two in the series

**BY HONOR BOUND (IM #1111)**
and
**RETURN OF THE PRODIGAL SON (IM #1123)**

*Available at your favorite retail outlet.*

*Where love comes alive*™